THE POLICE PROBLEM
IS NOT A SIMPLE ONE . . .

Even the simplest case was maddening.

Take the proxy murder, for instance. Ten and Roban had collared a suspect—Ladras, one of the Silents on Egar—who claimed innocence despite having the means, the opportunity, and an acknowledged grudge against the victim.

A solid case, by Earth standards—but this was Egar, where witnesses were telepathic Normals, who knew barely enough verbal speech to be questioned, and didn't care a bit about mere physical descriptions. Where producing merely one suspect might simply mean the Terrans did not understand Egarad murder motives.

Moreover, if there was even a chance the suspect was innocent, Ten and Roban had to know, because in court, the cops wouldn't just be prosecuting Ladras —they also had to defend him!

DEADLY SILENTS

Lee Killough

A Del Rey Book

BALLANTINE BOOKS ● NEW YORK

For DAVID HOLM, who wanted
so much to see this story
written,
and for PAT, who loveth
and sustaineth.

Chapter One

STEVEN KAMPACALAS felt as he had at the age of eight seeing the St. Louis earthquake ruins . . . breathless, all eyes and ears, trying to look everywhere at once. For the moment, Ten forgot all about the crisis that had brought him here. Every sense told him he stood on an alien world. The 1.2 gravity dragged noticeably harder on him, and the air, smelling of a faint, pleasant muskiness, touched his skin with such a dry chill that he instantly visualized the vast arid plains that dominated Egar's surface, landlocking the scattered seas. D'shenegar's travelport terminal lay low and broad around him, its lines and angles subtly different from Terran architecture, lighted through numerous skylights by the large bronze sun and marked with signs bearing Chinese-like characters.

And of course he saw aliens, Iregara, although fewer than Ten had expected to see in a facility serving the world's third largest city. As holos of them showed, and like one Ten had seen in Kansas City, they stood in about the same range of height as Terrans, but uniformly stockier and more muscular, with four-fingered hands, short torsos, and heads large in proportion to their height. Wide violet eyes dominated their flat faces, and intricate designs patterned their velvet-textured fur. Ten saw the designs easily because except for a few individuals in overalls, most, despite a temperature that raised goosebumps on Ten, wore only calf or thigh-high boots and multi-pocketed tabards or pouched belts.

Behind him, a flat Terran voice said, "This is sure mighty different from Dallas."

Another voice replied, "I'd be disappointed if it looked anything like Earth."

Ten turned to grin at the speakers, a muscular, sandy-

1

haired young man near his own age and a taller, older one with the dusky skin and wiry black hair of Afro ancestry. He had met Pol Wassom and Roban Adeyanju in Switchpoint, where they came through shuttleboxes from their respective cities to connect with the D'shenegar shuttlebox. Recognizing the undefinable but unmistakable stamp of leo—law enforcement officer—on each other, the three had drifted together and, after discovering they were all headed for the same job at the same destination, joined forces to wait their turn through D'shenegar's shuttlebox with a load of computer components, ski equipment, and bicycles.

"Does it look like home to you, though?" Ten asked.

Roban's dusky face lighted up. "Yes, as a matter of fact." In the process of exchanging personal histories in Switchpoint, he had told them he was brought up on stories of Egar told by his grandfather, who was born in Lushanah when Roban's great-grandparents were there as members of the Terran trade delegation.

Pol cocked a brow. "Well, homeboy, would y'all do me a favor, then? I know they all look alike to me now, but isn't there *really* a way to tell the men from the women here?"

Roban grinned, shaking his head. "My grandfather swears not . . . unless a female is pregnant or nursing, or a male feels"—he extended his thumb, pointing it skyward—"like loving. Don't worry about it. Iregara themselves ignore gender most of the time."

They walked on through the travelport, with Ten finding delight in every new object and scent. Of course, once he and Pol knew about Roban's grandfather they had plied the Afro with questions about Egar, but nothing he told them in any way diminished the child's sense of wonder Ten felt now. He was glad he had not let his partner Avel Siem talk him out of coming. She might recoil from living on an alien world, but with each passing moment, Ten looked forward to it more.

At the entrance, they hurried outside, eager for a look at the city, but to their disappointment saw no sign of it. Instead, they appeared to be in the wilds. The only habitation visible was a couple of building complexes on the eastern side of the valley where the travelport lay and another small complex on the rim of hills to the south.

"That should be lion country," Pol said. "The travel instructions said the stationhouse is three klicks south of the travelport."

Ten eyed the distant building. "Shall we hike or take the monorail?" Three kilometers was not far; he ran a longer distance than that for physical qualification every month, but carrying luggage in this gravity made it another matter.

"It's called a skyrail here," Roban said.

"And we're supposed to have a free ride, so let's us take advantage of it." Pol headed for the skyrail platform.

Following, Ten wondered if Pol's drawl were really that heavy, or had been acquired, like so much "local color" since the Regionalization craze swept the United States of North America.

They boarded the next train south, and as it climbed the hills and followed the crest, Ten saw D'shenegar at last. Rather than a city, however, it looked like a collection of tiny villages nestled among the hills, all separated from one another by a kilometer or more of fields and woods, linked only by narrow paths and the shining silver strands of the skyrail. The villages stretched east to the sea and to the horizon in all other directions, which made them a very imposing collection. They looked peaceful, too, with nothing visible to suggest a desperate people under siege.

"How big do y'all suppose it is?" Pol asked.

"Fifty klicks square," Roban replied promptly.

Twenty-five hundred square kilometers for three hundred thousand people? Ten whistled. That *was* spreading them thin!

"It's going to be a mighty big area to patrol," Pol said.

The happy light in Roban's eyes faded. He grimaced. "I'd planned all my life to come here some day . . . but I never dreamed it would be to work as a police officer."

"I think everyone was surprised when the Iregara started advertising for leos," Ten said. "What did you think when the notice went up in your department?"

"That it was a mistake, or a joke. I thought it was impossible for telepaths to have crime."

Maybe they never used to, Ten reflected, but that had changed. "You applied anyway?"

Roban gazed out the window. "The job was on Egar." After a moment he looked around at Ten. "What about you?"

Ten shrugged. "Well, the salary was more than I could hope to earn in the Shawnee County P.D. and after a close call one watch, I decided that whatever the situation, it had to be better than street war and finding excuses to give the high holies for not attending church."

He still felt that way, although Devane Brooks, the department director, had explained the seriousness of the Egarad problem when he interviewed Ten. What irony, that people faced with a situation nothing in their history ever prepared them to expect or handle had to appeal for help to the only other intelligent species they had met during interstellar colonization, even though it was on the others' world where the problem began.

Ten knew *that* part already. He had learned in school about the discovery of a Terran colony which led to the Iregara locating Earth four hundred years ago and establishing cautious, then gradually more friendly communications between the races, ultimately resulting in the exchange of trade delegations. Each delegation was to live on the other's planet and help carry on trade through fast, unmanned tachyon freighters. Unfortunately, although Terrans knew about Egarad telepathy and Iregara were aware that Terrans broadcast without generally being able to receive, neither side thought to correlate that with population densities. So when the Egarad ramjets landed in Terran cities after a near-century-long trip, Iregara who had never been in contact with more than five hundred other minds at once suddenly found themselves surrounded by millions of alien thoughts. Something burned out in them and around Earth, eight thousand trade delegates became instant telepathic deaf-mutes . . . Silents.

But not until Devane Brooks told him had Ten heard of the equally tragic sequel. After development of the Equipotential Transfer Portal, the shuttlebox, provided instant star travel and made possible the repatriation of trade delegate descendants who wanted to return home, Silence did not end. It perpetuated. Without a prenatal telepathic link to her fetus, a Silent woman, even on Egar, with telepathic neighbors, could bear only Silent children.

Ten thought about that, looking out the skyrail window. How had both races failed to consider what might happen to growing numbers of Silents in a society geared for telepathy? Why was it that only by looking back on the past seventy-five years since repatriation anyone could see the growing Silent frustration with the difficulty of communication and at having so much of their own culture inaccessible to them . . . frustration that had eventually erupted into uncontrollable and, for the first time in Egarad history, unpredictable violence?

"I considered it a five-year vacation from Earth," Pol said, breaking into Ten's thoughts, "or however long it takes to organize and teach the job to the locals. And I reckoned they might appreciate what I was doing."

Amen to that, Ten thought.

Disembarking at their station, they found themselves with a hike after all, half a kilometer west to the stationhouse. They arrived, panting, in the forecourt of the sprawling, X-shaped building with its handsome red-gold stone and smoky-dark windows and roof tiles, but excitement buoyed Ten—they were *here*—and without pausing even to catch his breath, he headed for the double doors opening beneath a large yin-yang symbol worked in dark green and umber. Inside, a receiving area stretched before them, open and full of light, like the travelport.

A woman behind the circular desk in the center raised her brows at them. "Officers? Put your hands over the scanner on the edge of the desk, please."

While he let the scanner read the I.D. code imprinted invisibly into the cell structure of his hand at birth and flash the data to the computer, verifying his identity, Ten eyed the woman. Even nicer than the building. He particularly liked her clothes. Colored like the symbol outside, and with a patch version of it on the upper left sleeve, the jumpsuit fit like skin rather than hanging loose and shapeless, hiding the human form inside as fashions at home did.

"Roban Simue Adeyanju, Denver; Pol Gregory Wassom, Dallas; Steven Jason Kampacalas, Topeka," the desk officer read from her computer screen. "Welcome to Egar. I'm Sergeant Loros." She looked up at Ten and a corner of her mouth quirked. "The uniform fascinates you, sweetface?"

Ten tried to ignore the flush heating his face and studied the jumpsuit with a more critical eye. "Uniform? What does the patch mean?"

"It's our badge. The Iregara adopted it from Earth, I'm told, because they like the concept it embodies, but I've never asked how they apply the complementary coexistence of opposites to police work.

"The three of you will be sleeping in detention room

Twenty until you find a place to live. That's in A wing. The exercise room is on the way. Report there for outfitting."

They headed in the direction she pointed. A short way down A wing's central corridor they found the exercise room. The door bore an Egarad character but under it someone had stuck a piece of tape lettered in English. Inside, more officers in green and umber piled their arms full of equipment and uniforms, including an equipment belt with a sidearm sleeper and the smallest belt-buckle computer tie-in Ten had ever seen.

"Do the uniforms all fit so tight?" Ten asked.

"Yes," one of the officers replied. "Our new bosses don't like to waste fabric. It offends you?"

Ten hesitated. He rather liked it, as a matter of fact, though he could well imagine how a high holy would condemn it as lewd. "I'm just wondering how I'm going to put an undersuit beneath it."

"You don't need to. The fabric has a high enough insulation quotient to keep you warm in about any weather here."

Ten frowned. "How about alive?" He was not about to work anywhere, even here, without the protection of a paragee shield, and the undersuit contained the wiring for generating the deflective field.

"Paragee circuits are woven right into the uniform. You'll find the control plate in front under the collar. From here you report across the corridor to the infirmary."

Ten struggled across the corridor with the equipment and his luggage. He dropped them gratefully for the few minutes it took the medic to plant the tiny radio button deep in his left ear, then groaned as the medic helped load him up again and dismissed him with the comment, "You're a bit lightweight for this gravity. Work on building more muscle."

He went in search of his room.

Farther down the wing a heavy metal grille lay across the corridor. Roban eyed it with distaste as they passed through the open gateway. "After all the playing with psychological restraint and force fields, we always come back to bars, it seems, like barbarism we never quite outgrow, and now we're even exporting it to the rest of the galaxy."

"Bars survive power failures," Pol said.

Ten groaned. "Can we find our room before my arms break off?"

"Sixteen, Seventeen, Twenty," Pol counted, reading the tapes under the Egarad characters. "I don't know what happened to Eighteen and Nineteen, but here our room is, podner."

At that point Ten did not give a damn about Eighteen and Nineteen. He staggered into Twenty and dumped his armload on a mat lying in one corner, then dropped onto the end of the mat and lay back against the wall, panting. Sunlight slanted through the window and across him, blessedly warm.

Roban and Pol chose mats, too. Pol said, "Aside from what looks like sleeping on the floor, I wouldn't mind spending cage time here."

Ten looked around. The room did seem more like one to be found in a dormitory than a jail, though the lock on the outside of the door and the mesh embedded in the window material stood as reminders of its function as a cell.

Two women jogged past on a track in the walled court-yard outside. They waved.

Pol waved back. "Change into exercise clothes and let's join them."

Leave his sunwarmed spot? Ten shook his head. "I'm sure the brass will start us on physical training soon enough."

"Hey, podner, unless you've managed to arrange for something on Egar already or plan on celibacy, those she-lions are all we'll have for female companionship the next few years. Now is a mighty fine time to get acquainted."

"Later, maybe," Roban said.

"Well, I'm going. I'll be sure to brand some fillies for y'all, too."

Ten watched Pol rummage in his luggage for exercise clothes and disappear into what must be the bathroom, then closed his eyes, savoring the heat of the sunshine. "I don't know about Texas she-lions, but even with the high holies preaching womanly submission from the pulpit four times a week, my partner would have broken the fingers on any man, lion or not, who claimed to be branding her."

Roban chuckled.

Someone rapped on the edge of the open door. "Hi, leos."

Ten opened his eyes. He looked up to see a tall, dark-haired young woman in the doorway. "I saw you come in and thought I'd introduce myself. Jael Meadin, Chicago."

The sun and mat still felt good, but Officer Meadin crackled with infectious energy. Ten found himself standing up to respond, introducing himself and Roban.

They were getting acquainted when Pol came out of the bathroom wearing exercise clothes and an expression of disbelief. "Did you know there's just a sink and a sandbox in there?"

Ten and Roban rushed to peer into the bathroom. As Pol said, a sandy material instead of water filled the low, wide commode. Roban said, "My grandfather never mentioned this."

Jael chuckled. "It's different, but logical when you realize that on this world, water isn't something to be used wantonly. You'll get used to it."

"You sound like the voice of experience," Ten said.

"I lived in D'shenegar for five years as a kid. My father bought fabric from the textile mills for fashion houses on Earth."

Roban's eyes lighted up. "My grandfather was born on Egar."

Soon he and Jael had become engrossed in exchanging Egarad anecdotes, oblivious to everyone and everything else. Rolling his eyes, Pol headed for the door. "I reckon I'll leave these two singing their rendition of 'I'm Home, Sweet Jesus, I'm Home' and go meet me some fellow tourists." He glanced back at Ten. "Sure you don't want to come too, podner?"

"I'm sure."

Ten sat down, listening to Roban and Jael talk, but he only half heard them. Instead, he could not stop thinking about the bathroom fixtures. A sandbox, but no shower or tub. *Alien,* it occurred to him, meant more than a different colored sun and more or less fingers on a hand. It meant differences in even the simplest things, things he had never thought to consider. He began wondering, with a touch of uneasiness, just how *alien* Egar and the Iregara might prove to be.

The intercom in the communications console on Devane Brooks's desk chimed and flashed yellow. He passed a coffee-colored hand over the light. "Yes?"

"They're all in, director."

"Thank you, Sergeant Loros." Devane waved his hand over the intercom again. "Communications."

After a moment a new voice replied. "Communications here."

"This is Director Brooks. Ask all sworn personnel to report to the reception area in fifteen minutes."

When the dispatcher acknowledged, Devane waved the intercom off and sat back in his chair. Day One. Well, that was not quite true, perhaps. He had been here thirty days already and the command officers—the sergeants, lieutenants, and captains—for fifteen, but they had all been working toward *this* day, when the field officers arrived. Now the job would begin in earnest.

He grinned, feeling a bit like a kid on Christmas morning. He had dreamed of a job like this for all of his police career, through sixteen years of rising from patrolman through Investigations to Research and Planning in the San Francisco P.D. He knew what he felt a police department should be and had somehow managed to keep the vision despite the bitterness of experience and the inability to try any of his ideas, even after he should have been in a position to do so, because of tight budgets or lack of manpower or a workload that left no time for anything but trying to stay alive while providing the citizenry with some measure of security. Then like an answer to a prayer, word had come that five cities on Egar wanted to establish police departments, and the police board of D'shenegar had approved the plan he submitted and asked him to be director. He had his chance now. It began today.

Devane picked up the sheet of notes outlining what he intended to say in introduction. He had written most of the notes in Egarad characters, determined to set an example for the rest of the department from the beginning, but he occasionally had cheated with an English word. The object, after all, he rationalized, was to remind himself of various points. He could lose complete track of his thought train attempting to interpret the still-unfamiliar characters, which represented concepts rather than words, with elements expressing not only tense, subjects, actions, and objects but also all the accompanying sounds, scents, and emotions.

He ran a hand over the short, kinky thatch of his hair. Paradise was not without its serpents, unfortunately. Not everything he had to say would meet with approval. Lately he had had periods of dismay and doubt himself, and long hours convincing himself, as well as his command officers, that the situation must be accepted and would work out. He would make it work out. But, he thought with a sigh, he would feel a hell of a lot more confident if the entire police board was supporting him, instead of knowing that two of the five had volunteered for their positions expressly to limit the police.

Those two had already managed to convince the rest of the board that they should be able to summarily cancel the program any time within the first year if it was not producing substantial results or it became obvious Terrans could not work within the Egarad culture. Devane's bitter protest had gone unheeded.

So why did he still feel as if he were opening the biggest and best Christmas present of his life? Meda teasingly accused him of being a hopeless romantic. Maybe she was right.

He smiled as he always did at the thought of his wife, visualizing her at work in the chem section of the Criminalistics lab across the building—slender, with toffee-gold skin and hair like chocolate fleece, so glowingly beautiful she looked even younger than her twenty-seven years. Perhaps Meda made the difference in his determination to make this department good, despite all that boardmembers Gemun and Lishulir might do. Her presence had a way of making anything more bearable. With her, he thought, he could be bound in a nutshell and still count himself king of infinite space. As soon as things were a bit more organized, he must start giving her more time than he had been able to these past few months.

A rap sounded on his door. Captain Tova Craig put her head in. "Ready?"

Devane nodded. Taking a last look at his notes, he stood up. "Maybe we ought to have the service department heads here, too. Will you round them up?"

"Will do."

Devane walked through the outer office and down the corridor to the reception area. Heads turned as he approached. *Here goes,* he thought, and used the desk chair to climb up onto the desk top.

Ten stood near the warmth of the front doors with Roban, Jael, and an officer from Toronto named Jean Broussard who had appeared an hour ago to share room Twenty with them. He could not see Pol.

Ten stopped looking for the Texan as soon as Devane Brooks stepped onto the desk. The director looked just as he had during Ten's interview in Kansas City, moving with the controlled grace of a panther. Outwardly, the meeting had been casual and chatty, with Brooks letting Ten know the situation on Egar and then wanting to know everything about Ten: what police work in Topeka was like; what his interests outside his job were; what his two older sisters were like; what his parents did; did he see them often; whether he preferred a needler or sleeper as a sidearm; how he would characterize his relationship with other ethnic groups in his jurisdiction . . . but all the while, despite an easy, crooked grin and deep, rich voice, Brooks's obsidian eyes dissected him.

From the top of the desk, Brooks looked around as though recording each face and checking it for name and history in a mental file. He said nothing, however, until a female officer with salt-and-pepper hair brought two more women and a man to join the knot of command officers to one side of the desk. Then he glanced at some notes in his hand and smiled out across the reception area.

"Welcome, officers. You're a very special group of men and women, about to embark on a unique experience. Some of you are already somewhat familiar with the planet and its people for one reason or another, while others know only what they've read or learned in school. By the time you leave, however, you'll know the planet, people, and city intimately, and you'll have performed a great service for them all."

"Nice of us, considering we caused the problem in the first place," Roban murmured.

Ten silenced him with a sharp elbow in the ribs.

"The job won't be easy," Brooks said. "We have almost twenty-five hundred square kilometers to cover, and if you've been curious enough to count heads here, you'll have noticed the tally is just three hundred."

Ten blinked. *Three hundred*? For a city of *three hundred thousand*? How could Brooks expect them to produce effective law enforcement with a ratio like that?

"The number was set by the police board, who are reluctant to be invaded by an army of Terrans. However, I'm not trying to pass responsibility; after some contemplation,

I've come to agree with the number. D'shenegar has only about eight or ten thousand Silents, and of them, only a small percentage are violent deviants, no more than five or ten percent. So you see, the ratio is actually quite favorable."

Ten did not consider five to ten percent a small number, despite the director's reassuring smile. From the muttering around him, he guessed few other leos did, either.

"Our problem, because of our numbers, is one of effective patrolling. We intend to solve this in several ways. First, the average patrol will cover a single cluster, consisting of a shopping mall and its twelve surrounding *ishen*, housing areas, along with several business and industrial malls. The main patrol vehicles will be Isinhars and Chehashas. If you're not familiar with the local car makes, those models are comparable to a Kyrios or Fricke-Porche on Earth."

Around Ten, leos whistled happily. He felt his own interest pick up. He loved good cars, particularly fast ones.

"These vehicles are small, precision maneuverable, and lightning fast. They fly at a hundred thirty kilometers per hour with no strain and considerably faster on demand. They'll be backed up by Iraths, larger workhorse vehicles ideal for transporting prisoners and specialized squads. Patrol areas will be adjusted according to activity as mapped by the computers. That will keep us on top of hot spots.

"Another way we'll make the most of our personnel explains why you're all cramped into detention rooms, the exercise room, and the infirmary right now. I want you to find living quarters all across this city."

"We won't be living in the Terran Enclave?" someone near the front asked.

Brooks looked back steadily. "No." Above a rumble of surprise he said, "We need you out there. You'll learn to know the people and cluster where you live, which means you'll know when something is wrong. You may be able to spot potential trouble before the computer maps it. There is also the matter of cultural differences."

Ten thought of the bathroom fixtures.

"We can't teach you about the culture; your supervisors and I don't know any more than you do. We're all going to learn together. What we can do, though, is give you a start, and part of that is living with Iregara and part is what we'll be doing for these next eight days.

"You may have noticed the strange symbols on the doors around the station, the unalphabetical designation of the wings, and some missing numbers. They're all Egarad." Brooks took a breath. "We're working for these people, and working toward training them to take our place, so in eight days, when orientation is over, written English and Translan will disappear from this station. From that point on, all notices on the bulletin board will be in Isegis, the local language. All reports will be written in the same language, all numbers figured for base-eight, and measurements expressed in local terms."

No murmur met those statements, only a dismayed silence.

Devane smiled. "It won't be that bad. If you're stuck on a measurement or number conversion, use your computer tie-in. Your command officers and I have had the same Quickteach sessions you'll be taking. We know what you'll be experiencing. Practice is the important follow-up, practice to set the synaptic connections and turn short-term memory into long-term memory."

Ten rubbed his thumb down the cleft in his chin. Learning new writing and measures might not be so bad, but new mathematics? Counting became almost a reflex; changing a reflex could be a struggle.

"And finally . . ." the director said, "like rookies, we're on probation this first year. Poor performance could result in our dismissal at any time, so . . . take your job seriously. Work hard. Let's give our citizens some careful, impressive work."

He motioned to the group of officers nearest the desk. "I'd like to introduce your command officers. Captain Lenard Titus, Uniformed division; Captain Dane Basanites, Investigations; and Captain Tova Craig, Services." He pointed to each in turn, then introduced the lieutenants and sergeants.

Ten lost track when Brooks went through the eight sergeants and barely heard the director introduce the three nonsworn staff members who headed the service departments of Data, Communications, and Criminalistics.

"With a few exceptions, all other clerical, laboratory, and garage staff are locals. You'll be meeting them as you work with them," Brooks said. "It's been a long day for you. With a thirty-six-hour rotation period, or forty-four by local counting, all Egarad days are long. And some of you may be wondering right now how tight those contracts you all signed are. They're tight. It cost to travel around interviewing you and to bring you here and outfit you. The citizens want a return on their investments. A meal is being served in the canteen in E wing. Eat and get a good sleep. At least the nights are long, too. I'm not worried about your performance; I know you'll do well. You've been chosen out of six thousand applicants. You're class; you're the best."

With that, he stepped down off the desk and left the reception area. Captain Titus raised his voice, calling, "Orientation starts at thirteen hundred hours, Egarad counting. Meet here for division into orientation groups."

Then the command officers were gone too, leaving everyone else to straggle toward the canteen in a roar of voices.

"He's wickers," someone near Ten said. "We can't possibly patrol this city with just three hundred officers."

"I knew the salary was too good to be true," someone else moaned.

Jean Broussard looked thoughtful. "The credit, she is very good, but not, perhaps, worth this. We are allowed a psychological discharge from the contract. I think I visit the psyman."

"Don't panic," Jael said. "Give yourself a chance."

Roban grinned. "Personally, I'm looking forward to this, even without the incentive of the credit." He looked at Ten. "What do you think?"

Ten smiled wryly. "I think I'll do like the man suggested, eat and sleep. I'll think about tomorrow at thirteen hundred hours."

Chapter Two

THE HOUSE followed the hillside like stairsteps, rising from the living room and outside deck to Gerel's room at the top. Along with its gayly colored neighbors in Blueside Shen, named for the blue velvet-leafed, ivylike groundcover that grew everywhere on the hillside it was allowed to, the house's smoky-tinted Sunsorb windows looked east toward the sparkling waters of Rahelem Bay. With very little effort, Devane and Meda could imagine they were back in San Francisco—one of the reasons they had taken the house. Devane did miss the ocean sunsets, though. Coming down the winding steps from the skyrail stop on top of the hill, he struggled with a nagging feeling which insisted the sun should not be going down behind the hills at his back but slipping away instead over the waters of the bay and the Iseg Sea.

Watching the first of Egar's three moons rising out of the water, Devane said, "I hope the plumbers came in today like they promised."

Behind him, Meda sighed. "I wish you'd let me stay home. I don't like the idea of letting people wander in and out of the house as they want with neither of us there to watch them."

Having a front door with no lock made Devane feel uneasy, too, but he turned to smile reassuringly back at her. "If they tried to take anything, someone else around would know."

"I suppose."

Still, she ran past him, up the steps of the deck and in through the front door. She glanced quickly around as she mounted the four steps to the cooking/dining area and the longer flight to their bedroom. Moments later Devane heard her exclaim in delight and she reappeared grinning.

"No more sponge baths. There's now a shower in the bathroom."

"In the san," he corrected.

Her grin became impish. "Well, if you want to be picky, the actual Egarad word is *eb*, but I don't care what we call it as long as I can take a real bath there." She came down to the dining level and waved across the phone on a central post. Her fingers touched the colored buttons on the face. "Runah? This is Meda Brooks. Will you please send Gerel home now?" She disconnected with another wave. "It's handy having a First-Level school right here in the shen, and a teacher willing to keep Gerel until we get home."

Devane watched her take off her coat and move into the cooking area. "All ishen have First-Level schools." He shed his own coat. "Well, how are you liking the lab?"

She shrugged. "It isn't quite as interesting as my job back home, and given a choice, if I have to work with Iregara, I think I'd rather work with Silents." She leaned down to open one side of the counter-high refrigerator. "I can't understand the Normals. Do you really expect us to mix socially with these people?"

Devane frowned. "We have to try. I think—"

A high yell interrupted him. "Hi, Daddy." His son Gerel charged in through the front door.

Devane scooped him up into a hug. "Hi yourself, cub. What did you do at school today?"

While Devane helped him out of his jacket, Gerel launched into a recitation so rapid Devane could hardly understand half of it. Devane gathered, however, that Gerel found his classmates somewhat strange but that they could certainly hit the ball hard playing *chanach*.

"What's *chanach*?"

"You hit a ball against a wall and it bounces off other walls. I'm not five years old anymore, either."

Devane grinned and raised a brow. "Just how old *are* you?"

Gerel held up eight fingers. "Ten." He raced back to the front door and pushed it open. Outside stood a young Egara about Gerel's height with fur of the same toffee-gold color as Gerel's skin. "This is D'ne. Can we play in my room?"

"Of course."

"Come on." Gerel ran up the long stairway past his parents' bedroom toward the small room at the top of the house. D'ne followed.

"You see?" Devane said. "Mixing with them isn't all that hard."

Meda continued taking out food for supper. "How do you think your officers will do, now that you've seen them en masse?"

"I think they'll do just fine. Of course"—he smiled—"I did see the two sexes eyeing each other. I expect we're going to have a few more problems with personal entanglements on the job than most departments, but that's to be expected under the circumstances."

"Maybe you shouldn't have insisted they all be single." She arched a brow at him. "After all, you brought a wife with you."

"Rank ought to have some privileges."

Saying it, he reached for her. She tried to duck away, protesting, "Dee, there are no drapes on the windows and Gerel's just upstairs."

But he pinned her against the counter and wrapped his arms around her. "This isn't Earth. No one hides love here. It's all in the open."

She pushed at him. "Dee, let go. I have supper to fix."

He nuzzled her ear. "Man shall not live by bread alone."

She snorted, then giggled. "You're terrible." Her arms slid around him. "Why do I let you talk me into such shameless behavior, Director Brooks?"

Against her hair, he said, "Because I'm irresistible, Mrs. Brooks."

A clapping noise startled them. "Director," a voice said in Isegis.

Meda flung away from Devane, face flaming. Devane turned with a frown. "Yes?"

An Egara, brown face and arm fur bleached into gold tiger stripes, stood in the open front door. "Need."

Devane looked at the impassive face and solemn violet eyes with their vertical oval pupils. "What kind of need?" Behind the single word, he knew, lay images and concepts on several thought levels, but without telepathy, he could not begin to guess what they were. "You'll have to specify for me." He went ahead and spoke English since the Egara could understand his meaning no matter what words he used.

The Egara's face remained expressionless, but the eyes narrowed with the effort of slowing thought down enough to put more of it into words. "Neighbor Sinin needs. Trespass. Come."

That part was clear enough. The leo instincts in him rose up, sniffing the scent of blood. He reached for his jacket. "I'm on my way. Meda?" He glanced back at her.

She bent over the counter, face averted. "I have supper to fix."

Devane followed the Egara out of the house and down the hill. They circled the bath house then passed through several communal gardens, terraced and planted with thorny, flowering hedges and grape-scented blue flowers.

"Where are we going?" Devane asked.

"There."

Devane saw it a moment after the Egara pointed. The house had been dug into the side of the hill and a small area before it filled to make a flat terrace. Some dozen Iregara stood in a group on the terrace. They stepped back as the tiger-striped Egara appeared and Devane saw they had been surrounding a small, pregnant, red-furred Egara and an Egarad child.

"Sinin," the tiger-striped Egara said.

The pregnant Egara looked up at Devane, then pointed toward the door of the house. "Trespass."

Devane worked his way past her through the group to the doorway. There, he looked in and swore softly. The house had nearly been destroyed. Every piece of cushion furniture lay slashed open, spilling its stuffing onto a black-stained carpet. Personal belongings such as book cassettes and seashells lay smashed below the wall shelves from which they had been swept. The kitchen cupboards stood open and empty, their contents broken or dented on the floor. Clothes smoldered in the middle of the kitchen's tiled floor.

Devane stepped inside and walked around each room, examining the damage without touching anything. Whoever vandalized the place had made a thorough job of it. He tried to imagine the frenzy that could have possessed someone to do this.

Then, in the doorway of the bedroom beyond the kitchen, he stopped short. "Oh, dear god." In the middle of the slashed sleeping mat lay the remains of what had once probably been a luras. Now, however, Devane could not even tell what color its fur was. He had the impression that before the little animal was thrown down, it had been used as a brush to paint the walls and floor with its own blood.

In all the years he worked Homicide, with the needler shootings, stabbings, and hatchet murders, in his years on patrol pulling dismembered and eviscerated bodies from wrecked cars, he had never seen anything that hit him quite like the wanton slaughter of one small pet animal. He retreated abruptly toward open air.

In the front entryway, he ran into Meda staring horrified at the destruction. "Who could—" She broke off, looking up at him. "Dee, what is it? You look ghastly." She peered past him toward the sleeping area. "What's in there?"

He pushed her outside. "I thought you were cooking supper."

"Gerel and D'ne came tearing down the stairs not a minute after you left, Gerel yelling something about D'ne reading trouble. I came after them."

The children outside were crying. The adults stood hugging and comforting them, eyeing Devane.

"Images," the tiger-striped Egara said.

The images of what he had seen inside? So that was what upset the children. Devane sighed. "I'm sorry, I—" How did one turn off thought? He swung toward Sinin. "Do you know anyone who—"

He broke that off, too, as Sinin stared unseeing at him. "Reason?" She buried her face against the top of her child's head.

Her helpless bewilderment moved him. This was something he and his officers would have to help these people do, to cope with their experience. "I don't know exactly why it happened to you, Sinin. Maybe we'll know when we learn who did it." He looked around. "Did anyone read anything here in the last couple of hours? I need a verbal answer, please."

The tiger-striped Egara said, "No."

"Did anyone *see* any strangers around here?"

A burly Egara with mathematical symbols bleached into chestnut fur stepped forward. "I."

That was luck. "Tell me what you saw."

The Egara considered. "Silent."

"Yes, but can you describe the Silent's appearance?"

The violet eyes regarded him solemnly. "Never looked."

So much for luck. Devane turned back to Sinin. "My

Criminalistics people are working only days. I'd like you to seal up the house. You and your child spend the night with a friend, please. And I know you're hurt and confused, but will you try to think of all the Silents you can remember having recent contact with? Write the names down tonight. Tomorrow we'll examine the house for evidence and I'll send an investigator to talk to you. We'll see if we can find who did this."

Sinin looked up at him. "Yes."

He patted her shoulder. "I'll have my people clean up the—"

The children whimpered.

He tried to think of something other than the luras. "I'm terribly sorry this happened." He looked around for Meda and found her hugging Gerel to her, as the adult Iregara were doing with their children. Crossing to her, he picked up Gerel. "Let's go on home."

"What made D'ne cry, Daddy?" Gerel asked.

Devane decided he could hardly tell the boy about the luras. "Sinin is upset. When one Egara hurts, all Iregara around him hurt."

"Why is Sinin upset?"

"Because someone whose pain Iregara can't feel did some bad things to Sinin's house. You'd feel bad if someone broke all your toys, wouldn't you?"

"Why did someone do bad things to Sinin's house?"

Devane sighed. "I don't know."

They reached the steps of their deck and Meda asked, "Is that the kind of thing they've brought you here for?"

He opened the door. "Yes."

She shuddered. "What kind of an—" She broke off, glancing at Gerel. "What are these Silents?"

"People with social circuitry gone skewers."

"People who do this kind of thing."

And worse, he thought, but did not say so aloud. "Yes."

She looked at the door. "I want a lock, Dee. I won't live here another day without a lock."

Thinking again, unavoidably, almost compulsively, of the luras, Devane nodded. "I'll have it installed tomorrow."

Chapter Three

THE SERGEANT who outfitted him had been right about the
uniform's insulation, Ten discovered. Sheathed in the
green-and-umber jumpsuit, he felt warm enough to believe
heating circuits had been built in along with those for the
paragee shield. The fit pleased him, too, smoothly snug
without a bind or uncomfortable crease anywhere. Looking
around the Investigations squadroom that had become his
orientation group's classroom, he decided they looked like
a prime outfit.

Seated on a desk facing them, Lieutenant Marin Hasejian
said, "Let's begin with the basic philosophy of this department."

Ten aimed his kinecorder at her and tapped the machine
on. Around him, twenty-three other leos did the same and
sat back comfortably in their chairs.

"So, as of now, you need to delete the terms *leo* and *lion*
from your vocabulary."

Twenty-four young police officers straightened in their
chairs, staring at Hasejian.

"On Egar," she said, "we're peace keepers, not law enforcement officers, and we have to stop thinking of ourselves as leos."

"That's reasonable, since there aren't any laws to enforce," Jael murmured to Ten and Roban.

Hasejian looked at her. "Why not share your observa-
tions with the rest of us, Officer Meadin?"

Jael shrugged. "I just said we can't enforce laws that
don't exist. D'shenegar has a loose, informal city council,
but it only administers the city and passes a few traffic and
trade ordinances, *mala prohibita* kinds of things. The Iregara are a cooperative but individually autonomous society. There's no formal government to pass real laws."

"Oh?" Hasejian almost purred. "You mean the violence the Iregara want stopped isn't legally wrong?"

Jael eyed the lieutenant warily. "Even without legislation there are still what we'd call *mala in se* offenses."

"Adroit answer. Now, have you anything else instructive to add, or may I have the floor again?" the lieutenant asked dryly.

Jael flushed. "No, ma'am—I mean, I'm through."

"Thank you. As I was saying, our objective is keeping the peace. If that can be accomplished without arrest and prosecution, that's ideal. Arrest should be considered a last resort except, perhaps, in cases of premeditated murder."

Last resort? Ten frowned. What did they do, then, make the perpetrators promise to be good and let them go?

Hasejian smiled. "I know what you're thinking. Of course this goes against everything we've practiced until now, but it's our baseline . . . keeping the peace. Part of the reason is very practical; there are no prisons aside from our detention wing, only care facilities for the mentally ill and incurable antisocials. Also, the Iregara don't consider violent Silents as criminals. We're supposed to think of them the same way, as social deviants, who are nonetheless held responsible for their actions, and to consider their behavior something we want to correct, not merely punish."

Ten raised a hand. "I understand that, lieutenant, but what's wrong with calling ourselves leos? It's what we *do* that's important, isn't it . . . not what name we give ourselves?"

"The name is very important, Officer Kampacalas. The name is everything. You know this is a telepathic society, don't you?"

Ten frowned in puzzlement. "Of course."

"Do you *comprehend* it? Why do you suppose telepaths bother to talk at all?"

Ten looked around for help. Jael and Roban wore knowing expressions but only grinned at his discomfort. Finally, with a helpless shrug, he said, "I don't know."

"The spoken word directs a listener's attention to the appropriate images and thought levels. A word raises mental images and the Iregara read the images. There are no masks possible here, no 'yes, sir, no, sir, have a nice day, sir' smiles covering thoughts like: 'I hope the high holies catch you flatdancing your secretary, you nago.' " While the class grinned, she went on, "We have to think and feel what we say, or else say what we feel. All of which brings me back to the matter of police nomenclature. What do you think about when you say *leo*, Kampacalas?"

Ten shrugged. "Nothing in particular. Just us."

"Oh? Is that why *leo* and *lion* are interchangeable, and why we call police stations *lion dens* or *lion country*?"

"Oh." Ten felt the flush heat his neck. "I guess I do think of the animal."

"Not a very appropriate image for a peace keeper, do you think?"

"What do we call ourselves, then?" someone asked. "*Keepers* makes me think of prison guards."

"Fortunately our employers have a solution." A smile flickered around the corners of Hasejian's mouth. "It seems a member of the police board has read a great deal of Terran literature, including history texts. The boardmember discovered that back in the thirteenth century, the king of England appointed a number of knights as Conservators of Peace. The boardmember, reading more contemporary history, said that by the twentieth century, the position had apparently become more commonly known by its acronym." The smile tugged harder at her mouth.

Ten worked out the acronym. COP?

"But criminal justice history says *cop* means *constable on patrol*," Pol said.

"Or that the term comes from the copper buttons on the early uniforms," Hasejian said. "No one really knows for certain. Perhaps the boardmember is right. At any rate, boys and girls, the police board has adopted the term. We are to be known officially as Conservators of Peace. They've tried out the name and the term *cop* on our fellow Terrans in the Enclave and found satisfactory, or at least neutral, images."

Ten tried the word. *Cop*. It rang flat and alien in his head, an arcane, obsolete term from ancient history, like *teamster* or *squire*. Cop. He could not feel it had anything to do with him or what he did at all.

Despite the warmth of his uniform, he found himself chilled. What were the Iregara trying to do to him? They wanted him to work here, to protect them, but in order to do so he had to give up his language and mathematics. He had to forgo living with his own kind. And now they wanted to take away his professional identity. Would they leave him anything of himself?

He only half listened to the lieutenant explaining department structure and the chain of command. The kinecorder was recording it all; he could replay it later. He groaned with everyone else on learning each watch would last twelve hours, but was pleased to hear that debriefings would be group meetings, not just soul-baring with a computer simulation hologram of an appropriate father figure.

"We need a give-and-take exchange of information," Hasejian said. "You won't all be in the same room; you'll be participating via holocom from storefront stations, but we hope to achieve the same result as a single group meeting."

"Storefront stations?" Jean Broussard asked.

"We've established a small station in the shopping plaza of each ishen cluster. There's a communications booth outside with a direct connection here for the benefit of the public, but the stations themselves are locked and unstaffed, intended mainly as supply depots and for briefings and debriefings. Working out of a storefront near your home and in your patrol will save you the time and transport energy of coming into the stationhouse every watch."

At seventeen hundred hours, still well short of midday, Hasejian ended the session for the morning and sent everyone but Jael, who already knew Isegis, down to Data for a Quickteach language lesson. In Data, Garith Hall, the department chief, led them back through the clerical and records sections to the Quickteach booths. There he handed them over to a black-furred Egara.

"Brithe is one of my best technicians," Hall said. "She'll set you up in the booths and monitor your session."

Ten eyed the Egara. She? He would not have known just by looking, though having been told her sex, he found himself reading femininity into her choice of bright yellow hip boots and the matching pouched belt slung low around her hips. He found her fur decoration feminine, too. Somehow she had tipped the hair with reflective particles so that each movement sent coruscating rainbows across her coat.

"Sit down, please," Brithe said in Translan, pointing them toward the booths. When they were all lying back in the chairs, she worked her way down the line, adjusting the helmets and clamping the biofunction monitors to their wrists. "Remember, the first series of patterns and tones means nothing; they're merely to put you in a receptive state. In any case, don't make an effort to concentrate. Just let your senses follow the patterns and sounds."

A series of flickering, random color patterns began playing before Ten's eyes and equally random notes sounded in his ears. Before long, however, a visual pattern developed. The sounds became music, whose melody he could almost identify. His pulse and breathing fell into phase with what he saw and heard.

Then the visual patterns changed again. The rhythm remained but between the colors, images flashed quickly. He saw symbols, heard sounds for the symbols. Briefly, he viewed a vast umber dry plain; an inland sea surrounded by green waterland. He saw a bicorned animal, an *irath*, and the symbol for irath, then a more complex symbol for an irath used for meat, a more complex one for a female meat irath, for a brown female meat irath, for a running brown female. . . .

Light blinded Ten as his helmet lifted free some time later. He closed his eyes and pressed his hands against his temples. Inside his skull, his brain felt like his stomach after a Thanksgiving feast, sluggish and stuffed to bursting.

"Stay seated."

The voice was Brithe's, but this time she spoke Isegis and Ten understood the words. He opened his eyes and tried to answer but could not find the words.

"Read," Brithe said. She pointed at an Egarad sign on the wall.

Ten stared at it. After a minute some lines of the characters made sense. Gradually, more took on meaning. "It's the operating instructions for the booths." The lesson lay in his mind dormant, waiting for the proper stimuli to activate it.

Near Ten, Pol pushed up from his chair with a groan. "Lordy, I surely do hate these educational hangovers."

"My advice to you all," Brithe said, switching back to Translan, "is go read a book cassette or ask someone to speak Isegis to you."

"How about you?" Ten asked. "Join us for lunch?"

Brithe stared at him. "I cannot."

Ten felt like kicking himself. What was he thinking about? Of course she would not be interested in subjecting herself to the bombardment of all their thoughts. "I understand. We're probably a shangie group of minds. I'm sorry if I upset you by asking."

She stared at him a moment longer, rainbows glittering on her throat and arms as her cutaneous muscles twitched, then suddenly, she smiled. For the length of time the expression lasted, Brithe looked remarkably near-human, and very amused. "Your minds don't bother me; I'm a Silent, but I still can't join you today. I'll see you for your lesson tomorrow."

Ten smiled back. "All right."

Jael rejoined the group in the canteen and she talked at them in Isegis. Ten dug out meanings for most of the words, but that did not always help make sense of what she said.

"Come on," he pleaded. "Use whole sentences."

She switched back to English. "All I have available in Isegis is nouns and verbs. Verbal words aren't intended to convey ideas, only key the mental concepts."

Ten had a feeling Isegis was going to be harder to use than he had anticipated.

After lunch the orientation group headed back to Investigations for the groundschool preparatory to checking out in Egarad vehicles.

While they waited for their instructor, Roban said, "I have a lot of sympathy for the Silents spending their lives trying to communicate in that language. It makes me appreciate why some of them tip off."

Jael shook her head. "I have no sympathy for any member of this society who won't act responsibly. If they try, the Silents can find constructive outlets for their frustration."

Roban frowned. "If humans had acted responsibly in the beginning, there wouldn't even *be* Silents. I should have thought that you, Jael, of all people would understand—"

The entrance of Lieutenant Hasejian and the flight instructor cut him off. Roban continued to eye Jael doubtfully through the groundschool session, however, and Ten wondered if the pending argument would begin after class. From groundschool, though, the group changed into exercise clothes for physical training, and the trainer, a burly Afro, gave none of them a chance for any kind of talking.

"Got to build you up," Ogilvie boomed at them. "Got to help you run and climb in this gravity. We'll start easy, a half hour of warm-up exercises and a six-iyah run."

The warm-ups, however, proved to be strenuous calisthenics and the run a blistering five and half kilometers over paths through the hills around the stationhouse. Most of the group lasted the distance, but collapsed as soon as they returned to the station courtyard. Ten lay flat on his back among the others, gasping, his lungs aflame and stomach churning. He fought not to throw up.

Next to him, Jael rolled onto her side. "I think . . . we're finished for . . . the day," she said between breaths.

"Finished . . . is right," Ten agreed. He closed his eyes.

She managed a breathless laugh. "I have an idea what to do with the rest of the afternoon."

"Nurse our shin splints?" Pol asked. He groaned. "Lordy, I could sure use a tub of hot water to soak in."

"I think we ought to house hunt."

Roban said, "I'll second that."

Ten opened his eyes again and rolled his head to look at her. "House hunt? Already?"

She sat up. "We have to do it sometime and I don't know about you in the detention rooms, but I find the floor of the exercise room hard and not very private. We came to see the planet and people, didn't we?"

"Yes," Ten had to admit. "All right, how do we do it?"

"The director's secretary has a list of vacancies around the city and an eight-day skyrail pass for each of us. Liril and I talked while you were down in the Quickteach booths. We use the passes to ride out and look the various places over. We talk to the neighbors and let them read *us*. And when we find a place we want where the neighbors want us, too, we're home."

Evaporating sweat cooled Ten down rapidly. Even lying on the sun-warmed pavement, he found himself starting to shiver. He pushed to his feet. "That sounds simple enough. As soon as I've had a shower and warmed up, let's go."

Chapter Four

"FIND A place yet?" Jael asked.

She and Roban sat down beside Ten in the Investigations squadroom.

Ten shook his head. "I'm getting discouraged." Jael had moved out of the station the first afternoon. She did have the advantage of finding a vacancy next door to a childhood Egarad friend, and Roban had found a place in the same cluster the next day. All along the detention wing, rooms were gradually emptying, and here he sat, still homeless after four days.

"Haven't you found a place you like?" Roban asked.

"A couple, but . . ." Ten shrugged. "They didn't seem interested in me."

"Ishen are more than housing complexes," Jael said. "It's the basic social unit, even more important than family ties. You've probably noticed the variety in architecture. There's the same psychological variety. Just keep looking."

He had indeed noticed the architectural variations. One shen looked like a rabbit warren, with the buildings so close the spaces between became mere alleys, while another set each cottage in a separate garden and a third put everything under a single dome so that it became, in effect, a single house with several hundred rooms. One thing they all shared in common, however, was bare rooms in the vacant unit and Iregara who regarded him with solemn, impassive faces when he asked about *furnished* vacancies.

"None," was the invariable reply.

The previous day he had finally asked why not. The golden-furred Egara showing him the housing unit, who, much to Ten's embarrassment, casually nursed an infant while she walked around the unit, looked up at him and asked, "Feel?"

28

He frowned in perplexity. What did she mean?

She touched her breast, then stroked the suckling baby. "Wrong?"

Heat came up his neck and face. "I'm not used—at home that isn't—isn't done in front of anyone."

She looked intently at him, as though reading his mind with her eyes. "Strange."

Ten agreed. How could the high holies loudly praise the Lord's Works and simultaneously declare the human body, undeniably one of those Works, something shameful? That is, he agreed intellectually with the Egara's opinion. In practice, however, although his parents had done their best to bring him up as free of the church as possible, he still found himself affected by church hypocrisy.

Acutely uncomfortable, he struggled to change the subject by repeating his original question. "Why don't you have any furnished units?"

The Egara switched the baby to her other breast. "Individual." She paused, regarding him without expression while Ten shrugged helplessly, not understanding her, then she tried again. "Person is individual," she said slowly. "Furniture equals person."

Comprehension dawned. Of course. He should have guessed that people who decorated their fur in such highly personal manners and lived in the great variety of housing they did would consider their homes an expression of individuality, too.

"One thing, anyway," Ten told his friends at the stationhouse with a sigh. "I'm learning the skyrail system very thoroughly."

"Do you have possibles you're checking today?" Roban asked.

"Oh, yes; I'm working my way down the list. Jael, what are the Iregara looking for in me? Someone who thinks like—"

He broke off as Hasejian came in. "Good morning, peace officers. How do you know where to respond to a call in your patrol?"

An officer raised her hand. "Learn the names and locations of the ishen and malls."

"How do you know where to respond if you're called to back up someone outside your patrol?"

Everyone waited for Hasejian to provide an answer. She crossed to the wall map, which showed D'shenegar as a U-shape around one long finger of Rahelem Bay. "We lay a grid over the city." She pulled down a plastic sheet marked with crosshatched lines. "Numbers on the north-south axis and Egarad phoneme symbols on the east-west axis. The stationhouse, for example, falls in the G-13 square. The squares are two klicks or two point two iyah on a side. There will be copies of this grid on your patrol vehicle control panels, so when you call in a location, give both the shen or mall name and the grid coordinates. In the meantime, the computer has printed out hard copies for each of you and I suggest you begin memorizing some of the major locations, such as the travelport, textile mills, and copper refineries."

She passed them copies of the gridded map as she talked. Ten identified the places she mentioned, and went further by locating Jael's and Roban's ishen, too, at F-13 and F-12.

Hasejian had little more for them that session. She dismissed them early for checkout flights in the police vehicles they would be operating.

"Why don't you switch turns with me?" Roban suggested as they headed for the v-pool. "Then you'll have all day to house hunt."

And with Roban's checkout time closer to Jael's, the two of them would have most of the day at liberty together, Ten thought, somewhat wistfully. Perhaps when he had a place to live he could remedy the present lack of female companionship in his life.

"Adeyanju," the flight instructor called.

Ten stepped forward. "Kampacalas substituting."

When he had checked out in all three vehicles, he caught the skyrail north. An Egara boarded at the same time he did. Sitting opposite on one of the seats running lengthwise down the skyrail car, Ten recognized the bright rainbow from the black fur visible above the collar of the cape the Egara wore.

"Hello, Brithe," he said in Translan.

For a moment, she did not react, then she turned her head slowly to look at him. "Kampacalas, yes?"

"Yes." He moved across the car to sit beside her. "They give you the day off?"

"Yes." She eyed him. "And you?"

"I'm looking for a place to live. Do you have a vacancy in your shen?"

"No."

Despite the shortness of her answer, he smiled. "Too bad." He sighed. "I really need a place."

She toyed with her cape, pleating it in her fingers. "Perhaps . . . you could try Meem Shen. It's in my cluster and I overheard someone in our shopping mall mentioning Iregara leaving there."

"Meem Shen." He checked it against his list. Yes, it had a vacancy. "Thanks. I'll look."

She smiled, and as it had the times she smiled before, the human gesture removed some of the alienness from her face. Ten would have liked to continue the conversation, but Brithe lapsed into a private daydream, leaving him to look at the other passengers or beyond them out the window.

Trees blurred as the train passed through a belt of woods, and were replaced quickly by a meadow with the look of parkland and a small lake lying clean and blue in the center. Animals grazed around it. He pulled their names from Quickteach knowledge in his head: compact little prong-horn, yellow-spotted ichehasha, the namesakes of one of the vehicles the police would be using; their taller cousins the longlegs; bicorned, three-toed irirath. Then the train plunged through woods again and came out sliding to a stop near a shen with low, broad houses of blue-gray stone.

Ten followed Brithe through two train changes. He judged they must be headed for the northeast section of the city. Disembarking for the last time at a hilltop station, he could see the seacoast ten or twelve kilometers to the east, confirming his guess.

Brithe pointed down a hard-topped path. "Meem Shen is that way one and one-half iyah. When you come to the fork, go straight."

He set off at a jog down the path. It cut through a heavy belt of woods and climbed a hill. His uniform boots carried him along easily on thick, supportive soles, but when several bicycles passed him from each direction, he longed for one. A bicycle would be faster and easier transportation between home, the shopping mall, and the skyrail station.

The woods ended just over the crest of the hill and he came down across the meadow to the shen huddled in the hollow between the hills. At the edge, he stopped, eyes widening in delight. It looked like something out of a fantasy: duplex and triplex houses of pink, orange, blue, green, and yellow, free-form and cornerless, with arched doors and oval windows, sitting shoulder-to-shoulder behind flower-filled gardens. The ubiquitous smoky-gray Sunsorb tiles covered their round, mushroomlike roofs. And the air smelled purple.

On Earth that would have seemed a brainbowed notion, but here, in this village, beneath the bronze sun and a day-faded red moon, he found it believable. The air smelled purple.

An Egarad child sat on the doorstep of one house playing with a furry, sharp-muzzled creature whose eyes looked as large and violet as the child's. Ten pulled the name from his memory: luras. Iluras seemed to be another factor all ishen shared. Ten had seen the little animals everywhere.

"Where is number two-twenty-seven?" Ten asked the child.

Face buried in the luras' golden fur, the child pointed.

Ten followed a path spiraling in through the shen, converging with other paths around the communal bath house. Following the direction of the child's finger, he took another path that led off to the left. Before he had gone very far he saw the number he wanted carved into a stone post on the left side of the entrance to a garden. Beyond it sat a blue duplex with oval, diamond-paned windows and arched red doors.

Ten knocked on the left-hand door. When no one answered, he opened it and peered in. The barren interior informed him this was the unit he had come to see. Stepping inside, an odd feeling of *déjà vu* nudged him. He looked around the rooms, trying to decide where he might have seen them or something like them before.

Three steps led down into a roughly oval sitting area with a bright orange carpet, sunny yellow walls, and a round fireplace in the center of the floor. An opening cut in an inside wall looked up into a kitchen with a built-in triangular eating nook. Beyond the kitchen lay the closet and the san. Ten saw no separate bedroom, but decided he could accept that. An efficiency-type apartment would suit him just fine.

Then, looking out one of the oval windows, he recognized the house and laughed aloud. "A hobbit hole."

"What?" asked a voice behind him.

Ten turned. On the steps stood an Egara. Ten opened his mouth to explain what a hobbit was but the Egara said, "Understand. Myth. Help?"

"I'm looking at the house. I'm—"

"Cop. Feel?"

He had no idea what lay behind the query, but the word itself made Ten aware that the Egara's silvery-gray coat, unmarked by any design, was longer and finer than others he had seen. It reminded him of the Persian cat his sister Miral had had when they were children. In fact, now that he thought about it, the Egara's face, broad and flat with its snubby nose and large eyes, looked remarkably similar to a Persian's, too. He remembered how Underfoot felt to pet, and the warm silkiness of her fur against his skin when she crawled under the covers with him on cold winter nights. The Egara's fur looked as though it would feel just like—

He broke off the thought in horrified embarrassment as the Egara, expressionless, extended an arm toward him in a clear invitation to touch it. He backed away. "No, that's all right . . . I didn't intend—I wasn't going to ask—oh, shit!" He hated himself for blushing and wished desperately that he could hide his head somewhere, although he knew that was pointless; it would not stop his thoughts.

The Egara came after him and before Ten realized the intention, grabbed his wrist and started for the front door. Ten protested, pulling back, but he might as well have been a child for all the result his resistance had. The Egara hauled him relentlessly forward. He stumbled on the steps, but the Egara only lifted him onto his feet again and kept going, out the front door and in the door on the other side of the duplex.

The sitting area there was larger but otherwise similar to the vacant side. The Egara pointed Ten toward a rolled sleeping mat/chair and when he was sitting, scooped up a black luras from another pile of cushions and dropped it into Ten's lap.

The luras looked up at him. "Brrrt?" it said. It rubbed its head against his hand. Automatically, Ten began to pet it. The luras settled into his lap.

"Siyan," the Egara said.

Ten hunted memory for the word.

"Name," the Egara said. "Siyan."

"Steven Kampacalas. I—I hope I didn't offend you in there."

"No. Feel?"

Again, he was unable to guess what the Egara meant. He tried to reason it out. The language had no spoken words for the various emotions, just the keying word *feel*. Perhaps Siyan wanted to know if he felt he had been offensive. No, the Egara would have already read that in him. Was the intended question *how do you feel*, then?

"No . . . feel improved?" Siyan asked.

Oh. "Yes, I feel better." Much better, in fact. Remembering the way Siyan had thrust the luras at him, he looked down at the creature. "Are you responsible?"

"Brrrt?" the luras said.

Siyan said, "Buffer."

The luras acted as a buffer? No wonder he saw so many around. But *he* was not telepathic; how could the luras affect him? He was about to ask Siyan when he saw something that made him forget all about the luras . . . a table with a stack of what he recognized as Egarad sheet music. He set the luras on the floor and crossed the room to the table. "Do you play a musical instrument?"

"Sing."

Ten smiled. "Sing?" How could they sing when they lacked language enough to speak sentences?

Siyan demonstrated. The Egara used no words, simply voiced notes as *ah*'s and *da*'s.

Ten did not recognize the musical passage but found it lovely. "Once I was a music major, back before I decided I could serve society more as a leo. I didn't sing, though; I played the piano and synthesizer." He picked up a sheet of music. "Do you sing professionally or for your own pleasure?"

"Professional," Siyan said. "City philharmonic."

Ten regarded Siyan with increased interest. "Really? What do the other people in the shen do?"

"Artists. Musicians. Dancers."

Was it like an artist's colony? This might be a very interesting place to live . . . if they would have him.

"I propose," Siyan said.

Siyan would? Ten smiled gratefully. "Thank you. When do I need to meet the others?"

"Not necessary. Read."

He did not try to figure out the thoughts behind that word. "When will I know about living here, then?"

"Tonight."

Jael and Roban were still at the station waiting for Roban's checkout flights when Ten returned. Jael collapsed whooping after he told her about the shen.

"Meem? That's delightful. The imeem are the Egarad version of the Little People. I hope you're accepted."

Ten hoped so, too, and he sweated out the long hours left in the afternoon and evening until thirty-six hundred hours, when the radio in his ear paged him to the phone. He took the call on the extension at the detention guard's station, waving a tense hand over the activator cell. "Kampacalas here."

"Siyan," came the reply.

Ten waited for Siyan to go on, missing the visual contact of Terran phones. Iregara needed their phone screens for writing, though. Idly, he wondered how advanced their technology had been before they learned to converse beyond telepathy range. Then lines began appearing on the screen, forming an Egarad character. A second and third character appeared, crowded onto the screen. Ten frowned, working at deciphering them. Even with Quickteaching, his reading skills were still slow.

He found the symbol for meeting in the first character, and pieced together the other elements to find they indicated general mood and numbers. What was this second character, though? He dug hard into his memory until recognition came: *drana*, whatever that concept meant. It had no Terran translation. The elements appeared to have something to do with variety. Shrugging, he went on to the last character, and there it was, easily read . . . a mind reaching out, a door open . . . invitation.

"Receiving?" Siyan asked.

Ten grinned. "Receiving," he replied in Isegis, then picked up the light scriber on the side of the phone and pushed the *clear* button. On the cleared screen he wrote a character of his own: *gratitude*.

Chapter Five

LITTLE HILLS Shen reminded Ten of some residential areas back in Topeka. The roofs rose in grassy knobs across the meadow, with only chimneys and short windows at ground level to indicate they were underground houses. Like back home, too, many of the houses had small vegetable gardens beside them. Ten tried not to let his mind dwell on the similarities, though, because that caused an uncomfortable tightness in his throat and he refused to admit he could be homesick already. He had been on Egar only sixteen days—twenty by local counting—and on patrol just seven. They had been uneventful days, though, with little excitement to keep his mind off Earth, except for one incident two days before in which a kite-glider collapsed in midair, killing its rider, an Egara named Haritheen, in the fall. Ten had given the case to Investigations after his examination of the fallen craft revealed partially-sawn struts. Roban, who had been made an inspector, was busy now trying to find out who might have reason to want Haritheen dead.

From somewhere nearby came the high voices of children in the First-Level school at play. Just off the path ahead of him sat the bath house, a dome of smoky Sunsorb material, with two adults inside. One lay face down on a wooden bench while the other rubbed talcumlike cleansing powder into the velvety fur.

"Good morning," he greeted them in English from the open doors.

They looked up. "Cop," the one lying down said.

The term still sounded odd to him, but at least he no longer felt a mental wince hearing it. "Yes. Officer Steven Kampacalas. I'll be patrolling this cluster most days."

As a child he had once seen a picture of a twentieth-century police officer, a big, brawny man in a blue suit,

36

twirling his baton on a thong as he walked his beat, smiling at the shop proprietors and schoolchildren he passed. Ten knew from his mirror at home that he looked nothing like the officer in the picture, but he felt as though he should and kept seeing his image superimposed over that of the other.

"Walk," Lieutenant Dorn Robbie reminded the Day Watch every morning at briefing. "That comes from the director through Captain Titus. I know you have a large area to cover, but right now patrolling the entire cluster each watch is less important than learning to know your patrol, and you can't learn much in a car fifty meters up. So move your rears out and explore on foot. Walk the woods, too. Meet people; talk to them; introduce yourselves. And think friendly."

Walking and thinking friendly was easy enough. The trouble came in talking. For example, he had introduced himself but these two Iregara had not reciprocated. Asking them their names would sound interrogative, so what did he say now?

Feeling awkward, Ten sat down on another bench, in a bronze shaft of sunlight, and pushed up his faceshield. "I'm here to protect you and keep the peace." Lord, that sounds clumsy, he thought.

Communications murmured in Translan over his ear radio, giving a time check and warning units near the S-23 area that Traffic agents would be coming to aid two downed vehicles. Traffic control remained the responsibility of D'shenegar's already established Traffic Department.

The one Egara began brushing the powder out of the other's coat with a brush that reminded Ten of the rice-root dandy brushes used for grooming the ponies on his grandfather's farm. The Egara even worked with the same short, brisk strokes Ten had been taught to use.

"Function," the Egara lying down said.

Ten did not follow the meaning but suspected the comment had to refer to his thought about grooming ponies. He rubbed the cleft in his chin, wondering if he could ever become accustomed to having his mind read.

Before either Egara could answer that thought, too, he stood and headed for the door. "If you have trouble, call us. I'm only minutes away."

Oh, to have Avel here, or any partner, for that matter, someone to talk to who would talk back. He would even settle for an occasional meeting with a good friend in an adjacent patrol, but Pol worked a cluster in the south leg of the city, Jael stood the Evening Watch, and Roban had been put in Investigations.

"North Twenty-five," the radio murmured.

Ten tapped his ear to activate his microphone. "North Twenty-five."

"Assault, Gural Finesmithing, Crafter's industrial mall."

Ten raced for the car grounded at the edge of the shen.

The Crafter's mall lay on the southeast edge of the cluster, four kilometers from Little Hills Shen. Ten took advantage of the opportunity to open up the Isinhar and made the flight in a minute and a half. He also indulged himself by setting the car down in the middle of the mall, normally forbidden.

Ten had made a point of walking the mall each watch, partially because it enabled him to meet a great number of people in a single area and partially because the maze of crafter's workshops fascinated him. So Ten had a fair idea where Gural Finesmithing lay and quickly arrived in the workshop to find a graying Egara sitting on a bench surrounded by fellow Iregara. Blood matted the fur above the left eye and soaked a strip down the left side of the victim's face and neck.

"What happened?" Ten asked.

The group around the victim stepped back and drifted away toward their workbenches. The victim looked up. "*Shele.*"

The word meant nothing to Ten. "I'm sorry; I don't understand."

"Attacked," said a russet-furred Egara with chevron designs down both arms.

Ten looked down at the victim. "I know you were attacked. Tell me about the incident."

"*Du,*" the Egara said.

Ten looked at the chevron-marked Egara again.

"Told," Chevron said.

Ten sighed. "I need a detailed account."

"*Yafare,*" the victim said. "*Nil'mun.*"

"Wait a minute." Ten pulled off his helmet and ran a hand through his hair. What was wrong with him today? He could not understand a word the victim said.

Chevron said, "Speaks Fasisi. Born Yeshir."

That would be a city, Ten judged. Fasisi must be the

local language, and the victim spoke it even though now in D'shenegar. Well, why not? Ten still spoke *his* native language. It raised a point Ten had never considered before, however: that Iregara had no need to learn new languages when moving from place to place, and that he might meet hundreds of people in the course of his job here who spoke languages he could not understand. It was something to mention at debriefing.

"I'll need you to translate for me, then," he told Chevron. "May I ask who you are?"

"Sunubas. Supervisor."

Ten tapped on his kinecorder and aimed it at the victim. "What's your name?"

"Far," the victim replied.

"Position here?"

"Artisan." Sunubas picked a length of red metal chain off the workbench behind Far.

Ten recognized it as a section of body chain some Iregara wore as jewelry. So far, so good. "What happened?"

"Working," Sunubas translated for Far.

"Then what?"

"Threen attacked." Sunubas swung the chain in demonstration.

Ten's eyes narrowed. "Threen? That's the name of the assailant? You know this person?"

"Yes. Artisan."

Now they were getting somewhere. "Describe Threen."

"Silent."

Ten resisted a desire to sigh. Patiently, he asked, "What does Threen *look* like?" He glanced around into one pair of impassive violet eyes after another. "Height?" he suggested. "Weight? Color? What was Threen wearing?" he asked, beginning to feel desperate. How could these people work with someone and not notice *something* about him?

"Apron," Sunubas replied, pointing at the apron the other artisans wore.

That was not much of a description. "Where does Threen live?"

Sunubas did not answer.

Ten raised a brow. "You don't have employment records that list the address?"

"Records," Sunubas said. "Workingtime, work units earned."

Ten gave in to his sigh. "Nothing else?"

"No."

He stabbed off the kinecorder and slipped it back in a thigh pocket. No, of course not. After all, they did not have the government or regulation that demanded detailed records. For all its faults, the government back home did offer innumerable kinds of help to the police, he reflected.

A high electronic beeping outside announced the arrival of an ambulance. Ten watched the attendants examine Far's wound, then picked up his helmet and followed them when they took the Egara out to the ambulance, which bore the Namis Hospital insignia. Unlike on Earth, Ten noticed, no onlookers crowded around either the ambulance or the shop door, but he also saw that no one in the workshops was working, either. He felt them all listening hard.

As the ambulance lifted off, beeping piercingly, Ten looked around at Sunubas standing in the workshop doorway. "Threen must have talked to someone once in a while. Doesn't anyone remember a shen name being mentioned? Does *anyone* know information that might help me find Threen?"

"I." A pregnant Egara with silky dark fur stepped out of the pottery workshop next door. "Talked."

"Did Threen mention a shen?"

"Nayan Shen." She pointed south. "Visited."

For no logical reason, Ten found his eyes slipping to her swollen belly.

"Yes," she said.

Even in the midst of his embarrassment, Ten recognized that he had learned one useful fact: Threen was male.

"Reason?" Sunubas asked.

Did they never stop reading thoughts? Ten turned toward the supervisor. "Because description will help us iden—"

"Misunderstand," Sunubas interrupted. "Attacked. Reason?"

Damn, Ten thought. He had been distracted by getting Threen's description and had forgotten to ask about possible motives for the attack. "Did anyone notice an altercation before Threen hit Far with the chain? What were they doing?"

Sunubas considered. "Consulting. No argument."

Ten sighed. "You think about it. If you remember anything that might have caused Threen to attack, ask headquarters to tell me. I'll come back. Meanwhile, which way did Threen run?"

An Egara in the area outside pointed west.

Ten headed for his car, calling in the meager information he had. Iregara usually lived close to where they worked, so if Nayan Shen lay south, that probably meant in the nearest cluster. He asked Communications to notify Jone Weider, the officer in that patrol, just in case Threen went home. Ten took the Isinhar up and headed west. Threen had a big head start, but maybe Ten would get lucky.

Crafter's Shen lay closest, a bit under a kilometer to the immediate west. Between the mall and shen grew thick woods. Ten tried to guess Threen's mental processes. Would he keep going west toward the skyrail, or stick to cover and turn south for home? Would Threen even expect pursuit? Ten had not the slightest idea. He wondered if he would even recognize the Silent if he happened to see him. If only he could have gotten a physical description. Why did the Iregara spend so much effort bleaching and dying their coats if no one ever noticed the designs? For themselves alone?

Ten saw nothing but treetops between the industrial mall and Crafter's Shen, and nothing but semiwild ichehasha and irirath in the more open meadow immediately around the shen. He landed and walked through the clustered geodesic domes. He met a fair number of people on the way and talked to each, but none of them had noticed a Silent passing through. He stopped at the school, too, where he found himself the instant object of intense, unabashed curiosity. The children crowded around him, saying words with a question mark at the end of each.

"I'll come back and answer all your questions another day." Good public relations. "Right now, though, *I* have a question."

"Saw," three children called simultaneously.

Anticipated again. "A Silent, wearing a metal artisan's apron?"

"Yes."

"Where—"

They pointed northwest.

Ten raced back for the car.

He found an Egara only a short distance beyond, following a path down through the fields toward the shopping mall. Slowing the Isinhar as he passed over the Egara, Ten tried to decide if this were Threen. The Egara did not act guilty, but walked along at a leisurely pace, completely in the open. The Egara wore an apron, however.

Ten set the car down ahead of the Egara and swung out. "Threen?"

"Yes," the Egara replied in Translan.

"Police," Ten said in the same language. "I'd like to talk to you."

Threen bolted for the woods.

As Ten started after him, he mentally thanked Ogilvie for the killing runs around the station. Ten still noticed the heavier gravity, and wished for less, but he withstood it. He was almost on top of Threen when they reached the woods. Suddenly the Silent ducked and came up and around swinging a length of dead branch.

Ten's faceshield saved his nose. He grabbed for the end of the branch. Threen, however, did not try to pull free. He merely withdrew a step and came back, thrusting the branch forward end-on. Despite Ten's hold, the Egara's greater strength drove the branch into Ten's chest. The paragee field was no protection against that kind of attack. The force of the blow shoved him backward and off his feet. He landed flat on his back on the ground.

Threen hurled the branch down on him and whirled away again. This time Ten did not try to give chase. Instead, he drew his sleeper and fired. The narcolepsy induced by the frequency of the sleeper's beam folded Threen in his tracks. Rubbing the sore spot on his chest, Ten made his way over to the downed Egara. He hefted Threen experimentally. Heavy. Rather than try to carry the Silent back to the car, then, Ten pulled Threen's wrists behind his back and secured them with the wrap strap, then sat back to wait for him to regain consciousness.

"I didn't do anything," Threen said in a flat voice.

Ten spared only a glance for his prisoner seated beside him before returning his attention to the Isinhar's instruments. "So why did you run away from me?"

"I—I misunderstood. I thought . . . you were threatening me."

"You sound like you speak Translan well enough."

"I learned it from Silents to talk to other Silents, never a Terran before. Your accent is strange."

Ten raised a brow. "Silents use Translan to talk? Not Isegis?"

"Talking in Isegis is impossible."

"Why did you attack Far with that chain?"

Threen's impassive expression never flickered. "I didn't attack Far."

Ten rubbed the sore spot on his chest. "Far's head just started bleeding by itself, I suppose."

"I threw the chain at that insufferable fishbrain and walked out in disgust. Maybe the chain hit somewhere; I never looked to see."

Ten eyed Threen. Could that be possible? Sunubas said Threen attacked and Iregara were supposedly incapable of lying, but Ten had interviewed enough witnesses to know how deceiving one's perception could be. Threen's story had plausibility and he sounded sincere. He looked straight at Ten, unblinkingly calm, with none of the subtle signs that would have told Ten a human was lying. Threen not being human, though, Ten doubted he could apply the same criteria. Besides, he also knew humans who could tell blatant lies with the serenity of an angel. Ten decided he had no way of knowing for certain whether Threen was honest or only an earnest liar.

He set the car down just outside the Gural building. "Sunubas," he called, taking his prisoner into the workshop, "is this Threen?"

The supervisor looked up from some paperwork. "Yes. Reason?"

"I need a positive identification. Is this the person whom you saw—"

"Misunderstand." Sunubas looked at Threen. "Reason?"

"Misunderstand," Threen replied sullenly. "Explain."

"Far. Reason?"

Ten said, "I think Sunubas is asking why you attacked Far."

Threen pointed at Sunubas. In Isegis, Threen said, "Reason. You."

The supervisor's pupils dilated. "Me?"

"I asked, not partner Far, me. I misunderstand Far. Far misunderstands me." Threen looked at Ten. "And despite that," he said in Translan, "she still partnered us."

Sunubas stared hard at Threen. "Reason?"

Threen's ears flattened. "You know."

Ten noticed Sunubas was breathing harder, though the flat face remained impassive. "Not know. Asking."

Threen's hands clenched. "How does she expect *me* to know why she made me work with Far on that project?"

Sunubas snapped, "Misunderstand Far. Reason?"

The rising tempers brought Ten between the two of them. "To save further misunderstandings, why don't I answer the question? Threen and Far can't understand each other, supervisor, for the same reason *I* couldn't understand Far, because Far speaks Fasisi and Threen, like me, understands only Isegis."

Sunubas' pupils dilated. "Ah." Enlightenment filled the word.

"You mean you never realized that before?" Ten asked in astonishment.

"No. Understand."

Ten decided to take nothing for granted. "You understand what?"

"Far."

As any Normal would. So, Sunubas disregarded Threen's pleas of misunderstanding and assigned the two to the project. Ten could well imagine Threen's frustration under the circumstances. Given the same situation, Ten thought he might have lashed out with that chain, too. He regarded the Silent sympathetically, regretting the necessity of arresting him. "Let's go, Threen."

On the way back out to the car, he tapped on his radio. "North Twenty-five requesting a backup unit for prisoner transport."

"North Two en route," Communications replied a few moments later.

North Two? That would be Mete Lessman, his sergeant. Ten frowned. Why was Lessman coming? Sergeants did not usually make prisoner pickups.

"North Two requests a meet one *yah* east of Crafter's mall," Communications added.

A *yah* east? In the middle of the fields? That was not normal procedure, either. Ten flew to the meeting point with a knot of apprehension in his stomach.

When Sergeant Lessman arrived she first locked Threen in the back of her car, then walked Ten away from the vehicles. "I thought you'd rather talk out of range of listening minds," she said.

Ten eyed her warily. She reminded him in many ways of

Avel, a battle-scarred she-lion pared down to sinew, raw-hide, and long, sharp claws. "What did I do wrong?"

"Perhaps nothing, but Captain Titus, which means Director Brooks, wants arrest situations checked before actual booking. Give me all you have on this."

Ten told her everything, then handed her his kinecorder to play back. Lessman listened, watching the tiny screen thoughtfully. "You didn't record Threen's version of the incident?"

Despite her mild tone, Ten felt hot breath on his neck. "I was planning on taking a formal statement at the station."

"After booking? You think Threen is lying, then?"

He shrugged helplessly. "I don't know. I'm sure Sunubas and Far are sincere, so I feel I have to act on that."

"You're probably correct."

Ten still did not relax.

"However, there is one thing I've noticed on this playback that we need to talk about."

His stomach tightened. Here it came.

"All your questions are directed toward identifying Threen. You were anxious to start the chase, weren't you?"

"Yes," he replied slowly. "I guess so."

She sighed. The knot in Ten's stomach jerked even tighter. He knew that sigh. It was the same one his father always used before saying: *This is going to hurt me worse than it does you.*

"What's our primary function in D'shenegar?" Lessman asked.

He looked steadily at her. "Keeping the peace."

"And when responding to a call, to whom is our first duty?"

Damn, he had forgotten that in his eagerness to collect facts about the incident and assailant. "Sergeant—"

"To whom is our first duty, Officer Kampacalas?" she repeated.

Ten looked down at his boots. "The victim."

"To alleviate the psychological trauma by giving support and comfort."

Ten protested, "Aren't there doctors and counselors for that kind of thing? Don't we have enough of a job just tracking down the nagos who—"

Lessman interrupted sharply, "We have the primary contact with the victim. That period of time immediately after the incident is of critical importance in the future mental health of the victim."

Ten had heard it all before, first from Brooks during the job interview and then repeatedly during orientation. Somehow, though, it had sounded different then, progressive and humane, and a natural function. Here and now, Ten could only think how far Threen could have run while the responding officer sat nursing Far's psyche.

"Personally," Lessman said, "I think you did a good—" She broke off. "But it doesn't matter what I think personally. That's based on Terran standards of performance and this isn't Earth. I have my orders, and when we signed those contracts, we both agreed to play by Egarad rules, didn't we?"

And Devane Brooks's rules. Ten studied his boots, tight-lipped. "Yes, ma'am."

She put an arm across his shoulders. "Don't worry about this. We'll keep it off the record. I'll take Threen in and get a statement without booking him, then send someone over to—what was that hospital?"

"Namis."

"Over to Namis Hospital to talk to Far. This doesn't sound like a premeditated act to me. We may be able to settle it without an arrest. Since the workshop supervisor is aware of the problem between Far and Threen, it shouldn't happen again. You go on back to work." She patted his shoulder.

Ten did not find the gesture much of a comfort.

"I don't know how most of you deal with Normals all your lives without going over the brainbow," Ten told Brithe late that afternoon after he had gone off duty.

Brithe looked up from a printout. "You now pity Silents?"

The barb in her voice stung. For a moment Ten wondered whether he had been wise coming down to Data. Perhaps he should have gone on to the exercise room. "I don't pity Silents," he said, "and I don't excuse the deviant ones; I don't believe violence is ever a justifiable response to frustration, but . . . I'm beginning to sympathize with them."

"I despise them," Brithe snapped. "Most of them are cretins."

Was it possible for him to slink away before she ripped him apart? He started to back away.

"Why are you down here so late?" she demanded.

Too late to run now. "Well . . . I picked up a subject earlier today. I was interested in knowing whether he was charged with anything."

"Case serial number?"

He gave her the one from his call response report.

Brithe's hands touched the keyboard. "Hard copy?"

"No, thanks. That isn't necessary."

"No charge made," she read from the screen. "The victim declined on condition of payment of medical bill." She snorted. "That's a prime example of stupidity . . . attacking a coworker. Pure impulse and temper. There are better ways of dealing with frustration."

"Like you do?" Ten asked.

She stared hard at him for a moment, cutaneous muscle movement making rainbows across her fur.

"However you do it," Ten said. "You appear to cope well."

She smiled. "I think I do. Is there anything else you need?"

He liked her when she felt like being friendly. Could he prolong her mood? "No, but now I'm curious why you're working late."

"I'm developing a program to correlate complaints and determine which perpetrators and victims are repeatedly involved in incidents." She eyed him. "Can I answer any more questions?"

What a perfect opening she had given him. "One more . . . would you like to go somewhere with me this evening? I'd like to know you better."

"Go where?"

He tried to think of a place. The shen being the center of social life, D'shenegar had no clubs or bars, and its only restaurants served the guesting houses, small places nothing like hotel restaurants on Earth.

"How about a concert? My neighbor is singing in a symphony performance tonight."

"I never go to concerts," she said shortly.

He was losing her. Quickly, he suggested, "How about gambling?"

D'shenegar boasted twelve public and a number of private tracks running irirath, inege, and cars, and at least one chance house could be found in every shopping mall. Initially, Ten had wondered how telepaths could gamble, but understood when he found they did not play cards. Instead, they gambled on any race or game that was won by pure luck or physical skill. Going gambling particularly interested Ten. With everything similar being lion meat for vice officers at home, indulging here carried the spice of the illicit. "Let's go to a track."

"I can't tonight." She shut off her keyboard. Standing, she lifted her cape from a hook by the door. "Ask me another time."

"And get turned down again?" he muttered. But she was already gone and did not hear. Ten sighed. Why did he keep trying to be friendly? As much as he wanted to comply with the director's suggestion that they mix with the locals, was this worth it?

He trudged upstairs to the exercise room and changed into running clothes. Maybe a few fast kilometers would work out his frustration.

Out on the track, Pol came up alongside and fell into step with him. "Howdy, podner. Come to run off some mad?"

"I come because it's the one place in town I can find a shower."

Pol laughed. "Hell of a job, isn't it? Hell of a place, too. My folks were marines and we must have lived mighty near everywhere on Earth one time or another, but I've never been anywhere like this before."

"Amen!"

Pol laughed at Ten's heartfelt tone, then both fell silent, saving their breath for running.

At the end of five kilometers, they quit and headed for the shower. Under the steaming water, Pol said, "Running is good for the body, but you know what we really need? Bara Deem, that blonde from St. Paul who's South Twenty-seven on our watch, has been telling me about this wine she's found from the eastern Iseg waterlands. She says it's as good as any on Earth. Why don't I invite her to bring the wine and a friend for you over to my place this evening?"

That sounded like the best idea Ten had heard all day.

In Ten's ear, his radio murmured, "South Eleven, subject breaking windows in the Heerus shopping mall."

"Have fun, South Eleven. Better you than me," Ten said, and prodding in his ear with his little finger, deactivated the implant. The radio was one part of his job he could live without tonight.

Chapter Six

SOMEWHERE CLOSE a baby wailed. Ten fought his way up out of warm sleep into the cold dawn. Outside his window, the wail turned into a chorus of giggles.

"What—"

Breath tickled his chest beneath the blankets. "You don't have any windows open, do you?"

"Lord, no." The Sunsorb roof tiles absorbed enough sunlight to warm the house during the day and hold the heat most of the night, but by morning the temperature had always dropped enough to let Ten see his breath when he talked.

The giggles turned to wails once more. Ten sat upright, clutching at the blankets. "What the hell is out there?"

"Igelis." Phaedra Melandros flung back her side of the blankets and ran to the nearest window. "Come and look." She seemed unconscious of either her nakedness or the cold.

Ten watched her with pleasure, as he shivered in the chill air her exit had admitted and tightened the blankets around him on the sleeping mat to plug the hole. She looked as elegant as her name sounded.

"I thought you two might phase, both being Greek," Bara Deem had said, introducing them the night before.

Only Phaedra was real Greek, a marine biologist from the island of Kithnos, on Egar to study the adaptation of marine-life forms to the extreme salinity of evaporating old seas like the Iseg. She spoke Translan, but no English.

"There must be fifty or sixty in the troop," she said from the window. "You ought to see this."

"It isn't worth freezing for."

She turned to laugh at him. "Don't be a sissy. The cold will toughen you. Come *on*."

50

Gritting his teeth, Ten threw back the blankets and as goosebumps rose on him, dashed to the window. He wrapped his arms around Phaedra to take advantage of her body heat, then almost forgot the cold as he looked past her out the window.

The garden teemed with tiny life forms some fifteen centimeters high. Remembering the shen's name, Ten thought instantly of elves, elves with russet suits and golden manes of hair . . . only the "elves" here had long prehensile tails. One jumped up on the outside of the window and explored the edges with its tiny hands. A worried, wizened old man's face peered at them.

Ten grinned. "They're cute."

"They're vermin. Look at them . . . destroying your garden."

The flagstones lay littered with flower petals and with the red and golden leaves from Siyan's prized hegen'shu and medehela trees. Ten groaned. "Oh, shit; Siyan will—"

Siyan erupted from the other side of the house, barefurred, barefooted, and yelling, firing a sleeper in long, swinging sweeps. Siyan's luras launched itself past the Egara with a squeal of excitement and into the troop of igelis. Shrieking, the igelis dodged both the luras and the sleeper beam.

"If you'd left a window open, they would have been all over in here this morning," Phaedra said.

Ten shuddered at the thought. "How do we get rid of them?"

"Knock them down with a sleeper the way your neighbor is, or wait for the cavalry."

Ten blinked. "Cavalry?"

"There." She pointed.

Ten saw them, five creatures of three different species, coming up the path and across the gardens. But before he had time to identify them, they were on top of the igelis troop. The garden exploded into a melee of shrieking igelis and charging predators—black-maned and black-striped, tawny-striped, and white-spotted gray—mowing their way through the fleeing little primates with jaws snapping. Siyan snatched up the luras and fled for the house.

"My god," Ten gasped.

"When igelis leave the cover of the woods, it's picnic time," Phaedra said. "Here come iree, too."

Several species of raptors swooped down out of the sky

for their share of the game. In five minutes it was all over. The iree left clutching igelis carcasses in their talons; the dorsal-maned balach fled after gulping down several small bodies; and the white-eyed adu settled its stocky body in the middle of the bloodied flagstones to eat at leisure while the three irashuneg, who looked vaguely half-tiger and half-hyena, prowled snarling, snatching up carcasses the smaller but fiercer adu passed over. Ten whistled.

"Quite a wake-me-up, isn't it?" Phaedra said. "That's what comes with a city that has forest and wild animals in it."

She started to turn away from the window. What that did was turn her in Ten's arms to face him. He took full advantage of the position to kiss her. "It's only eleven," he murmured. "Day Watch doesn't start until fourteen hundred hours. We have plenty of time to climb back into bed and warm up."

She laughed. "I don't think you need more dancing to warm up, but all right, if you let me turn on the vid for the early news. You do have channel subscriptions, don't you?"

"Only two. I'm being well paid but I hate putting too much on credit before I see that first salary statement. Buying the house, furniture, and bicycle has me indebted enough for the time being." He snapped his fingers in front of the big wall screen's activator and pulled Phaedra back toward the mat. "It's on, but don't plan on having much chance to read."

She did not manage to do so for some time, but while he lay dozing in post-coital lassitude, she not only watched the news but read pieces out loud to him: about the plains fire around Anidel in the Gedin Drylands; the result of marathon-type races being run in Idin; a new underwater copper-mining site off the coast near D'shenegar; a city council meeting to be broadcast on the service channel that evening to discuss increasing donations and pledges for the city operations fund.

"Donations. These people are incredible," Phaedra said with a sigh. "At home they'd pass a new tax and just take the credit from us." Then she gasped. "Ten, look!"

He rolled over. On the screen green-and-umber uniformed figures milled around something on the ground. The picture flickered to a paragee stretcher being loaded into an ambulance. His eyes dropped to the text band below the picture but it rolled sideways too fast for him to interpret the characters. "What is it?"

"A cop was found dead outside the Harachad Textile Mill last night, an Officer Aaron Wofford. Found when——"

"A cop!" Ten sat bolt upright. He prodded his ear with his little finger, activating the radio, then jumped off the sleeping mat. "Does it say how he died?" Ten grabbed his uniform from the closet off the kitchen and pulled it on.

Something cold crawled up his spine. Officers died all the time on Earth, but . . . he had not expected it here.

"He was found in an pond near the mill."

Ten pressed the front seam of the jumpsuit closed. The cold moved through his back into his stomach and sat heavily. "Come on, get up; I have to go."

Together they folded the sleeping mat with the blanket inside and buckled on the long back cushion that turned the mat into a couch. Phaedra dressed while Ten wiped off his beard at the mirror on the san door. He listened for any radio dispatches that might tell him more than the vid news, but only time checks broke the air silence.

He unrolled his collar, making a hood to cover his ears until the day warmed up, then pulled on his helmet. "If this is high summer, thank god Egar doesn't have much seasonal variation or I'd hate to think what winter would be like." Opening the door, he stuck his head out and looked both ways.

Phaedra cocked a brow. "What are you doing? Making sure the coast is clear before sneaking me out? Don't you realize that everyone around already knows I'm here?"

Ten grinned sheepishly. "Automatic reflex."

Outside in the garden, a few bloodstains and scraps of hair were all that remained of the igelis picnic.

Walking his bicycle, Ten escorted Phaedra to the skyrail station. There, he pushed up his faceshield and kissed her goodbye. "I hope we can see each other again."

"Bara being my neighbor, I'm sure we will. Call me in a couple of days. You can ask your neighbors how much I enjoyed dancing with you." Then she laughed. "You're even cuter when you blush."

He jerked down his faceshield. "I'm *never* going to get used to having no privacy for *anything*."

She sobered abruptly. "Ten, I hope you can. You have to if you're ever going to be able to live here."

He was beginning to wonder why any Terran would want to.

The door of the storefront station in the D'she shopping mall scanned the code on Ten's palm and slid open to admit him. A wave of his hand activated the holocom, joining the storefront to the stationhouse briefing room. The dais at the front still sat empty, but uniformed officers milled around the rest of the room, walking through the projected images of the desks but apologizing when they accidentally encroached on each other. Ten estimated that most of the sixty-eight officers on the watch had arrived, including Pol, who stood toward the back talking to Bara Deem. For once, however, the innumerable conversations shared a single topic: Aaron Wofford.

Before long the room was full, a medley of green and umber, and as the chronometer above the dais registered 13:30, Lieutenant Dorn Robbie mounted the dais, followed by Sergeants Mete Lessman and Benne Cathcart. Conversation died away. The officers sat down, each finding the desk in his or her own storefront among the projected rows.

"Good morning, peace officers," the lieutenant said. He glanced down at the indicator lights on his lectern. "All storefronts are activated." His eyes moved around the room. "I don't suppose there's any point in trying to talk business until you've asked about Officer Wofford. So, in the hope of making this faster, I'll anticipate those questions and give you all the information we have." Robbie took a breath. Ten thought the breath trembled, but when the lieutenant spoke, his voice emerged flat and steady. "Last night at thirty-four-oh-seven Wofford was dispatched to the Harachad Mill to investigate a complaint of someone screaming. He reported arrival at thirty-four-fifteen. At thirty-four-thirty-one, sixteen minutes after arrival, Communications asked for a status check as procedure requires. Officer Wofford failed to respond. Communications called again and still received no response. Accordingly, Sergeant James Gerhardt, the south leg sergeant, was notified. Sergeant Gerhardt and two units proceeded to the scene to institute a search for Officer Wofford. At thirty-five-oh-two Officer Nile Paretski found Officer Wofford floating face down in a small pond one half kilometer east of the Harachad Mill. Workers in the mill who were questioned had read nothing unusual. Two reported Wofford within their perceptive range but read no fear or alarm in him. An autopsy is scheduled for this morning but as of now, it appears he drowned. That's all the information we have. When we know more, the grapevine will probably inform you long before official word reaches me," he said wryly. "So, shall we proceed to the business of this watch?"

Ten had a dozen questions but refrained from asking them. The lieutenant probably had none of the answers.

Robbie read off the list of violent incidents occurring during the night: two arsons, three assaults, and a half-dozen cases of vandalism. "As usual, we have almost no descriptions of even those perpetrators who were seen. When you talk to people today, keep stressing the importance of *looking* at the subjects committing these offenses. Keep trying to make people understand that we need cooperation if we're going to serve effectively . . . like this case: a Silent was observed cutting the spokes of bicycles in the Heemal Shen. That's in your patrol, Wassom. The witness says the suspect is named Ger'mal: G gelis, E erim, R ree, apostrophe, M meem, A adu, L luras. The suspect has a body-chain design bleached into yellow-brown fur and is believed to live somewhere in the area because the witness has seen the suspect in the shopping mall on several occasions."

"How'd we get so lucky?" Pol asked.

Robbie smiled. "If I interpret these characters in the report correctly, it was the opinion of the responding officer that sexual attraction may have caused the witness to notice the suspect more than normal." He shrugged. "Of course, we don't know which of the two is which sex. Anyway, Wassom, ask around. There are probably a hundred Ger'mals in D'shenegar, but see if you can locate this Silent one."

Pol sighed.

"You have some objection to that, officer?" Robbie asked sharply.

Pol stiffened. "Oh, no, sir, it's just—I know how these people feel, what they go through. I can understand why they tip off. Chasing them isn't much—" He broke off.

"Fun?" Sergeant Cathcart finished for him. "The victims don't find these incidents very much fun, either. Try thinking of them if you need incentive."

Pol's jaw tightened. "Yes, sir."

Robbie went on, "In response to incident levels charted by the computer, we're changing some patrols. I know," he said as the groans went up around the room. "You just memorized the names and locations in your cluster, right?"

But none of the changes affected Ten or other permanent patrols, however, only two floating officers in the west, who were shifted south to overlap patrols around the textile mills.

"From now on, the computer may also order impromptu checks of particular areas, so don't be surprised if you're suddenly sent off on a side trip in mid-watch," Robbie said. "All right, that's all. Go to work."

Devane sensed rather than heard Meda's sigh and hesitation as they stepped into the station forecourt. He glanced from her to the entrance with its large yin-yang symbol. "What's wrong?"

She shrugged. "Just resigning myself to another day of routine chemistry and one-word sentences. I wish we had more Terrans in the lab, or something more challenging for me to do."

He tugged at an ear. "Unfortunately, we're committed to filling all positions possible with local people. Can't you talk to Bioni Elanca?"

"She's the chief, Dee. She doesn't have time for casual chicha."

He eyed her as the doors opened for them and they stepped into the reception area. Meda probably did get bored and lonely around there in the lab; she had always been a talented chemist and a gregarious person. He could do little to improve the job, but perhaps he could help another way. He stopped at the point they usually separated to head for their respective wings. "Come round to my office when you take a break and I'll have some coffee with you."

She brightened. "Are you sure you have time?"

"I'm the boss, remember; I do what I want." He kissed her, enjoying the feeling of defying propriety by such a public display.

Meda stiffened but did not pull back from him. He noted her reaction with satisfaction. Egar must be good for her; she was relaxing, easing out from under her inhibitions. "Just come on around."

Turning away from her, he saw the wiry form of Captain Dane Basanites waiting for him by the U wing corridor.

"Morning, sir," the head of the Investigations division said. "Sorry to have spoiled your evening the way we did last night."

The warm thoughts of Meda disappeared beneath grimmer ones. "It's all right. Give me everything we know about Wofford so far." He headed down the corridor for his office.

Basanites kept pace with him. "Everything we have is what I gave you last night."

"What about the autopsy?"

"It's this morning."

"Who's doing it?"

"A Dr. Sherur at Methim Hospital."

Devane stopped, frowning. "An Egara?"

"Dr. Sherur is an experienced pathologist with some previous work on Terrans. Dr. Goodnight from our infirmary will be assisting, too, to help on anatomical questions."

"All right." Devane moved forward again. He passed through his outer office, greeting his secretary Liril, and went on into his office. "What about Criminalistics?"

"They're processing his clothes and car now."

Devane dropped into the chair behind his desk. "We might have to put a night crew in there. But that's Tova Craig's division; I'll speak to her about it." He ran a hand over his hair. "What do you think, Dane? Did he get careless and fall in or . . . was he lured out there and killed?"

Basanites shrugged. "I don't think we have enough to even guess about that yet. No witnesses sensed anything unusual and the preliminary medical examination didn't find any signs of violence."

"Which means we have to wait for results from the lab and post, I guess." Devane sighed. "Let's hope it was an accident."

"Lord, yes," Basanites agreed.

"Let me know the minute you have anything new."

"I will."

Instead of leaving, however, Basanites lingered by the door. Devane eyed him. "Is there something else?"

"Unfortunately, yes. Lieutenant Hasejian brought the matter up. It seems the inspectors resent being asked to build a case for the defense as well as the prosecution."

Devane leaned back, sighing. "Yes, I suppose they do."

"What do you want to do about it? You know what's happening, of course; they're working hard to find evidence of guilt and giving the suspect's side only half-hearted attention, if any. I can't say I blame them. None of us trained to work for the defense."

"We have to learn to do it, though. Our cases go before a mediator just like the civil suits," Devane said. "There are no lawyers for either side. We're all the defendant has to work for him. Try reminding them of that."

Basanites raised his brows. "You don't think that's going to convince them, do you?"

"If it doesn't, we'll . . . think of something else."

"Yes, sir." This time Basanites left.

Devane stared at the closed door for several minutes. Come to Egar and set up a police department. It had sounded so simple. Simple was not exactly how he would characterize the job now. On the other hand, he thought, touching a stack of hard copy on his desk, even the most complex machinery disassembled into simple pieces. Deal with the pieces and perhaps the whole machine would work. He picked up the sheets of printout and went to work on the pieces.

Liril appeared in the doorway some time later. "Visitor. Civilian. Dismiss?"

A secretary who knows how the boss feels and thinks could be an advantage sometimes. He smiled. "I wish I could let you do that, but . . . who is it?"

"James Booker Paulus."

Devane's brows rose. "Three names?" Liril usually announced people by the names they called themselves.

"Thinks," Liril said.

Devane tugged an ear. "And *what* is this person who thinks of himself by three names?"

"Deviant."

Devane straightened, startled. "What?"

"Zealot."

He relaxed, smiling. "Terrans can be highly emotional without being unstable. Show the gentleman in."

Nevertheless, as James Booker Paulus entered the office, Devane found himself thinking that Liril's assessment of the visitor had not been far wrong, after all. As Devane's profession stamped him indelibly for many people, so was Paulus marked by his: churchman . . . high holy.

Paulus held out his hand. "It's good of you to see me, Director Brooks. I know you're a busy man."

Devane shook the hand. "So you'll understand that I need you to be brief. What can I do for you?"

"It's more a matter of what I believe I can do for you. Your officers have been on Egar about three weeks, haven't they? And I haven't heard that you brought a chaplain. You must find this a spiritual desert."

"We've been very busy," Devane said carefully.

"Oh, I'm sure, but work and an alien world is no reason to slip into the habit of recusancy. I serve as pastor for the Enclave ESB church and I'll be very happy to hold a service for your men every day, too."

Devane wanted to toss the high holy out through the window. He kept smiling. "We have no facilities for a service," he lied. "The officers never meet here in a group; they're scattered across the city."

"What a pity. How desolate." Paulus sighed. "You know, I originally came out here to bring the Word, but Iregara refuse to listen. A most stubborn, godless race." He looked earnestly across the desk at Devane. "You can't leave your officers among these aliens without the armor of the Word. Tell them that we hold services four times a week in the Enclave, on Wednesday, Friday, and twice on Sunday. Tomorrow is the Friday service. All of them will be joyfully welcomed among us for any service."

The door opened. Meda started in, then stopped. "You're busy," she said in disappointment.

"We're almost through," Devane said. "Come on in."

She came over to stand behind his chair.

"I'll post a notice," Devane told Paulus, "though I'm not sure how you figure a week."

"Why, seven days is a week, of course. We keep God's time in the Enclave even though the aliens only count seasons." He smiled at Meda. "And who might you be?"

Devane introduced them perfunctorily and rose to show Paulus to the door, but Paulus held his place, smiling at Meda. "I was just telling your husband about the services we hold in the Enclave. I wish you and the director would join us tomorrow night."

"We'd love to come," Meda said.

Paulus beamed. "We'll look forward to seeing you."

When the high holy had gone, Devane waved his hand

over the intercom. He needed coffee. "Liril." He looked up at Meda. "What did you mean, we'd love to come? You were borderline Recusant at home, just like me."

"I don't care about the service, Dee; it's the people I want to see, *real* people, people I can actually carry on a conversation with."

Liril came in with two cups of coffee. "Rotgut."

"Better than that aqua regia you call tea," Devane replied.

The fur on Liril's shoulders rippled.

Meda began, "I like mine with cream and—" She broke off as she peered into her cup. "Did you put in sugar, too? How much?"

"Tab," Liril replied, holding up one finger. "Feel." The secretary left the room.

Meda sipped her coffee. "How did she know how to fix mine?"

"I probably thought about it when I called. Don't say *she*, though. I'm not sure Liril is female."

"You never asked?"

"Until it matters, why should I?" He lifted a brow at her. "And now, Mrs. Brooks, how has your morning been? Are you working on the Wofford case?"

"I wouldn't tell you if I were. We aren't going to talk business."

He pretended to cringe. "Yes, ma'am. Maybe you'd like to sit on my lap while we think of something else to do, then."

She frowned. "What if someone walked in?"

"They'll never get past Liril."

Even as he said it, though, Liril appeared in the doorway and clapped hands together twice, sharply. "Dane."

Basanites came in, nodding an apology to Meda. "You said you wanted anything new on Wofford right away."

Devane's whole attention fastened on him. "What do you have?"

"It looks like an accident. Hasejian talked to Goodnight at the hospital. They found Wofford's lungs full of pond water but no bruises or other marks to indicate he might have been forcibly held under."

"Anything from Criminalistics?"

"Just a verbal preliminary report. Wofford's boots were covered with mud like that from the edge of the pond and they found prints matching his boots crossing the mud."

"That settles it, then," Meda said.

"I guess."

Something in Basanites's tone set off a warning bell in Devane's head. "Except for what?" he asked.

"Well." Basanites rubbed the back of his neck. "That pond wasn't very deep, less than a hundred and fifty centimeters even in the middle. Wofford would have had to fall and not get up again in order to drown in it." He rubbed harder. "I worked Crimes Against Property back in Rochester, not Homicide, but I used to get this itch on certain cases . . ."

"And you have it now?" Devane felt an itch himself. "Put someone on it, then."

"Yes, sir. Thank you."

Devane sat back in his chair and sighed as the door closed behind Basanites. Meda squeezed his hand. He smiled up at her as he squeezed back, but inside he sighed again, heavily, and hoped to God the captain's itch was wrong.

Chapter Seven

TEN FELT strange walking around the shopping mall out of uniform, carrying a shopping bag like everyone else. The mall felt colder than usual, somehow, though the shopkeepers greeted him exactly as they did when he was on duty. He was halfway through his grocery shopping, picking over fruits whose tough green rind had the texture of orange peel, when he realized why he felt colder; he had simply grown used to the snug warmth of his uniform in this setting. His jacket felt warm enough, but beneath it his civilian clothes, woven for Terran wear, let the chill through to his body.

He dropped four of the green fruits into his bag and thought of his clothes with a frown of displeasure. When his sister Miral gave him this jumpsuit last Christmas, he had considered the blue color and clinging African styling rather daring. After his uniform here, however, and the bright tabards of the Iregara around him, the jumpsuit felt like a drab sack. That stung his vanity; he had always taken pride in dressing modishly.

He moved down the row of fruit bins, picking out two blue fruits and two red ones he had found to be very much like large Terran plums. He dropped them in the shopping bag. Was there anywhere he could buy clothes similar to his uniform? Not in this mall, he knew, and probably not even in the Terran Enclave.

Ten showed the fruit he had chosen to the shopkeeper and reached into his jacket pocket for a handful of the colored plastic disks that represented fractions and multiples of work units he was entitled to claim.

Picking out the correct number to pay for the fruit, the shopkeeper said, "Tailor."

Ten blinked at the Egara, forgetting for once to be flustered about having his thoughts read. Of course. The mall had a tailor and D'shenegar, of all places, had countless fabrics to choose from. Grinning, he shook the shopkeeper's hand. "Thank you very much."

The Egara's arm fur rippled. "Yes."

Ten left the shop humming.

Presently he became aware of the same tune coming from somewhere around him. He sighed. Did Iregara carry this mind reading even as far as echoing the music in another person's head? But moments later he realized that in fact the opposite was true; he had heard the music and unconsciously begun echoing *it*. He knew the piece, the Chorale Prelude "Wachet Auf" from Bach's Cantata No. 140. But who could be playing Bach in the middle of an Egarad city?

Coming around a block of shops, he found the source. Twelve Iregara stood before a small pond in the middle of the mall, singing. Ten recognized Siyan and several other neighbors among the group. They sang without words, vocalizing only notes, using their voices as instruments. Exactly as Bach intended, Ten thought. The old Master's work, which had already translated so well to countless instruments and arrangements across the centuries, now made a new transition, and remained just as vigorous, just as beautifully intricate even in the throats of nonhumans singing it beneath an alien sun. And even here, while he listened, Ten could not help but visualize the great European cathedrals Bach had written the music for, and feel the irony in his great enjoyment of music the devotedly religious Bach had written to glorify a god Ten himself assiduously avoided. But also as usual, he quickly forgot the irony, and the twinge of guilt it engendered, in giving himself up to the music.

He noticed other bystanders glancing at him, but did not wonder at it. He was, after all, the single Terran among them. After a few minutes, however, one of them with arabesque fur designs edged over beside him and murmured, "Stop."

Ten blinked. What?

"Interfering."

Ten frowned, holding his finger to his lips. It was Arabesque who was interfering, talking when Ten wanted to listen to the music.

"Images," Arabesque persisted.

He shook his head, not understanding, wishing the Egara would shut up. By this time everyone in the area had turned to stare at them. Then "Wachet Auf" ended and the members of the chorus came toward him.

"Ten," Siyan called.

Ten smiled hello. "Is this part of philharmonic work?"

"Fun," Siyan said. "Thank you."

Ten started to ask what for when Arabesque said, "Interfered."

Siyan looked back impassively. "*Drana.*"

"Imbalance," Arabesque said. Although the voice remained flat and the face expressionless, Ten received an impression of annoyance from the Egara.

The fur on the arms and shoulders of the singers rippled. Siyan said, "Yes."

Ten wished someone would explain this to him.

"Images," Siyan said. "Imbalance." The Egara's fur rippled again. "Strength."

Some explanation. Ten still did not understand. "Can you put two or even three words together at a time?"

He immediately regretted the sarcasm but to his relief Siyan did not appear offended. The Egara began, "Your images—"

Behind Ten someone said in Translan, "You interfered with the performance by upsetting the image balance. I expect that's what your neighbors find amusing, that one non-Egarad mind can produce images stronger than fourteen blended Egarad minds."

Ten turned around to find Brithe among the spectators. He looked quizzically at her. "Image balance?"

"Come with me; I'll explain."

He worked his way out of the group after her. She led him away from the pond area, toward the edge of the mall.

"You thought they were just singing, didn't you?"

He nodded. "And doing a beautiful interpretation of Bach, too."

Brithe stared off ahead of her. "The sound is only half the performance. What the performers think and feel, and the images the music produces for them, are the rest of it, the part people like you and me can never experience or appreciate. I've been told they try to blend their individual images into a single aesthetically pleasing combination. Whatever you thought while listening probably discorded."

"Siyan mentioned *drana*. That's something like counter-point, isn't it?"

"*Drana,* the different one. I suppose Siyan saw your images as the drana for their performance. After all, you're the drana for their shen, aren't you?"

Ten frowned at her, remembering the symbol on the phone screen the evening Siyan informed him he had been accepted into Meem Shen. "I don't know that I understand."

She glanced sideways at him. "Every shen likes to have at least one member different from all the rest, to add contrast . . . like eating something bland with spicy foods or something sour with sweet ones."

Ten bit his lip. "Something to prevent monotony." He had encountered a similar attitude before, on Earth: *I know the most fascinating people, my dears; why, I even know a police officer. Doesn't he look human? You'd never guess what he was out of his uniform.* As though he were a freak.

Brithe eyed him with concern. "You look upset. Did I say something wrong? I'm sorry. I never intended to hurt your feelings."

"You haven't hurt my feelings." Ten kept his voice level.

Her forehead furrowed. "Are you sure?"

"I'm sure."

But he was glad to be distracted by someone shouting. "Help!" A golden Egara with dark raindrop spots across head and shoulders ran into the mall. "Attack."

Ten forgot his wounded ego. "You were attacked?"

"No." Spots pointed beyond the mall. "Nadathin."

"Show me where."

The Egara ran back out of the mall and across the meadow into the woods, up a path Ten thought led toward either Chalu or Sunstone Shen. About half a kilometer away from the mall, Spots suddenly left the path. Following, Ten found himself in a small, stone-flagged clearing. An Egara in a bloodstained tabard sprawled groaning across a single wooden bench in the center.

"Nadathin?" Ten eased the Egara to the paving and swore softly. The attack had obviously been made by someone with a knife, slashing repeatedly. The Egara bled from at least a dozen wounds.

Ten prodded his radio on and tapped his ear. "Off-duty Officer Kampacalas requesting an ambulance and assistance at Sh-6." He looked up at Spots. "You get out in the open and watch for the ambulance and police. Before you go, though . . . did you see anyone around here?"

"No. Read."

The radio murmured, requesting North Twenty-five to proceed to grid coordinate Sh-6.

"I saw someone running just as we came up," Brithe said. "That way." She pointed north.

Ten jumped to his feet. "You wait with the victim. I'll—" But in his head Sergeant Lessman's voice cut through his words. *To whom is our first duty, officer?* He sighed, swearing silently, and knelt beside the victim again. "Tell me what the person looked like, Brithe, so I can have the description broadcast."

"I'll follow." Brithe ran for the path.

"No!" Ten shouted after her. "You don't know if the person you saw is the assailant, but if it is, that nago has a knife! You could be—"

She did not even slow down to listen. Short of going after her, Ten saw no way to stop her, and the Egara beside him was moving, holding arms up as if still fending off the attacker. "No. No."

"Watch for the ambulance," Ten ordered Spots. He took the wounded Egara's hand. "You're safe, Nadathin. A healer is coming. What can you tell me about what happened?"

Nadathin's head rolled in pain. The fingers closed hard around Ten's, almost crushing his hand. "Reason? Listening. Listening. Attacked." The Egara breathed with a liquid sound that suggested at least one wound had penetrated a lung. A bloody cough confirmed Ten's guess. "Reason?" Nadathin repeated.

Every muscle and nerve in Ten's body wanted to be chasing the assailant. He felt useless sitting there. There was no way to stop the bleeding, and what did *he* know about why Nadathin had been attacked? This was not like the incident between Far and Threen, and now was certainly no time for a discussion on the sociopsychological results of disenfranchisement. Maybe it had been a Silent Nadathin antagonized, or maybe it had nothing to do with this Egara personally; maybe Nadathin just happened to be in the way at the wrong time. "Don't worry about the reasons now. Just rest and wait for the healer."

He wondered if Nadathin even heard him. "No," the

Egara kept groaning, and between coughs, "Listening. Reason?" The grip on Ten's hand weakened steadily with every cough.

Ten shook the hand. "Help's coming. Don't give up. Everything will be all right; just hang on."

But the grip slackened and the coughing grew weaker until, with a final paroxysm, it and the liquid breathing stopped altogether. Ten swore, loudly and bitterly this time. A computer technician was chasing the murderer while the cop sat holding a corpse's hand. He put it down. Much good staying had done this victim; Ten had not even been able to keep the Egara alive. Sighing, he tapped on his radio and called for a Criminalistics unit.

He was sitting back on his heels brooding when Tom Duer, North Twenty-five for today, appeared in the clearing entrance with Spots and the ambulance attendants towing their paragee stretcher. Ten stood hurriedly. "Everyone keep back. A C-unit is on the way." On the woods path, out of the clearing, he told Duer everything he knew. "The victim died before I could learn how the attack happened. Maybe Spots can tell us."

"I asked a few questions on the way from the meadow," Duer said, then lowered his voice. "But I don't know if I understand the answers."

"What do you think you got?"

"A Silent came out of the woods with a knife and attacked without warning or apparent provocation while the victim sat listening."

Ten raised a brow. Nadathin had repeated that word a number of times. "Listening to what?"

Duer shrugged.

"Universe," Spots said.

The two officers looked briefly at the Egara, then at each other. *Universe*? Ten thought. He said, "Maybe we'd better hunt for Brithe, in case she caught that nago."

"You don't have to hunt her." Duer looked past Ten. "She brought the nago back to you."

Ten turned. Brithe came up the path behind him with an unconscious Egara slung over her shoulder. She dumped her burden at Ten's feet and handed him a dagger with a short, wide blade. "The cretin not only still had this, but tried to use it on me. I hit back with a much longer tree branch."

Duer looked up from feeling the Egara's head. "You hit pretty hard."

Brithe's forehead furrowed. "I'm sorry, but I didn't know what else to do." In a worried voice, she asked, "Will I get in trouble?"

The Egara groaned. Duer put a wrap strap on the limp wrists before the suspect could regain consciousness. "I'd give you a medal, sweetheart."

After all was said and done, Criminalistics come and gone, statements taken, body removed, the consensus appeared to be with Duer . . . Brithe had done a nice piece of work and she ought to apply for the department when they began training Egarad officers.

Sergeant Lessman said, "If there's any question, you struck in self-defense."

Which appeared to settle the matter. Ten and Brithe headed back for the shopping mall to find the groceries Ten left behind when Spots came for help. The bag still sat where he had put it. Checking the contents, Ten found them undisturbed.

"Theft isn't one of our problems," Brithe said.

Ten smiled. "I can't fight twenty-four—I mean"—he thought fast, converting Terran to Egarad years and Egarad numbers—"forty-six years worth of reflexes." He searched for something more to say, to prolong the conversation. He hated to go home. The shen had something planned for the evening but after hearing about drana, he no longer looked forward to mixing with his neighbors. Let them break their monotony with another freak. "What was that place in the woods? The Egara who took us out there said something about the victim listening to the . . . universe?"

"Yes," Brithe said. "The Tharshanists consider that every person and rock and tree is simultaneously a separate individual and an integral part of the One, the universe. We're all supposedly vital to some vast pattern. They build their retreats outside the range of other people's minds and try to hear the collective mind of the One. They think that by doing that, they can sense the Great Pattern and learn their place in it."

So even Iregara asked the question: *why am I here?* "So a Silent wanting to kill someone could be reasonably sure no one would hear the mind of someone attacked out there?"

"Reasonably."

Ten ran a hand through his hair. The police had been lucky, then. The victim might have died alone and laid out there until another Tharshanist came to meditate. The murderer might never have been caught. "How many of those retreats exist?"

She looked at him. "I cannot guess . . . several in each cluster, probably. Tharshan and Lesed are the largest philosophical followings on Egar."

So now they had more places they needed to check out regularly. He would mention it at the next briefing.

She started to turn away. He reached out to stop her. "Brithe, don't go. I really would like to know you better."

For a minute he thought she was about to refuse his company again, then the fur on her arms and neck rippled, shooting light and color at him. "All right," she said.

At her insistence, however, they moved to her house to talk, where she could, she explained, introduce him to genuine Egarad food. That turned out to consist of a local tea brewed strong enough to dissolve the table, a salad mixing fruits and vegetables, and poultry baked with something that smelled and tasted much like sauerkraut . . . all of it eaten with the prong-ended spoon that seemed to be Egar's chief table utensil. To Ten's surprise, the poultry/sauerkraut combination tasted quite good.

He found her house even more interesting than the meal, though. Outside, it looked like the others in Sunstone Shen, low and broad, thick-walled and small-windowed, a miniature fortress in buff-colored stone. Inside, chairs of red and black leather woven across heavy frames of red wood furnished it and the walls blazed red or orange where not obscured by shelves. Brithe had many shelves, all filled with book cassettes. Looking them over after dinner, Ten found an entire section of Terran mystery novels in Translan, and even some bound-page facsimilie reproductions of classic twentieth- and twenty-first-century suspense fiction.

"I didn't know you knew English."

"Only to read," she said.

He smiled. "You like that old literature?"

She regarded him impassively. "I find it much more . . . imaginative than the work of modern writers."

"Is being a mystery buff why you came to work for the department?"

She thought a minute before answering. "Perhaps." Rainbows played along her arms.

Ten had read very little mystery fiction. In fact, he found he knew almost none of the mystery and speculative fiction she had. He remembered others only as names from some long-ago literature class.

"You ought to read them. I'll pick out some books for you," Brithe said. "If you don't read, what do you do in your idle time?"

"I read, but mostly professional literature, and I attend exchanges and workshops. I also exercise and practice firearm, baton, gas, and open-hand techniques so I can keep qualified. Back on Earth I practiced the piano regularly, too."

Brithe froze. She stared at him. "You like music?"

"I love it." He grinned. "I almost became a professional musician."

She looked blindly through him. "What prevented you?"

He cocked a brow, puzzled by her intense tone. "Nothing. I took a night watchman's job to earn money for college and that hooked me on law enforcement, so I switched my major from music to criminal justice. What makes you think something prevented me from going into music?"

She did not answer for a moment, but then said abruptly, "Come with me."

She led the way up a short flight of stairs to the bedroom. On a chest against one wall sat a Sweeny synthesizer with small, model-P amplifiers. Ten looked at it with delight. "May I try it?"

"Yes."

He touched the keys. They responded with the clear, clean notes of a flute. Almost without conscious volition, his fingers found the haunting theme from the "Virgo" movement of Leitner's *Zodiac Suite*.

"You play well," Brithe said without inflection.

He shrugged self-consciously and backed away from the keyboard. "I'm rusty. Let me hear you."

"I play for no one."

He eyed her. "You can't possibly be as bad as some of the alleged musicians I've heard. Please play."

How alien she looked, he thought, how Egarad, her face

impassive as a Normal's, revealing nothing of what might be happening inside her head.

"Please," he repeated.

Stiffly, she stepped up to the keyboard. The first selection was Egarad and unfamiliar, but he recognized the expert performance of it; then, as she finished it and moved into Bach's *Two-part Invention in B Flat Major*, something as electric as the Sweeny jolted his nervous system. Goosebumps rose all over his body and he listened breathlessly. Brithe made his playing sound like the fumbling of a tonedeaf novice.

After she finished he could only stare at her until he had worked the knots out of his throat. "Why in god's name are you running computers?" he asked hoarsely. "You should be giving concerts."

Now her face and voice carried emotion . . . bitterness. "Who would come? I might execute with technical brilliance, but my performance has no soul."

"No *soul*! What idiot ever told you that?" Ten demanded. "You're great!"

"I'm Silent."

"So?" he began, then remembered the chorus in the mall. He stared at her in disbelief. "You can't mean you aren't allowed to perform just because no one can read your mind?"

She looked down at the Sweeny. "Yes."

Outrage welled up through him. "That's a stupid attitude!"

She touched the keys again, producing a last, sad chord, then spun away. "It dominates this society," she said flatly.

He bit his lip. "Are many jobs closed to Silents?"

"All the performing arts, all teaching positions and most in business, anything dealing with communication . . . roughly two-thirds of the possible jobs. But computers need no telepathy and they have a keyboard."

Despite the lack of expression in her voice, Ten felt the acid burn of her bitterness. "Why do you tolerate it?" he asked. "You could emigrate, join a colony on a new world where the society could meet Silent needs."

She came around on him with eyes of purple flame. "You insufferable cretin! This is *my world*! I refuse to be exiled, to be driven away from what's mine, just because I'm different!"

Talk about insensitivity and thoughtlessness, Ten reflected, cursing himself; he had demonstrated shameful examples of both. "I'm sorry, Brithe," he said in apology. "It was a stupid thing for me to say."

Her face went blank. She looked through him. "Yes."

Feeling about a centimeter tall, he edged toward the stairs. "I think I'd better crawl out of here. Thank you for dinner. I'm sorry I ruined the evening."

He had his foot on the first step when she suddenly said, "No, don't go. You haven't ruined the evening. I'm as foolish as you, overreacting that way. The idea of emigration upsets me. The Normals keep hinting and sometimes outright demanding that Silents should leave Egar. They want to be rid of us. No matter that we served Egar well on Earth for centuries; now they want us to go away rather than make the effort to live with us." She smiled. "Please stay."

The gesture, so human on the inhuman, Persian-cat face, touched him as always. He let himself be dissuaded from going, and acquiesced when she refused to hear further apologies. Still, he felt it was high time to change the subject. "Let's talk about music. Better yet, will you play for me some more? I'll beg if necessary."

That touched a responsive nerve in her. "You don't have to beg. I'll play."

Chapter Eight

"I DON'T know why I let myself be talked into this."

Meda guided her bicycle around a hole in the path. "Think of it as a social occasion rather than a church service."

"It's a social occasion," Devane repeated dutifully, then sighed. "But it's still a church service."

Meda laughed at him. "Listen to that pout. Times like this I think I have two sons instead of just one. Speaking of which, I wish you'd let Gerel come, too. It would be good for him to see other human children."

"He didn't want to come. You heard him; I gave him a choice and he said he'd rather do homework with D'ne this evening." Which secretly pleased Devane, because if Gerel had not chosen that, Devane would have had to order him to remain at home, which might have initiated unpleasantries with Meda.

Devane watched the headlights of their bicycles bobbing on the path ahead of them. Going anywhere else, for any other reason, he could have enjoyed the ride. Though cool, the twilight temperature remained comfortable. Most of the four-kilometer path from Blueside to the Enclave followed the hilltops, giving them a fine view of the bay and the half-disks of the moons Adayan and Chabed rising from the sea. In the west, the third moon, red Nishim, was already well above the horizon, heading east to meet its sisters. Devane wondered absently if the ancient Iregara had found religious significance in the moons' crossing. Had there once been Egarad priests saying: "Be sure to be at the ceremony for the midsummer conjunction of moons, or your crops will surely fail and your hunters return empty-handed."

". . . for homework," Meda said. "He's only five."

Devane pretended he had been listening. "The Iregara might have the right idea, starting children learning early, when their minds are most receptive and they're eager to learn." Maybe early training in an Egarad atmosphere could save Gerel the nagging guilt and hypocrisy the high holies had impressed on Meda and him so long ago.

The path left the hilltop and turned down. Below them, just above the land's final plunge into the bay, rose the Terran Enclave.

Rose. Looking down on the Enclave, the humanness of that description struck Devane. Egarad structures characteristically sprawled. They reached outward, spreading across the land. Terrans built up, piling on top of one another, huddling together. Anthropologists and psychologists no doubt found in that some profound statement about the nature of the two species.

At the gate, he swung off his bicycle and tapped the call button. Meda eyed the silver shimmer between posts set at three-meter intervals around the perimeter of the Enclave. "A barrier field?"

"I've been told it's to keep the children in and the wild animals, particularly igelis, out." Privately, however, he wondered if it was to keep *all* of Egar out.

A security guard peered out of the gatehouse. A moment later the silver shimmer disappeared across the path. While Devane and Meda walked in and parked their bicycles, the guard directed them where to find the Reverend Paulus. The barrier shimmered again behind them as they started into the Enclave.

Meda pivoted while they walked, staring around in amazement. "It looks just like home!"

Eerily so, in fact, Devane reflected. He had been in the Enclave only twice before, but each time it struck him as somehow profane. Except for the heavier gravity, which he scarcely noticed now, and the presence of the bronze sun or the three moons overhead, he found almost no signs that he stood on an alien world. He might have been on the edge of almost any large Terran city, albeit one built in four-hundred-year-old architecture. From the street to the apartment towers to the plants, everything was Terran. Even the air failed to smell Egarad, the normal faint, pleasant muskiness overpowered by the scents of Terran plants and the sharp, acidic odor of humanity.

In the center stood a shopping area of more contemporary vintage and the Enclave's two churches, the Ecumenical Southern Baptist church and a small all-faith chapel/synagogue/mosque. Paulus met them at the door of the ESB church with an effusive welcome. "I'm so glad you could come. A number of your officers are attending, too. It supports my belief they're suffering from spiritual thirst."

Or homesickness, Devane thought. He shrugged out of his jacket. The Terrans certainly kept their church warm. Or did it only seem that way after solar-heated Egarad buildings?

"Be sure to stay after the service and meet the other members of our congregation."

"We will," Meda promised. "Otherwise it's a wasted trip," she added in a whisper as she and Devane moved on into the church.

Devane grinned.

They found seats. Up front a board bore a date, Friday, Summerday Nineteen. Devane grimaced. Today was actually the Twenty-third. The Enclave not only imposed weeks on the Egarad calendar but used Terran numbers as well. He switched his body to automatic and retreated from the service into his head.

What was he going to do about the inspectors? He had shamelessly used Liril to eavesdrop in the squadroom and his secretary confirmed Basanites's report of deep resentment at having to act as defense investigators. There must be some method of convincing them of the necessity of it, and persuading them to accept it, however contrary to previous training.

A series of random visits to Communications had also revealed another problem, a pattern of frequent meets between certain officers of the opposite sex in adjacent patrols. Each meet was always properly called in, but checking the dispatch logs and car and radio transponder positions on the map, Devane found the "meets" overly long, up to an hour each, and all held in secluded sites like the meditation retreats. He decided to have their lieutenants warn the officers to conduct their sex life off-duty, and if that did not work, he would resort to imposing days off without pay and/or switching them to new patrols far enough apart to make meeting impractical.

Statistics. He hardly wanted to think about those; doing so gave him a headache. Clearance rates on complaints ran only about ten percent so far. Lack of suspect description was probably the largest factor in that, followed by the difficulty of developing definitive associative physical evidence. Criminalistics could use laser diffraction to identify hair, and could type dust and cast footprints, but the papillae on Egarad fingertips varied too much throughout life to make any kind of fingerprinting possible.

Fortunately they had a few successes. The Silent who probably vandalized Sinin's house and killed her luras in Blueside had been found and was waiting for a court appearance. They had bad news, too, though. Checking out the pond where Wofford drowned, Criminalistics had found prints leading into and out of the water . . . probable footprints, but they were so blurred as to be unidentifiable, even to the extent of determining how the foot was shod and whether it was Terran or Egarad. That made both Basanites and Devane itch.

Meda elbowed him. He came out of his reverie to find the service over and everyone filing down a corridor toward the fellowship hall. There, while they drank coffee, Paulus introduced Meda and him to the Enclave's ESB inhabitants. Devane acknowledged each with a nod and a smile, but his eyes kept moving beyond the Terrans, searching for his own people. They would have been easy to identify, even if he had not known them by sight already. Little by little, as Terrans met them and drew back—"Leos? How . . . interesting"—the dozen or so officers sifted out into a small group apart.

"What is it like directing an alien police department?" one woman asked.

Devane raised a brow. "It isn't alien. My sworn personnel are all Terrans." He had better talk to the ones here, too, he decided. They had begun eyeing the other Terrans with increasing resentment.

However, his inquisitor persisted. "But I understand you have furries in clerical positions, and even a furry secretary. How in the world can you understand what they mean when they talk?"

Furries! Anger flashed through Devane. So they had found a pejorative for Iregara, too. "I don't employ *furries*," he said with a smile, "just as I'm not a *dusky*, nor any of my officers *tacos, slants, sand rats,* or *pastas.*"

The woman blinked. "I beg your pardon? Of course I'd never call another person one of those despicable names."

His smile and easy voice never changed. "I wonder if Iregara think of us as *baldies*."

Meda touched his arm. "Dee, please don't."

The woman finally realized she had been reprimanded. Red flared in her cheeks.

Paulus realized it, too. "Really, director," he said in a conciliatory tone, "there's no need to insult Mrs. Hanke over a group of aliens."

Devane turned his smile on the churchman. "Mr. Paulus, here *we* are the aliens."

Spinning on his toe, he strode out of the church. On the steps he stopped to suck in long, slow breaths and debate how foolish he might have been. Was one word worth anger, worth risking the displeasure of a churchman?

He could not be sure whether he regretted walking out, but he did regret leaving without his jacket. After the stuffy heat of the church, the outside air seemed colder than ever. With sundown, the temperature had begun falling. He leaned against the stone wall of the church to take advantage of the warmth it still radiated.

Footsteps clicked over the floor inside. Meda, he thought, but rather than his wife, he found himself surrounded by his officers.

"I never heard anyone tell off a high holy before," one of them said.

Devane smiled wryly. "You may never hear it again, but let me find out that any of you have called an Egara a *furry* and I won't hesitate to turn *you* inside out. Is that clear?"

"Yes, sir."

No one said anything for several minutes. Devane finally broke the silence. "Well, did you slake your spiritual thirst?"

A round of profanity answered him.

"Nagos," one young woman spat. "I thought that maybe here, away from Earth, people would be different—you know, everyone standing together in the midst of strangeness—but . . . they're just like back home."

"Churchgoing isn't mandatory here," Devane said. "You don't have to subject yourselves to this again if you don't want to. I'd rather have you involved in activities that are part of the local culture, anyway."

A young man stared broodingly past Devane. "We don't belong there, either."

Devane watched them leave, then looked up with a sigh at the three bright half-disks overhead, two silver, one red. More steps sounded inside and this time it was Meda. He heard her voice and those of other women as they approached the door.

"I admire your presence of mind," one said. "Personally, I could never live out there among them. How can you bear having your neighbors know everything you're thinking and doing?"

Meda replied hesitantly, "I . . . don't think about it."

"But what about . . . at night? Doesn't it bother you knowing they're listening to your and your husband—you know."

Devane stepped into the doorway. Meda's color had darkened with embarrassment. "Did you bring my jacket?" he asked.

She seemed relieved by the question. Her normal toffee color returned. With a nod, she handed him the jacket.

He lost no time bidding the women goodnight and towing Meda down the street toward the gate. She came readily, but silently. For most of the ride home, too, only their breathing, turning to panting on the hills, broke the silence.

She did not speak until they neared Blueside. "You didn't need to attack Mrs. Hanke that way, Dee."

"I think so," he replied easily.

"Everyone was very understanding, though. They don't hold it against you."

Save him from righteous understanding! Aloud, however, he said only, "Good."

"You know, they have everything in there, including schools at all levels. Don't you think it would be a good idea if Gerel—"

"No, I don't. Aside from the fact that we've already paid his tuition, one change of friends in a year is enough."

"But he isn't going to live on Egar all his life. He ought to mix with *some* humans."

"Would you like to have him come home calling our neighbors *furries*?"

She sighed. "No."

"You can visit the Enclave if you want, and there's no reason Gerel can't go occasionally, too, as long as it isn't to church, but he will continue to attend school where he is. Understood?"

For a moment, Meda did not reply.

"Is that understood?" he repeated.

Slowly, she replied, "Yes, sir."

Chapter Nine

TEN ASKED the question several times. "Do I look all right?" He did not want to give the judge, or rather, mediator, cause to fault him on personal appearance his first time in court here. Maybe appearance was not as important as on Earth, but like there, he had had to turn his patrol over to a relief officer and use up a day off for court, so he preferred not to take chances on other details, either.

Roban eyed him. "You look good. Where did you manage to find a jumpsuit that fits like our uniform?"

Ten checked a sleeve to be sure the yellow-striped seam ran straight down his arm. "I'm having a tailor make them for me. The material is the same as our uniform, too. What's a little more debt on top of the rest?" He tried to see his reflection in the smoky windows they passed on the way through the Ubre business mall to the courts of Mediator Nafee. "Do you think yellow and orange are too bright?"

Jael, along officially to help Ten keep charge of the prisoner but privately to lend moral support, grinned. "Well, you'll never be able to wear it in Topeka." She switched to Translan and asked their prisoner, "Are we going too fast for you, Ladras?"

"No." The shorter-legged Egara stopped dragging against Jael's and Ten's grip and speeded up.

Jael returned to English. "Personally, though, I love the style. If you didn't have a fur fetish, I might ask you midnight dancing."

Ten eyed her. "Fur fetish?"

"Your buddy Brithe."

"What's wrong with being friends with Brithe? The director says to mix with the locals."

"But three out of the last six evenings?" Roban asked. "That's a lot of mixing."

Jael winked at Roban. "Brooks hasn't asked for miscegenation."

Ten felt his face heat. "We just talk!"

Jael raised a brow. "What about?"

"Our jobs, and the differences between Terran and Egarad culture."

They exchanged personal histories, too, though he had learned little about Brithe beyond the fact that she grew up in Subath, a fishing-industry city in the fresh-water Rachad Seas area, and that she had studied music, then computers, in the Lesed-supported university city of Hadaya before coming to D'shenegar. The reluctance with which she spoke of her childhood made him suspect that as a Silent, she had found it painful beyond his imagining.

Mostly, though, they talked about music, both Terran and Egarad, and they played her Sweeny. He had not realized how much he missed music until he met Brithe.

"What differences between the cultures?" Jael persisted.

Ten shrugged. "Oh, like the fact they have no marriage, nor even much cohabitation. Women have never been dependent on men here. Egarad society evolved from women banding together for hunting advantage and mutual protection. The males didn't join on a permanent basis until later."

Roban rolled his eyes. "Fascinating."

"But not perverted." Jael sighed. "Damn."

Ten was profoundly relieved when their arrival at the courtroom stopped the conversation.

An Egara in a small outer office, acting in a kind of bailiff/receptionist capacity, inquired their names and checked them against an appointment list. "D'shenegar/Ladras. Wait."

They sat down in chairs against the walls. Ten had trouble feeling that this was a court appearance. It felt and looked more like a doctor's appointment. At intervals the bailiff spoke to a group of the other people waiting, all Iregara, and showed them into the inner room. When they came out, another group entered.

"I didn't kill Haritheen," Ladras said. "You can't find anyone who ever saw me near that kite-glider."

Iregara around the room slid glances at them.

Roban rolled his eyes. "Tell the judge."

"What?"

"Mediator," Roban corrected himself.

"But the mediator can't read my mind, only yours, and you believe I'm guilty."

"Yes," Roban said.

In English, Jael murmured, "You don't sound much like a defendant's investigator."

"Would you like to know what I think our glorious director ought to do with his defendant's investigator directive?"

Ten waited with amusement to see how the Iregara would react to *that* image, but surprisingly, only a few looked in Roban's direction, and those with only mild surprise. Thinking about it, though, he recalled that in all interaction he had seen between Roban and Iregara, none of the locals ever reacted as strongly to Roban as to most other Terrans. For the first time, it struck Ten as odd.

"What are you people talking about?" Ladras asked. "I didn't kill Haritheen."

Roban went back to Translan. "You threatened her. You even attacked her once."

"Slapped. I admit that. I told you that before. Slapping is not killing."

The bailiff pointed at them. "D'shenegar/Ladras."

The inner room looked nothing like a courtroom, nor even like a judge's chambers. A woodland mural covering every wall of the small room, including the door through which they had entered, gave it the look of a Tharshan retreat. In the center of the shaggy green carpet sat a ring of pillow chairs, one occupied by an Egara with a lap board and writing tablet and another by an Egara whose liver-colored fur had been decorated with blond and bright auburn flame designs spreading out across the chest and shoulders and down the arms.

"D'shenegar opposing Ladras," Flame said. "Summerday Thirty-one; year 10,150."

The Egara with the lap board and tablet wrote. Ten craned his neck to watch, fascinated by the speed with which the recorder drew the characters.

"Sit," Flame said.

Flame must be Mediator Nafee, Ten decided. He sank down into one of the pillow chairs.

"Yes," Nafee said. "Identities?"

They dutifully gave their names and roles in relation to the case. For Ladras' benefit, they spoke Translan.

"You know court procedure?" Nafee asked. The mediator spoke slowly, making an obvious effort to use sentences, and kept his eyes fixed intently on Roban. "Say charge. Say D'shenegar's facts. Say Ladras's facts. Answer questions. Understand?"

"Yes, mediator," Roban said. "The charge is murder. On Summerday Seventeen, a professional proxy named Haritheen was killed in a kite-glider fall. Evidence indicates that the defendant Ladras engineered that fatal fall. Officer Kampacalas responded to the initial call and referred the case for investigation. Ten, tell the mediator why."

Nafee sat back in the pillow chair in a relaxed attitude. Ten shifted uneasily in his. Without lawyers to question him, he felt unsure of himself. "At twenty-four seventy-two hours on Summerday Seventeen, I received a call directing me to city grid coordinate H-5. I was advised there had been an accident of an unspecified nature resulting in two injuries. I arrived—"

"No," Nafee said. "Details unnecessary. Be general."

Now he felt on even more unfamiliar ground. "I . . . arrived in an area between Chalu and Sealight Shen. I found a kite-glider on the ground in a very damaged condition and one person under it, dead. I found several people around a second, unconscious person nearby. Several bystanders who read the accident and came out to it identified the dead Egara as Haritheen and the unconscious one as Shumar. Shumar came to before an ambulance arrived and I managed to conduct a short interview." Lord, what a job that had been, between Shumar's fragmentary, dazed replies and the confusing "explanations" of the bystanders.

"Results?" Nafee asked.

"As I understood it, Shumar was watching Haritheen fly the glider. Shumar saw it collapse in midair and fall. The shock of experiencing Haritheen's death caused Shumar to faint.

"After the ambulance took Shumar to the hospital, I examined the glider."

Ten remembered the meadow clearly, the golden sunlight, the pleasant muskiness of the chilly air, the dark green of the grass underfoot. Most particularly, though, he remembered the gay blue-and-gold kite-glider lying in the middle of the meadow, crumpled as if wadded up by some giant hand, with the still, equally broken body of Haritheen beneath it. In his memory, he turned over an edge of the wing and once more saw the sabotaged metal strut.

"I found that in no less than eight—I mean, ten places, the struts had been sawn halfway through. It was at each of these points the frame had folded. I immediately notified Communications and referred the case to Investigations."

Nafee sat up and looked intently at Roban, as though trying to read his thoughts visually. "Investigated?"

"Yes, mediator. If you agree to hear this case, some of the witnesses will be experts from Criminalistics but I'll just summarize their findings for now. They determined that a fine-bladed metal saw had been used to cut the struts, and from residue found on the cut edges, concluded that wax had been used to fill in the cuts and hide them. They identified the wax as ski wax, an imported Terran brand named Genet.

"Interviews with friends and neighbors of Haritheen revealed that the defendant Ladras, who works as a mechanic and services the race cars Haritheen flew for various clients, had disagreed and argued with Haritheen on several occasions, had threatened her, and had once, in fact, slapped her in the presence of her two children. She had no other disagreements of a violent nature with either Silents or Normals.

"On the basis of that, we visited Ladras and asked permission to search the house. We found a tool box with a metal saw of the type used on the struts and a container of Genet ski wax. When not in use, the glider had been kept in a shed adjacent to Shumar's house in Sealight Shen. The shed was freely accessible to anyone, with no lock or other security device on it."

"Not sabotaged car?" Nafee asked.

"A sabotaged car would have pointed directly to Ladras."

All of which, Ten thought, made a prima facie case against Ladras, and, except for the lack of witnesses to the Silent's ever being in Sealight Shen, a fairly strong case, too.

Nafee glanced briefly at Ten, then returned gaze and attention to Roban. "Continue."

Roban turned palms up. "That's all."

"Ladras's facts?"

The dusky color of Roban's skin deepened. He cleared his throat. "Ladras claims to be innocent."

"Blameless," Ladras said in Isegis.

"No alibi can be established, though. The glider could have been sabotaged at any time since its last use eleven days before the accident. On the other hand, the evidence is only circumstantial. Criminalistics cannot establish that Ladras's metal saw was *the* one used on the glider, just that it is of the same type. Also, skiing is a popular sport. I understand that Remer, a city several hundred iyah north in the Iseg Mountains, is one of the largest ski resorts in this hemisphere. Investigations of the sporting goods shops reveals that Terran ski waxes are in demand, and Genet wax is the most common of the imported brands."

What a hell of a job, Ten thought sympathetically. He would hate to have to testify for both sides and oppose himself.

Nafee's eyes flickered toward Ten, then fastened hard back on Roban. "No witnesses."

"That's true," Roban agreed reluctantly. "There are no witnesses who can place Ladras in Sealight Shen at any time during the period when the glider would have been tampered with." He shrugged. "That's absolutely all the evidence we have for the defendant."

"Poor," Nafee said.

Roban flushed again.

"You . . . restricted." The mediator's ears twitched with the effort of putting into words ideas that could no doubt have been so quickly and easily communicated to another Egara. "Questions. Alternatives."

Roban looked at the mediator helplessly. "I don't understand."

Nafee sighed. "Recorder . . . transcribe."

The recorder drew rapidly, then handed the tablet to Roban. Looking over his shoulder Ten and Jael read along with him. The characters for *mistake* and *possibility*, expressed as queries, combined with elements indicating color, scent, and sight to communicate a picture of the meadow as Ten remembered it, only with Shumar beneath the fallen glider.

"No," Roban said, shaking his head. "Shumar could not have been intended to die instead. The neighbors in Sealight told me that Shumar never flew the glider, only hired

Haritheen to do so, then experienced the flight through the proxy from the safety of the ground."

"Possibility . . . Shumar victim?"

Roban sighed. "I just told you that couldn't be."

"Intent not death; intent, injury."

"Injury? How?" Roban asked.

Jael started. "My god," she exclaimed. "As much as you discussed the case with me, I never thought of that, and I should have."

Roban turned toward her. "Thought of what?"

"The whole idea of employing a proxy is to experience what a person can't do himself for fear of it or lack of enough skill, something like that. During the episode, the vicarist's mind virtually merges with that of the proxy. Whatever happens to the one becomes the experience of the other, too."

Ten stared at her. "Shumar fainted from the shock of Haritheen's death and is still in the hospital!" He looked at the mediator. "Could someone count on a person suffering a severe psychological injury from an experience like that?"

"Yes."

The three officers exchanged chagrined looks. Here lay an entirely new possibility, a whole avenue of investigation left unexplored. But who would have thought to consider such a thing?

"Iregara," Nafee said.

But Terrans, Ten thought, whose society did not include professional proxies, would not. How many other motives might escape notice because they lay hidden in Egarad culture? How could the police conduct satisfactory investigations until they had learned all those cultural differences?

"Experience . . . learn," Nafee said. "No hearing. Investigate alternatives, possibilities."

They filed out in silence. Wheels turned slowly and thoughtfully in Ten's head. As distasteful and strange as was the idea of investigating for both sides, he saw the sense of it. The adversary system of the USNA could not possibly work in these courts.

When they were in the car, headed back to the station, Ladras asked, "What happens to me now?"

"We'll ask," Roban said.

"I don't envy you reporting to Hasejian," Jael said in English.

"She's going to tear me apart," Roban agreed gloomily.

Ten turned the Irath west to avoid two private cars flying abreast at treetop height, well below the required seventy-meter altitude for northbound vehicles. He asked communications to advise the Traffic Department of the location and description of the cars, then told Roban, "We could be worse off."

"How?"

"We could have been caught trying to suppress minor evidence that hurt our case against Ladras here."

"If you talk about me, use a language I can understand," Ladras demanded.

No one paid any attention. Jael's eyes widened in understanding, but Roban's forehead creased in a puzzled frown.

Ten asked, "Remember how Nafee picked up the fact that we have no witnesses placing Ladras in Sealight? We can't choose the evidence we want to present. With a telepathic judge, *everything we know* is before the court."

Roban stared. "I'll be damned. Of course . . . and that means that any flaws in the investigation benefit the defendant. Why the hell didn't Basanites tell us that? Working *for* this nago is the only way we're going to make a tight enough case to get a conviction." Unexpectedly, he laughed. "What a wild blue yonder job this is turning out to be. If it doesn't drive me over the brainbow, I'm going to love it."

"Let's hope Hasejian and Basanites are also amused," Jael said.

The lieutenant and captain were not, nor was Devane, receiving a report on the hearing from Basanites. "Get Inspector Adeyanju in here."

"Sir," Basanites began.

Devane smiled. "I don't want excuses from him, captain; I want him here in front of my desk in five minutes."

The mild, almost absent tone did not deceive Basanites into underestimating Devane's seriousness. "Yes, sir." He left quickly.

Devane leaned back in his chair, closing his eyes. Damn. He could have gone all day without this. The sound of feet on the carpet brought his eyes open again to catch Liril setting a cup of tea before him. "I don't remember asking for that poison."

"Calming," Liril said, but removed the cup.

"I'm calm. Do you hear me raising my voice? I have nothing to excite me except an officer whose cause of death is still inconclusive, police board members like Gemun and Lishulir wondering if we're worth our generous salaries and threatening to pack us back to Earth because we haven't put a dent in the violence statistics yet, and asynaptics who claim to be investigators turning loose the few deviants we *do* manage to catch."

Liril stared solemnly at him, sipping the tea.

Devan let acid etch his voice. "Anything interesting in my head?"

"Meda."

He stiffened. "Did I hire you as a secretary or psyman?" He constructed a deliberate image of Liril chained to the desk in the outer office, buried beneath mountains of paperwork.

Liril regarded him impassively for a moment, then with fur rippling, left the room.

Devane sighed. Unfortunately, Liril was right. His irritation this afternoon did not stem from having a case thrown back at them, but had begun much earlier, with Meda. Or perhaps the original fault lay in attending that damned church service in the Enclave. Ever since, Meda had been quiet, tense, and untouchable. At first he had attributed it to anger at him for refusing to let Gerel attend the Enclave school, but Meda did not usually stay mad long and when after five days she still held him at arm's length, he started to worry. When she retreated to her side of the bed again last night, he had asked what the matter was.

"Nighttimes are cold enough without having the temperature as frigid in bed as out."

She huddled deep under the blankets. "Is that your chief concern, what happens after bedtime?"

He recognized quicksand when he saw it. "No. I hate seeing you unhappy . . . though I have to admit, I don't like solo dancing, either."

She moaned in the dark. "Please don't be vulgar. The neighbors will hear."

So *that* was it. Those Enclave women had infected her with their damn paranoia.

"I feel the minds out there, listening to me all the time, knowing everything I say and think and feel . . . and what we do together." She sat up, clutching the blankets around her. "I want to live in the Enclave, where we can have some privacy."

He frowned. "We've never had privacy before. The apartment walls in San Francisco were thin enough for us to hear the neighbors snoring, so you know they heard us, too, but that didn't stop us from making love and a son there."

"That was different."

"Why? Because everyone pretended not to listen? What makes you think anyone here reads us in particular? We're just two of almost five hundred people in Blueside."

"But we're different from the others. We're Terrans," she said. "Of course they listen to us in particular."

"And what if they do?" he asked in exasperation. "What's wrong with them knowing two people love and enjoy each other?"

He should never have said it. He realized that just one second too late as she came back furiously, "Oh? You like the idea of performing for a crowd?"

The fight had lasted the rest of the night, no less bitter for being held in low hisses to keep from waking Gerel.

Devane rubbed his eyes. So now after a sleepless night, he had to deal with a cop whose reluctance to accept a new system had resulted in having another case thrown out of court.

From the doorway, Liril clapped twice. "Dane."

Basanites brought in a tall, dusky-skinned officer. "Inspector Adeyanju, director."

Devane reached into his memory. "I remember interviewing you," he began with a smile. "Denver, wasn't it? You worked Juvenile. You have a grandfather who was born on Egar."

"That's right," Adeyanju replied with caution.

"And today," Devan went on, still smiling, "your case against a killer came flying back in your face."

Adeyanju stiffened to attention. "Yes, sir."

"Do you have an excuse?"

The investigator appeared to debate with himself, then said tentatively, "Sir, I don't see how we could have thought of the motive the mediator proposed."

"Aren't you an Egaraphile, inspector?"

Adeyanju bit his lip. "Yes, sir."

"Grew up on stories about Egar, you told me, but . . .

it seems you don't know that much about the culture after all."

"I—it takes—" He broke off with a sigh. "No, sir."

"And are having to learn about it the hard way, apparently. Why haven't you taken Captain Basanites and Lieutenant Hasejian seriously when they urged the inspectors to act for the defense, too?"

"I didn't understand—"

"Apparently not," Devane agreed mildly.

"It won't—"

"Are you aware of our present clearance rate?"

"Yes, sir."

"Not many cases reach court. Yours was the fourth to go before a mediator, only the fourth, and was the fourth thrown out." Beyond Adeyanju, Basanites frowned. Devane saw but ignored the Investigations chief. "One or two I could accept, but *four*? I would have thought that by this time you would be giving your investigation methods some serious re-evaluation."

"I think Officer Kampacalas was the first to realize what court *is* here. I promise you, sir, the next case will be tight. I realize the—"

Devane leaned forward. "Oh, I think we can do better than tight, inspector; I think we can bring these cases in hermetically sealed."

Adeyanju's jaw tightened. "Yes, sir," he said through clenched teeth.

"The police board hasn't been too impressed with our performance so far. I'd hate for our department to be declared a failure and disbanded. I can't tell you how bitterly that would disappoint me, not to mention the adverse effect it might have on our future careers. I hope you spread the word about your court experience among your colleagues, inspector, because the next officer who slops through the case and doesn't investigate it *completely* won't be just ass-kicked in court; I'll personally preside over the drawing and quartering." He smiled. "That's all."

Adeyanju looked as if he had something more he wanted to say, but he turned and marched out.

Basanites looked after him. "Do you think he deserved that? He learned his lesson in court today, I think."

"Knowledge is like a nail, my father used to say, not worth much until it's driven home with a few hard knocks."

"But a sledgehammer?"

Devane eyed Basanites. "Maybe I should start the mayhem with the head of the division."

Basanites slid toward the door. "I think I'll go back to work."

Guilt stabbed Devane. What was he doing taking out his irritation on everyone in sight? He sighed. "Dane, forget what I just said." He rubbed his eyes, grimacing. "Want to trade jobs?"

Basanites shook his head. "Do I look wickers? No, thank you."

The sun balanced on the western hills, reddened and bloated, casting dusky shadows across the path where Ten and Roban ran. Ten still remembered the agony of running those first days on Egar, but now he moved in relative comfort, his breathing measured, his feet light on the path that would take them north up the valley, around the travelport, and back to the station. He hardly noticed the cold, either, even though he wore only a running suit. Roban, however, ran with effort, fists clenched and jaw set.

"Would you rather have played a few rounds of *chanach*?" Ten asked.

The Egarad game, faster and more complex than handball, which it resembled, had become increasingly popular for physical training.

"No," Roban said.

Ten glanced sideways at him. Since coming out of the director's office several hours ago, Roban had said almost nothing, and then only monosyllables. It bothered Ten. Anything, even profanity, would be better than silence. Destructive things happened to officers who stayed locked up in their own heads. "Want to talk about it?"

Roban ran a minute before answering, then he began with a snort. "One thing hasn't changed from Earth. The brass are still bastards."

Ten welcomed the bitterness. At least it came in full sentences. "Did Brooks sharpen his claws on you?"

"And took a few practice swipes for good measure. Remember what he was like during your interview with him on Earth?"

How could Ten forget that casual dissection? "Yes."

"This was more of the same . . . the smile, the friendly

voice, but he hardly let me finish a sentence and he sure as hell never let me tell him anything I'd learned!"

Roban relapsed into silence. Ten became too busy thinking to push conversation. In moods like this, his partner Avel had gone looking for heads to break. Earth had enough vulnerable heads for her to get away with it, but here that could only cause trouble. The question was: how did he pull Roban out of his hole?

"Don't try telling him," Ten suggested. "We'll show him. Sealight Shen is in my patrol. I'll talk to everyone in it, check out all Shumar's neighbors, friends, and acquaintances. We'll sift this case so fine it'll pass through a semipermeable membrane. We can start tonight."

"Tomorrow, maybe. Tonight I don't want to show anyone anything. I'm not interested in working for Brooks or any other Terran cop."

"Shall we go somewhere and do something then? The track? A chance house?"

"I'm not in the mood for company."

Ten eyed him. "You ought to talk to someone."

Roban stretched his stride. They passed other runners. "Don't use psyman cant on me."

Ten thought again of Avel. "I want to help, Ro."

"Being mother-henned by a green kid isn't going to help me a bit," Roban said venomously. "I want to be *alone*. You glim?"

He sprinted ahead. Ten stretched to catch him, then slowed again. Forcing himself on Roban would accomplish nothing. Maybe Roban knew what he was doing. Everyone did not necessarily react like Avel.

By the time Ten reached the exercise room at the station, Roban had showered and left. Pol, Bara Deem, and two other officers, all drenched with sweat from playing *chanach* doubles or working on baton and open-hand fight techniques, had seen him go.

"Mighty riled about something," Pol said. "He made an Egara seem plumb garrulous by comparison."

Ten told them why.

Bara grimaced in sympathy. "I wish I'd known when he was here." She headed around the partition separating the men's and women's showers and shouted over it at Ten. "I'd have invited him to come with us tonight. Would you like to? I'll call Phaedra and ask her to join us, too."

Ten stripped off his running suit and turned on a

shower. The water scalded him at first, but as he became accustomed to the temperature, he stood blissfully in the jet, letting it stream over him. He called back to Bara. "Phaedra left two days ago for some sea up north on the equator and won't be back until mid-autumn." He peered through the steam at Pol under the water of the next showerhead. "Where are you going?"

Pol, looking past Ten, forehead creased in thought, did not answer. Ten repeated the question in a louder voice.

From the other side of the partition, Bara replied, "Naramim Concert Hall. I found out today they have holo showings of Terran plays there."

"Holos of plays?" What, Ten wondered, did Iregara get out of those?

"Recorded during performances in the best theaters on Earth and shown with Egarad subtitles. I'm advised that fiction fascinates the locals . . . because it's an alien concept, do you think?" Bara called.

Ten washed thoughtfully. Fiction *would* be alien to them. Being essentially untruth, it could not exist here. An idea might be presented as speculation, as a possibility, but not as "reality." He imagined that plays, and actors in particular, people pretending to be other people, must seem very exotic and puzzling. As exotic as proxies were to him, perhaps?

"Will you come?" Bara called.

It tempted him, for the opportunity to see Egarad reactions if nothing else, but thinking about proxies reminded him of Haritheen and Roban's case. "I can't; I have to work."

Pol's eyes focused on Ten. "The mediator reads *everything* you know?" He asked the question without his usual drawl.

"More than the average Egara, anyway." Ten enjoyed the hot water a few moments longer, then turned it off with regret and grabbed fast for a towel. "Coming back, Ladras told us mediators are deep-readers, like healers."

Pol closed his eyes and let the water stream over his head. "Then we'uns all better think *mighty* clean thoughts when we go to court, podners."

"Don't try to hide evidence, at least," Ten said.

Dressing and leaving the exercise room, he began considering how to go about reaching everyone in Sealight. If it was like Meem, people lived on all possible schedules.

D'shenegar ran forty-four hours a day. Well, he would just have to keep going back until he finally caught everyone.

It occurred to him that in light of the fact that cultural ignorance had made him extra work, a native might provide useful insights into what questions to ask. Brithe had been working late the past two or three nights. Maybe he could catch her here again. He headed down to Data.

He found Brithe at a keyboard of the computer with eyes fixed on the screen. Only her hands moved, dancing across the keys.

"No time," she said in response to his plea for her help.

"You can keep me from overlooking obvious questions I don't know enough to ask."

She looked up. Her impassive expression told him he had come the wrong day to ask favors. He started a retreat. "But perhaps I can handle it by myself. See you another time." He lifted his chin in greeting to the Normal Evening Watch technician and escaped.

Brithe certainly had her moods. Climbing the stairs, Ten congratulated himself on an unbloodied withdrawal. What was it with her? Hormones? He had had a girlfriend in college who spent one week a month snapping or crying at the least thing. Perhaps, he thought wryly, Egar's three moons made Egarad females three times as moody as Terran women.

He checked his chron. If he left the station now, he would have a twenty-minute wait on the skyrail platform for the train, twenty minutes in the chilly night. Better to wait and leave at the last possible minute. He passed the time talking to the desk officer and flirting lightly with her . . . lightly because Jenann Eads kept company with Lieutenant Trey La Flore, the Evening Watch supervisor.

He had been talking to her for about five minutes, letting her wheedle him into giving her the name of his tailor, when Brithe hurried up the stairs and across the receiving area with cape billowing about her.

"Brithe," he called.

"Late." She sailed out through the doors.

Ten checked the desk chron against his. Both read the same. If Brithe intended to take the skyrail north, she had plenty of time. Perhaps she just wanted an excuse to avoid him. He sighed. She did not have to make up excuses. He could accept that she preferred to be left alone for the time being, although he found it rather discouraging to be told that by two different people in the same evening.

In the end, he was the late one. He had to run all the way to the skyrail station, arriving sweating and out of breath just as the train slid to a stop. He did not look for Brithe but sat catching his breath and listening to the traffic coming over his ear radio: broken windows and trampled flowers in Ramun Shen, arson in the Filid business mall, a fight in Hillrock Shen. He did not look for Brithe at any of the transfer points, either. By the time he left the train at its stop by his cluster, he had forgotten her in thinking about Ladras, Shumar, and Sealight Shen.

He backed his bicycle out of the station rack and took the path east past Sunstone and Chalu to Sealight. There, music attracted him to the center of the shen, where a party appeared to be in progress around the bath house. While some neighbors groomed each other, others danced to music provided by a bowharp, drum, and Y-shaped twohorn. Thanks to his exposure to Egarad music through Brithe, the alien rhythm and scales sounded less dissonant than they once might have. Thanks to the Silent, too, he was able to identify the music as the folk type rather than the more formal symphonic music Brithe preferred.

Then the music dwindled into silence and the dancing stopped. All eyes turned on him. Ten was pleasantly surprised at the number of individuals he recognized, by sight if not by name. It reduced his feeling of self-consciousness.

He picked out an Egara whose name he did remember. "Good evening, Gubir. Sorry to interrupt your Gathering, but I need to ask some questions about Shumar."

Now not just eyes but attention focused on him. He almost felt their minds crowding his, peering in.

"Ask," Gubir said.

"It's been suggested that the person who caused Haritheen's death might have really—"

"Understand."

Ten tried not to feel flustered. "Then you understand I need to know of any disagreements or—"

"Yes."

He sighed. "Since you understand what I want, I don't need to ask the questions. Can anyone give me some answers?"

"Complainant?" one asked.

Ten blinked, nonplussed. What did the Egara mean? Then the radio murmured in his ear and he understood. The Egara had read the radio traffic from Ten's mind and confused it with what Ten actually wanted to know.

"Overlap," the Egara said, fur rippling.

"I'll shut the radio off."

He reached for his ear . . . and froze in the act. Over it came a new message. "North Five, patrol unit South Four down, NN-11 coordinates. Investigate and report status."

A car down! Ten forgot all about asking questions. He listened intently to the radio instead.

Minutes later, the dispatcher said, "Go ahead, North Five." Static crackled in the dead air while North Five spoke, unheard. Communications said, "North Two, meet North Five at NN-11," and a short time later, "North Five, ambulance dispatched."

Ten rubbed his thumb down the cleft in his chin. South Four must be injured. Who was South Four on Evening? Ten could not remember. He wished he could hear North Five's end of the conversation.

He heard nothing more for a while and started to talk to Sealight neighbors, but then Communications spoke again. "South Two, meet North Two at NN-11. North Two, South Two, the supervisor, and a C-unit have been dispatched."

A knot of apprehension tied in Ten's gut. The lieutenant, the south sergeant, and Criminalistics going to the site, too? What the hell had happened?

Chapter Ten

THE MUTTERING brought Devane's head up from the reports spread across the table. He smiled at his son sprawled stomach-down on the sitting-area carpet. "What's the homework tonight?"

Gerel frowned at a printed list. "Solar system. Listen." Crossing his hands, he looked up at Devane and rapidly recited the names of the system's nine planets, indicating which were small planets, which gas giants, and which ringed.

Devane nodded approval. "That's very good."

"Moons, too. Hamun's:—"

Devane glanced at his chron. "Not tonight. It's almost thirty-five hours, cub, and I promised your mother to have you in bed on time."

Gerel regarded him solemnly. "Moons first?"

Devane pointed toward the stairs. "Now."

"Take me?"

Devane hesitated. Meda usually insisted that Gerel undress himself. "You carry him around and baby him too much," she would tell Devane. However, Meda was not here to object tonight. He pushed away from the table and went down the steps into the sitting area to scoop up the boy.

Getting ready for bed took much longer than Meda would have approved of. The process became a wrestling match that had the two of them rolling on the floor together, Devane laughing and Gerel squealing in delight. In the midst of the romp, however, the triple-note chime of the phone sounded downstairs. With a sigh, Devane left the boy to finish changing and went to answer it.

He waved his hand over it. "Brooks."

A dispatcher's voice came back at him. "Captain Basanites has ordered a car sent for you, sir."

The lighthearted warmth left over from playing with his son evaporated abruptly. Devane's jaw tensed. "What's happened?"

"A patrol unit went down. The officer may be dead."

Cold apprehension spread through him. Another one? He swore. "Tell that car coming for me to burn sky."

Waving off, though, he looked up the stairs and ran a hand over the woolly cap of his hair. What could he do with Gerel? Meda was not due back from the Enclave for several hours and he could hardly take the boy with him.

The sharp report of clapped hands sounded at the door. "Devane."

He opened the door to find the brown-furred Runah, Gerel's teacher, who lived just below them on the hill. Runah said, "I," then when Devane blinked, puzzled, added, "Tend Gerel."

He gratefully stepped back to let Runah in. "Thank you. I'm sorry to impose, but . . . you understand it's an emergency."

"No imposition. Parent."

Devane blinked. What was Runah talking about? He did not understand. However, he had no time to work through an explanation just now, so he merely nodded and hurried back upstairs to Gerel. He explained briefly that he had to leave for a while. "But Runah is downstairs if you need anything."

Gerel frowned. "Come?"

Devane lifted a brow. "What kind of question is that? Of course you can't come. You don't mind staying with Runah, do you? You like Runah."

The boy nodded. "Parent."

Devane kissed the boy good night. When he had time, he would have to find out what they meant.

Lem Cole, the officer who came after Devane, knew nothing except what he had heard over the radio, and that he dutifully repeated to Devane. It set the skin on Devane's spine crawling, generating more questions than answers. Devane chewed a knuckle and speculated while he looked down at the city slipping beneath them, the ishen glowing in scattered patches of light amid the dark of the woods and hills. Just one moon shone in the night sky, red

Nishim. Eyeing it, Devane wondered wryly if it were an omen.

Transponder lights blinked on the control-panel grid, directing them toward the correct site, but as they came down, the car settled not onto a meadow or near a shen but into a hole nearly half a kilometer wide, down past irregular rock cliffs to rest on a grassy floor. Devane pushed up the door and ducked out under it to find himself in the middle of a small Officers' Exchange. Following Basanites to meet him came Captain Lenard Titus, Lieutenant Trey La Flore, and Sergeants Green Brynche and James Gerhardt.

Devane looked from them up the rock walls. "What's this place?"

"An old quarry," Titus said.

"What the hell happened?"

Basanites pointed. "This way."

In the middle of the quarry floor, surrounded by the glare of field lights, sat a patrol car, its body crumpled and splintered around the bottom. Devane stepped into the circle of light. Criminalistics technicians at the car backed off so he could peer inside. An officer sagged in the flight harness . . . silent, motionless, unbreathing.

Devane walked back to his command officers and let the technicians return to work. "Forget all the official language; tell me fast and simple."

Titus talked. "The officer is Karal Ashe, South Four. Communications saw him leave his assigned patrol, then his car transponder went out at this coordinate. Twelve minutes later a citizen reported a downed car to Traffic, who called us since it was one of ours. North Five, Officer Mirre Howe, was dispatched to investigate. She asked for Sergeant Brynche, who sent for Gerhardt, because Ashe is—was one of his squad, and for La Flore. La Flore called me and I called Basanites."

"Why?"

"I thought Ashe's neck looked broken," Brynche said, "but you can see from the damage to the car that it probably didn't fall much farther than from the height of the quarry walls. Ashe should have walked away. Also, the citizen who called came back to wait until Officer Howe arrived because of an observation the citizen thought worth reporting. After listening, I wanted backup."

At the edge of the lighted area on the far side of the car

Devane saw a dun-colored Egara with the heavy breasts of a lactating female standing beside a slim, fair-haired female officer. "What did the citizen have to say?"

"There's one of those meditation sites down at the far end of the quarry," Titus said.

Devane could not see the end in the dark so he took Titus's word for it. "A Lesed retreat, you mean?"

"*Tharshan* retreat, sir," La Flore corrected. "Lesed is the group that builds schools and laboratories and funds athletic events."

"A retreat, anyway," Devane said. "I presume our citizen was there?"

Titus nodded. "The name is Duma. Duma heard the crash. Ashe didn't die instantly. Duma felt Ashe's mind still functioning after the car came down, but at a reduced level indicating marginal consciousness. We're about a quarter of a kilometer from the retreat and by the time Duma arrived here, Ashe was dead. According to Duma, the mind didn't fade as it should have done with coma and then death, though; it stopped suddenly."

Basanites, who had been shifting with nervous impatience, broke in. "Duma saw someone run away from the car."

That was not cause for just an itch; it could lead to a full-blown case of the hives. Devane's eyes narrowed. "Any readings from the subject, or was it a Silent?"

"Duma couldn't be sure," Basanites said. "There's some psychological trauma in experiencing another person's death, I gather. It can distort perceptions for a few minutes afterward."

"We didn't get a description, either, I suppose."

"In the dark and at the distance Duma saw the subject . . . no, sir," Brynche said.

"It doesn't prove anything, of course," Basanites observed. "The subject may have been no more than another witness who decided to leave when Ashe died, but . . . it makes me think of Wofford."

Devane understood the reasoning. Both officers had died about the same time of evening, out away from the population in relative isolation, and in circumstances that did not look completely accidental. To proceed on the assumption that the deaths were *not* accidental, however, perhaps even linked in some way and part of a pattern, would initiate something Devane hoped to keep off Egar . . . the fear they had all lived with on Earth . . . the constant looking over the shoulder, the suspicion of hands out of sight near them, the automatic distrust of anyone beyond the police family circle. Just thinking about it made his back feel naked and vulnerable, made his hand want to reach for the place over his collarbone where the paragee field controls of a uniform would have been located.

He looked back steadily at Basanites. "I find it hard to believe anyone could have known in advance that Ashe would be here, out of his patrol, at just this time, or that someone could force the car down."

"A meeting could have been arranged."

"Get his log out of the car and see what excuse he gives for the trip." As Basanites went to the car, Devane eyed the lithe officer, Howe, still standing beside the Egara on the far side of the accident site but deep in conversation with Officer Cole. "Could she have been the reason he came?"

"I don't think so," Gerhardt said. "I've noticed that involved officers pair up at briefings and debriefings, but while Howe's interests are widespread, none of the men with her has ever been Ashe. Besides, Communications located her on the far side of her patrol until dispatched here."

The Criminalistics technicians began packing their equipment. Devane wandered over to where the police doctor knelt examining Ashe's body. "What do you think?"

Goodnight looked up. "He broke his neck."

"Any odd bruises in the area?"

"No." The doctor lifted a brow. "You expecting some?"

Devane shrugged. "When can you post him?"

"I'll see if Dr. Sherur can do it in the morning." He smiled. "A few more of these and I'll be able to claim expertise in pathology, too."

Devane stared down grimly at Goodnight. "Don't say that even in fun, doctor." He looked over at Basanites reading through Ashe's log. "Do you have anything?"

"Maybe."

Basanites handed the log to Devane. Devane skimmed down the entries, which had times and notations written in precise Egarad characters. At the last line, he frowned. According to the log, the computer had ordered Ashe out of his regular patrol for an impromptu check of the quarry.

"The computer didn't notify Communications of any impromptu for this area," Basanites said.

"Double-check it."

Basanites called Communications. The answer came back promptly. The computer denied having ordered any impromptu.

Titus frowned. "A false entry, do you suppose, to cover the real reason?"

If so, it was careless of Ashe. Such a lie would be caught as soon as the log was checked against Communication's log after the end of the watch. The possibility existed, of course, that the computer had glitched. Devane looked at Basanites. "Talk to Data in the morning. Get that computer fundi of Hall's to help you, the Silent with the rainbow fur, Brithe. Let me know what you find out, and bring me the path and criminalistics reports as soon as you have those, too. And now," he went on, raising his voice, "if Officer Cole will fly me home, I'll let him return to his patrol and leave the rest of you to your job here."

Cole headed back for his car. After lifting off, he said tentatively, "Howe and I were talking down there. We've been on patrol just fifteen days and lost two officers already."

Devane heard the questions running around in Cole's head as clearly as if both men were telepaths. He replied, "It could be coincidence. We'll conduct an inquiry to determine whether deaths were due to human error or, in Ashe's case, to equipment failure."

Cole said nothing, but Devane sensed the officer did not accept any theory of coincidence. He looked sharply at Cole. "Let's not jump to unfounded conclusions."

After the words were out, Devane cursed himself. One of his objectives in setting this department up had been to encourage freer communication between field and command officers. The habits learned over sixteen years were difficult to break, though. This was two good opportunities those habits had ruined today, Adeyanju this afternoon and now Cole. He sighed. Ordering Cole not to be paranoid was futile, too. If anything, it had only convinced him the brass were hiding something.

Devane tried to repair some of the damage. "I think the biggest danger we face here isn't from people, or even from the planet and wild animals down there. It's inexperience, our own ignorance. Ashe could have crashed because the gravity makes these cars handle differently from Terran cars."

"Yes, sir."

The scrupulously respectful reply indicated to Devane that he had accomplished nothing. With an inward sigh, Devane let the rest of the flight pass in uncomfortable silence.

As Cole let Devane out on the hilltop above Blueside, however, Devane paused to look back into the car. "Be careful. Before you do anything—leave the car, respond to a call, interview a subject, or even take a personal—let Communications know."

Cole looked back with a slightly startled expression. After a moment, he said in solemn sincerity, "I will. Thank you, sir."

Devane stood watching the car lift off. He ran a hand over his hair. They were so alone out on patrol. All of them were, here . . . even more so than they had been while being feared and hated and shunned on Earth. At least they had known and understood their enemies there.

He shook himself angrily. He had told Cole not to jump to conclusions, but look what *he* was doing. Maybe Wofford and Ashe had died accidentally; the evidence did not rule that out. The wise course was to wait for Basanites to give him the path and lab reports. Then he could decide whether to panic.

Chapter Eleven

THE REAL estate agency, run by a Sealighter named Refenal, had broad windows looking out across a plaza portion of the Neer business mall. Ten stood with his back to them, soaking up the morning sunlight while he talked to Refenal. The process was an unusually slow one, marked not only by numerous backtracks but also complicated by the red-furred Egara's apparent reluctance to talk to Ten. Refenal answered slowly and even more tersely than most Iregara, making no effort to help Ten understand those replies.

Ten stifled a sigh of impatience. "You don't know of any disagreements Shumar might have had that would cause someone to strike through Haritheen?"

After a long pause, Refenal replied, "No."

"There are three Silents living in Sealight. Do you know of a disagreement of any degree Shumar might have had with one of them?"

Again Refenal paused before answering. Ten counted the seconds: one, two, three. "No," Refenal said.

Everyone Ten had talked to said the same thing. He had trouble believing it, though. Even Normal Iregara became angry at each other on occasion. Normal/Silent exchanges almost always resulted in some irritation on one side or the other.

Ten saw Refenal glance at a table chron. "I'm sorry this is taking so long," he said in apology, "but it's important."

This time Refenal answered promptly. "Unimportant."

Ten stared at the real estate agent. "Refenal, Shumar is still in psychological shock because of Haritheen's death. You don't believe it's important to find the person responsible for that?"

"No." Refenal looked pointedly at the chron again.

Ten ignored the hint and let his thoughts run the direction Refenal's last answer sent them. If Refenal did not care about finding the person who injured Shumar, perhaps Refenal had cause for wanting Shumar injured.

Refenal's eyes snapped back to Ten. As he hoped, the unspoken accusation stung the Egara into volunteering information. "Indifferent."

That gave Ten something more, anyway. He regarded Refenal grimly. "How can you not care what happened? Shumar is your neighbor."

The Egara looked back without expression. "Price."

"What price?" Ten's eyes narrowed. "Are you saying the injury was the price of something Shumar did? That it was deserved?"

"Yes."

The idea, and the calmness with which Refenal delivered the judgment, outraged Ten. "Did Haritheen deserve to die, too?" He heard his voice rising but made no effort to lower it. "Do Haritheen's children deserve to be orphaned?"

Refenal paused, then said, "Neighbors parenting."

As though nothing beyond the care of Haritheen's children mattered. Ten scowled. What about Haritheen herself, and Shumar? What had they done to bring such condemnation on themselves?

"Incomprehensible," Refenal said.

"Try me," Ten suggested.

But Refenal looked at the chron again. "Good-bye."

For a moment Ten wished that the ploys Avel had used to wring cooperation from reluctant witnesses could be applied here. He spent the walk out of the office resenting his impotence. Once in the plaza, however, pulling on his helmet, anger gave way to wry amusement. As often as he had criticized Avel's methods while working with her, he should not be longing for their leverage now. He had no real desire, he knew, to see power used here as police at home were pushed into using it by the general public's frenzied demands for security above all else and the high holies' righteous crusade against Sin and Evil.

Ten sucked on his lower lip. What Refenal would not tell him, perhaps he could learn from someone else. He pulled his list of Sealighters out of his thigh pocket and ran a finger down the names. Four others from Sealight worked in Neer during the day. He would find out what they had to say.

Two hours later he came out of the last office trying to evaluate all the answers. Like Refenal and the Sealighters he had talked to last night, the latest four said Shumar had only minor conflicts with Silents or other Normals, nothing of a great degree, nothing beyond normal disagreements.

"Were any of those with Refenal?" he asked.

There the answers became ambiguous, even the one that had to be written because the Egara came from a city in the Sith Lir Mountains and spoke a language Ten could not understand. *Yes*, they said, *no . . . in a matter of speaking.* But when Ten asked for clarification, nothing they offered resolved the confusion.

Still looking for a question that could be answered clearly, he had said to one, "Refenal seems to think Shumar deserved what happened. Do you have any idea why?"

"Vicarist."

Ten noted that it was the same word that Jael had used for Shumar. However, that still did not explain Refenal's disapproval.

"An'nafus," the Egara said.

Which answer did not help, either. Ten sighed.

The Egara echoed it with almost human impatience in the sound. "Good-bye."

So now Ten stood with his helmet tucked under his arm, wondering what he had accomplished, and what he ought to do next. By rights, he should walk through several ishen. He had not been through the Thelis industrial complex today or checked the Third-Level school down near Lus and Skyline Shen. But he felt he ought to pursue this disapproval of Shumar, too. Whatever the cause, it might be reason enough for murder in someone's mind.

He touched the computer tie-in on his belt buckle and tapped his ear to activate his radio transmitter. "Computer."

The computer's voice came back promptly in his ear. "ID."

He passed the palm of his hand over the tiny scanning cell on the buckle.

"Proceed," the computer said.

"What's the meaning of the word 'an'nafus'?" He spelled it.

"An'nafus, proper name, twenty-seventh-century teacher

and philosopher, originator of the An'nafus Principle: *All necessary work is honorable work.*"

Ten walked slowly back toward his car. Now how did that apply to Shumar? Shumar worked as a sandman, cleaning and replacing the filler in san commodes. According to the An'nafus Principle, Shumar should be well thought of for performing such a necessary job, not killed over it.

A shout broke into his thought. Moments later he realized he actually heard no sound, but the several Iregara in his vicinity had all paused and looked one direction, and Ten's perceptions interpreted the action as a response to a cry. He reacted nonetheless, pulling on his helmet as he ran in the direction the Iregara looked.

The business mall had been constructed in a figure-eight, with an arcade through the central row of offices connecting the two plazas. Coming out of the arcade into the other plaza, Ten saw an Egara sprawled coughing on the paving and another nearing the edge of the business mall on the far side of the plaza. He looked helplessly after the fleeing Egara. He doubted he could run fast enough to catch the Egara before the fugitive disappeared into the woods, but several people near the Egara right now could probably make a capture, if only they would, instead of coming in to the injured Egara.

Abruptly, three Iregara whirled and raced after the fleeing Egara.

Ten stared, then shouted, "Be careful," and hurried to kneel beside the injured Egara. "Let me help you."

The victim wore a bright purple tabard with a neckline twisted tight at the throat. Ten loosened the tabard and with the help of an auburn Egara who wore a white star design above each eye, sat the Egara up. The victim's coughing eased.

"That one try to strangle you?" Ten asked.

"Yes." The Egara's voice emerged as a thin wheeze.

"Do you want a healer?"

"No."

"Then if you feel up to it, I'd like to ask you some questions. Maybe we can learn why this happened. Don't try to talk, though; just nod for *yes* and shake your head for *no.* If you need to use a word, let someone else answer for you." He looked up at the starred bystander. "You?"

Star squatted beside them. "Yes."

The story emerged slowly and circuituously. The victim, named Beem, was an assistant to the real estate agent Refenal who owned the business mall. Beem had been telling the assailant, a Silent gardener from the greenhouse in charge of the business mall's landscaping, about some desired changes in planting. In the midst of telling the gardener what new flowers to put in, the gardener suddenly grabbed the neckline of Beem's tabard and began choking Beem with it.

"You had no warning the gardener might attack you?"

"No."

"Was the gardener shouting at you?"

Beem nodded.

Ten sighed. And despite being yelled at, Beem never anticipated violence.

"Caught," a bystander said.

Ten looked up to see three Iregara coming across the plaza with a fourth who wore a gardener's coverall, knee pads, and tool belt.

Ten waited until the group reached him, looked the suspect over for a minute, then asked, "Was the problem something Beem couldn't make you understand or something you couldn't communicate to Beem?"

The Silent's eyes fixed on Beem, but the gardener said nothing.

A crisp voice behind Ten said, "Tell."

He looked around to find Refenal there. "Please let me handle this," he told the real estate agent.

Refenal glanced at Ten. "Alien." The violet gaze went back to the Silent. "Our problem. We tend."

Now Ten understood Refenal. Only part of the earlier interview's difficulty had been caused by Refenal's disapproval of Shumar. The rest resulted from a dislike of Terrans, and perhaps a belief they should not be serving a police function.

As Refenal approached the Silent, Ten stepped between the two. Defensive reaction to Refenal's hostility put an edge on Ten's voice. "I said, let me handle this. You people haven't tended to your problem so far or I wouldn't have to be here."

Refenal stopped short.

Ten's anger faded. Pulling off his helmet, he ran a hand through his hair and said more mildly, "You won't contribute anything to bringing peace by being here, so please, go back to your office and let me do my job."

Refenal stared impassively at Ten for a long minute, then backed away and left the plaza.

Ten turned to the Silent. "What's your name?"

After a pause, the gardener replied, "Sihithe."

"All right, Sihithe, tell me what made you so mad you attacked Beem."

"I was supposed to put in new flowers there." Sihithe pointed at a planter area. "But the fool didn't know the name of the flowers to ask for."

"Did you ask for a description?"

"Oh, yes, but the only way Beem could describe them made them sound like either the hisisith or the nus sahigan. The trouble is, that spot needs low, sunlight flowers and the hisisith is a shade plant and the nus sahigan is a flowering hedge, not a ground plant. I told Beem that and suggested using a miminithe planting—that's a flowering ivy—but that . . . that fishbrain wouldn't listen and wouldn't understand!"

Ten looked at Beem. "Did you read that in my head all right?"

Beem stared at Sihithe. "Yes."

"Maybe you two should try looking at pictures of flowers. Beem can pick some likely ones from there and Sihithe can say whether they're appropriate. And why don't you try writing when you have trouble understanding each other, as if you were on the phone?"

They discussed that for a while, through Ten, and the matter was almost settled before Ten thought to ask if Beem wanted to make a formal charge and take Sihithe to court. Beem declined. Which *did* end it as far as Ten was concerned. He left them with a sigh made up of equal parts weariness and relief and headed for his car a second time.

"Well done, supercop."

He looked up to find Roban beside him. "How long have you been here?"

"Since you dismissed Red. That was clever, having the Silent talk to the Normal through you. You ought to mention it at debriefing."

"I will." They walked back through the arcade and across the other plaza toward the cars. "Do you want to know what I've learned about Shumar?"

Roban nodded. "And I hope it's something useful. I checked the employer, Remech San Services. Shumar was a good worker, by all reports. No trouble of any consequence. Sandmen work in pairs and part of the time Shumar's partner was a Silent. As far as I could learn, the Silent was being truthful about getting along with Shumar. Everyone else says the two of them worked peacefully."

Ten twirled his helmet by the chinstrap. "Did you feel any kind of general disapproval of Shumar?"

"No. Why?"

"Your grandfather ever tell you about something called the An'nafus Principle?"

Roban thought. "I can't remember that he did. Again, why?"

Ten told him about the conversations with Refenal and the other Sealighters and about his query to the computer. Roban listened with lips pursed in thought, but at the end, he could only shake his head. "It doesn't make sense to me. You think it's significant?"

"If we don't check it out, we'll just be kicked out of court again."

Roban had to agree that that possibility existed. "Do you have any idea how to find out more about this An'nafus Principle?"

Ten considered. "Go to an expert on Egarad culture . . . Brithe."

Roban grinned. "Not bad thinking for a green kid."

"Green kid reminds me," Ten said, thinking back to the evening before. "You must have gotten your mad all worked out last night."

Roban's grin faded. His eyes flickered away from Ten's. "Yes. When do you plan to talk to Brithe?"

Ten eyed him in sudden concern. That sounded like an evasion. Anxiously, he asked, "You didn't go break someone's head, did you?"

Roban stiffened. "What business—no, of course not." His dusky color deepened. "I . . . went home and . . . got drunk. Why don't you call Brithe right now?"

Ten still studied Roban. That sounded like a lie. What had Roban really done last night? And, he asked himself, turning away toward a public phone, was it any of Steven Kampacalas's business? He debated the question while the station answered and transferred the call to Data, and during the long wait for Brithe to come on the line. He had just decided not to pry when he heard Brithe's voice. To his relief, last night's bad mood seemed to have passed.

"Hello, Ten. Sorry to keep you waiting, but I had to do some work for Captain Basanites. That officer who died last night logged an impromptu and I had to see if the computer ordered it."

"Did it?" Ten's nerves twitched. He had almost forgotten Ashe in the press of his own work.

Her voice lowered. "Don't tell anyone I told you, but no, it didn't. He must have gone to that quarry for his own reasons. Now, since you've never called me in the middle of the day before, this must be business. How can I help you?"

He told her about the problem with Shumar and Haritheen and the An'nafus Principle. As he reached the end of the recitation, Brithe snorted. "Stupid Normals. There are single words that can explain volumes, but they never use them. If that Normal had called Shumar a parasite, wouldn't that have meant much more?"

"It certainly would have!" The Iregara took great pride in their individuality, in developing that in each of them which was unique. By living vicariously, Shumar negated individuality. "I'm overwhelmed by enlightenment. What about Haritheen?"

"That's the application of An'nafus's philosophy. Proxying is not a necessary occupation, even though a number of people practice it because it can be very lucrative. I don't know if I can make you understand why it's considered dishonorable. Normals experience many things through the other minds around them, but . . . normally they don't *pay* to share the experience."

Ten could think of a very good parallel on Earth— prostitution. If Iregara considered proxies as humans did prostitutes, could that be a motive for murder, or for wanting to injure the vicarist who used a proxy? "How strongly do Iregara disapprove of proxies?"

"Normals don't disapprove *strongly* of anything. Strong emotions cause pain, so Normals avoid them. If they don't, other Normals avoid *them*."

What about Silents? Ten wondered. Or would the disapproval of proxies and vicarists be felt by people to whom the relationship was impossible? He supposed it had to be checked.

"Is there anything else?" Brithe asked.

There was still Ashe. "Did Basanites say anything about how Ashe died or what the lab found when they processed the car and crash site?"

"No. He just asked if the computer could have ordered an impromptu and not notified Communications, too. All I know about Officer Ashe is station rumor. I'll try to find out more if you like." She paused. "I can tell you what I've learned tonight if you'd like to get together."

It was the first time she had ever extended an invitation. He accepted quickly. "Let's meet at my place."

Then he went back to Roban and passed on what he had learned.

Roban pursed his lips. "Egarad prostitution. Sounds more like a motive for killing Haritheen than slagging Shumar's mind. If we were home, I'd start dragging in the holy abers and brainbows, but there's no such things as Leagues of Decency here."

"Thank god. So I think that means we need to check out Silents both of them knew." Ten pulled his Sealight list out of his thigh pocket. "Here are the three in Sealight and where they work. They're yours. If you need help, call me, but better give me a chance to walk through a few ishen and malls first so my people won't think I've abandoned them. And be careful, will you? Don't walk into any Tharshan retreats without looking first. I don't want you ending up like Wofford and Ashe."

Roban snorted. "You mean you believe those rumors that they were killed?"

"You don't think they were?" Ten eyed him in surprise.

"I think they got careless and killed themselves."

Watching Roban climb into his car, Ten pensively twirled his helmet by its chinstrap. Now that was cold kelvin, throwing rocks at brothers' graves. Roban must still be feeling a bit anti-Terran, anticop today—or could something else be happening to him? He was certainly evasive about last night. Feeling a vague but disturbing uneasiness, Ten watched Roban's car lift off and disappear west.

Chapter Twelve

"No GLITCHES in the computer?"

"No glitches." Basanites shrugged at Devane. "Brithe and another tech checked everything. On the basis of plotted activity alone, the computer wouldn't have ordered that impromptu; the cluster is one of the quietest in the city."

"So we still don't know what Ashe was doing at that quarry." Devane raised a brow. "What *do* we know?"

Basanites unfolded notes from the autopsy he had attended earlier. "It was one hell of a way to start the day. I fainted at the first three autopsies I ever saw and I've never liked them since—one reason I chose Crimes Against Property when I went into Investigations." He frowned at the notes. "There's a lot of technical jargon but what it amounts to is Ashe died because his head was twisted so hard it dislocated several vertebrae and severed his spinal cord."

"His head was *twisted*?" Devane leaned forward in his chair. "What do the doctors have to say about possible causes? Could it have happened naturally?"

Basanites rolled his eyes. "You know doctors. To use Sherur's word, it's 'atypical.' Goodnight says the common injury in crashes is a compression fracture, which may paralyze but usually doesn't result in immediate death."

The noncommittal adverbs and adjectives did not rule out the possibility of accident. Devane ran a hand over his hair. Would the cause of Ashe's death remain inconclusive, too? "What else do you have?"

Basanites had reports from Criminalistics and the vehicle pool. All fingerprints on the car had been identified as either Ashe's or those of other officers using that vehicle. A few other smudges found were of undefinable origin. The grass-covered ground around the car yielded no footprints of any kind. However, a wider search discovered one interesting bit of possible evidence. The quarry wall directly east of the crash site showed skid marks and freshly dislodged stones, indicating that someone had made a recent rapid descent at that point. The ground at the top bore several blurred prints that in the lab's opinion had been made by soft-soled boots.

Devane's nerves crackled. Someone on the quarry wall? It fit. He almost expected it. Aloud he said, "I don't suppose we'll be able to use the footprints for identification. Half the population wears footwear with soles like that," and looking at Basanites's uniform boots, added, "including our own officers."

"It could have been the person the witness saw running away."

"That still doesn't give us a killer. The person could have seen the crash and gone down to help."

"And helped by breaking Ashe's neck?"

Devane's mouth tightened. "Maybe it was a deviant Silent who took advantage of the situation to vent his anger."

"Instead of attacking whoever happened to be in the retreat?" Basanites frowned. "It's possible, I suppose." He paused before going on. "The mechanics are still examining Ashe's car, but so far they haven't found any signs of mechanical failure to explain the crash." He looked at Devane. "You want to bet they don't?"

A diplomatic man, Dane Basanites, Devane thought. Instead of saying, "*You don't expect me to buy that bullshit about a passing deviant Silent or an accident, do you?*" he carefully demonstrated all the suspicious aspects of the incident.

"No bets." He could certainly use something strong to drink—Liril's tea, even. "I thought about this case for a long time last night. Want to hear my midnight paranoia?"

Tension rippled along Basanites's jaw. "Go ahead."

Devane had not intended to think about Ashe. He had enough to do as director without playing investigator, too, but he had not been able to sleep. He lay awake, watching double shafts of silver moonlight slant down through the windows high under the roof to Meda's head on the far pillow, listening to his wife's soft breathing as she pretended to sleep. Anger at her and desire for her warred in him. He said nothing, however; arguing that she should accept the Iregara for what they were and let herself go had already proven useless. So when the ache of wanting her grew too painful, he had tried thinking of his job instead, and eventually, that had led to Ashe. While moonlight moved slowly across the room, he turned what he knew of Ashe's death forward, backward, and inside out. He compared it to Wofford's death at every point, asking himself how anyone could drown a physically fit adult male without a struggle and cause a patrol car to crash. Who would want to? He still had no idea *who*, but he had thought of a possible *how*.

"If someone wanted to shoot down a car, without having a weapon large or powerful enough to disable the car itself, the solution would be to disable the driver. Someone standing on the rim of the quarry could reach the driver with a sleeper beam as the car came down even with the rim on its way to check the quarry floor."

Basanites stared at him. "A sleeper. Wofford, too?"

Liril came in and set a steaming cup of tea before Devane.

He sipped it and grimaced. "That's certainly strong enough. Wofford," he said to Basanites. "Drop him in the middle of the pond and he'd drown without ever knowing what happened to him. Send someone to ask that witness if Ashe was unconscious before or after the crash."

"There's still the problem you mentioned of how anyone knew Ashe would be there."

Devane looked at Basanites over the rim of the cup. "When you were on patrol and bucking for rank or promotion to Investigations, how many meets did you set up with linnies, hoping one would tongue up something to give you a big, impressive wrap?"

Basanites frowned dubiously. "I can't see an informer system here."

"But maybe Ashe did . . . or someone made him think so."

"I'll check it out." Basanites stood and headed for the door.

After the Investigations chief had left, Liril remained, lingering by the door. "Patience."

Devane waited for an explanation.

"Meda," Liril said.

"I still haven't made you my psyman." But he said it without irritation and added, smiling, "Thank you for your concern."

Liril regarded him impassively. "Necessary. Pain reduction."

Devane had a quick vision of an Egara holding an aching head while hurrying to give analgesic to another Egara who actually had the headache.

"Yes," Liril said.

He considered his secretary thoughtfully. "Maybe one of your compatriots in the lab should treat Meda."

"Trying."

Although he felt sure Liril used the word to mean *attempting,* its other meaning, *aggravating,* sounded simultaneously in Devane's head. He said wryly, "Yes, she can be."

Liril's fur rippled with several waves of muscle contractions. Repeating, "Patience," the secretary left the room.

Oddly enough, Devane felt better about Meda. He smiled. Liril the luras. Now if only he could as easily stop worrying about the police board breathing down his neck, and settle the questions about Wofford and Ashe.

One by one, officers straggled into the storefronts for debriefing. Some struck up conversations with other officers but others walked straight to their desks, through the projected images of fellow officers, if necessary, and slumped tiredly in their chairs. The sitters almost equaled the talkers today, Ten observed, and even among those talking, the noise level remained low enough that for a change, no one needed to shout to be heard.

Ten debated whether to sit or to talk. He had no particular desire to take part; he would rather find Roban and hear how the interviews with the Sealight Silents had gone. Had Roban decided yet whether the killer was after Haritheen or Shumar?

Then Ashe's name drew his attention to a conversation between two officers near him. ". . . he was unconscious *before* he crashed," Mab Heier, a tall Afro woman, finished saying.

The words rang loud. Everyone dropped their own conversations and turned in Heier's direction.

"Who told you?" Ten asked.

"Barbara, from Investigations." She looked around at everyone. "A transponder blip came on my control panel screen this afternoon, and since I like to know what other officers are doing when they come in my patrol, I went for a look. It was Sergeant Barbara. He told me he'd been sent to ask that Egarad witness exactly when Ashe lost consciousness."

"And the witness said he was out before the car went down?"

Mental wheels ground audibly around the room and tension ran like electricity, jumping the spaces between them with a deadly hiss. Ten fingered his paragee controls.

At that moment Lieutenant Robbie came into the room with Sergeants Lessman and Cathcart. "If I can have your attention before we begin, I have some information on the investigation into Karal Ashe's death."

Ten knew that somewhere Andea Deathrage, the police psychiatrist, watched and listened, or let the computer record the debriefing for her to play back later and evaluate their every word and expression, but now he wondered if the lieutenant and sergeants listened too, making evaluations of their own, perhaps to choose a strategic psychological moment to join the group. No entrance could have been better calculated than this one. Robbie had the watch's instant and complete attention, and all speculation about Ashe waited while they listened. He effectively smothered any panic, even though he had little of real value to say, only the results of the autopsy and the information that no mechanical failure caused the crash.

"I'm North Five, too," Mab Heier said, "and I know that quarry. Has anyone considered that someone might have used a sleeper on Ashe?"

Robbie did not answer immediately. Instead, he looked around the room, studying each officer. He felt along the front row of desks until he found one that was solid to his touch. Sitting on it, he pulled his legs up and crossed them. "Why don't you all make yourselves comfortable?"

While everyone sat down he waited, concentrating hard on the boot top and pant inseam of one knee. Ten sat in the chair at his storefront's desk. The sergeants found places on the edge of the dais.

Robbie looked up again after the rustle of movement died away. "I know you're all very concerned about what happened to Ashe, and probably a little scared. I know I am. Given the nature of his neck injury and the lack of mechanical problem in the car, chances are high that someone deliberately killed him."

Ten felt cold, despite the insulation of his uniform. He pulled his arms tight against him to stop a shiver.

"So you're jumpy and you can't think about anything else. To answer your question, Heier, the idea of a sleeper is being considered. So is the possibility that a Silent on the way to attack someone in the retreat took advantage of Ashe's accident. And there are other theories, too, I'm sure. Right now, though, that's all they are. We don't *know* what happened, and we can spend hours here talking about it and we still won't know a damn thing more, so why don't we table the subject? Leave it to the investigators. I'll keep you posted on their progress. Meanwhile, we still have a job to do no matter what else is happening and we need to talk about that. I know it was a fairly active day. Kampacalas handled an assault in the Neer business mall very commendably. I understand you managed to enlist the aid of some citizens in capturing a suspect?"

Ten still wanted to talk about Ashe, to ask if that could be connected in any way with Aaron Wofford's drowning. A sleeper might account for the puzzling circumstances there, too. However, he saw reason in what Robbie said, and he felt the lieutenant was being honest. So he nodded. "Yes, I did."

"Normals helped wrap a Silent?" burly Nies Anders asked. "How the sweet jesus did you manage that? I've watched them let Silents go past them like they were invisible or something."

Ten related the incident in detail. Responding to nods of encouragement and approval from Robbie, he also told them about acting as a relay to help the Silent Sihithe communicate with the Normal Beem.

"That's good thinking," Robbie said. "That's adaptation." He looked around at the rest of the group. "As long as we're dealing with telepathic people, we ought to find ways to use their ability to help us where possible." He looked toward the back of the room with a sudden frown of concern. "What's the matter, Wassom?"

Ten turned around to see Pol at his desk, drawn and gray. But Pol drawled, "Nothing's the matter. I'm just fine, lieutenant."

He looked anything but fine. Robbie said, "If there's a problem, this is the place to talk about it."

"There's no problem!" With a quick look around, Pol

went on in a lowered voice, "I'm just tired." But this time, Ten noticed, the Texan spoke without his drawl.

Robbie eyed him, but said, "Very well," and turned to look at another officer. "Bridewell, what was your problem with that arson report?"

Ten did not think the lieutenant had dismissed Pol from his mind, however, nor believed Pol's self-evaluation. Tomorrow Pol would probably find a note in his storefront requesting him to report to Andea Deathrage as soon as possible, before his regularly scheduled visit.

Ten sighed, cursing the holocom and the storefronts that let them seem to be together but actually separated them. He could not pull Pol off into a corner for a private talk, where the Texan might mention what was bothering him. Ten could hardly talk to Pol at all until debriefing was over.

The session seemed to last interminably, but at last the talking slowed, and with a stretch, Robbie stood and dismissed them.

Ten headed straight for Pol. "You doing anything tonight? Come on over to my place. Bring Bara, too."

"I don't know." Pol frowned. "Bara and I . . . had a fight."

"Then bring someone else or come alone. All right?"

Pol shrugged. "All right." His hand reached out and he vanished.

The room emptied as one officer after another deactivated the holocom. Robbie and the sergeants winked out of existence, too, as Ten switched out of the network. It was then he heard someone breathing behind him.

He tensed. Debating whether he should go for his baton or sleeper, Ten slowly turned.

Roban grinned at him.

Ten sagged against the wall, limp with relief. "Damn you, Ro; don't do things like that. When did you come in?"

"Near the beginning of debriefing. I guess you didn't notice me in the crowd." He regarded Ten narrowly. "You seem a bit nervous."

"Aren't you, considering what happened to Ashe?"

"Or what everyone has convinced themselves happened? Why is everyone so instantly certain he died because of the uniform he wears?"

Ten frowned at him in disbelief. "Who are you trying to

jook? You've been in this business long enough to learn that *everyone* is out to slag us."

Roban's jaw set. "That's on Earth. Here we're cops, not leos, and the Iregara are a nonpredatory people."

Ten snorted. "Nonpredatory? What about the Silents? What about the person who killed Haritheen?"

"The Silents aren't home-grown, though; in a sense, they're a Terran import. As for who killed Haritheen—I still have people to talk to but I haven't found anyone yet who looks as good for it as Ladras. I think I'll ask to take that nago back to court if nothing better turns up in a day or two. Of course, maybe I'm not learning everything possible." Roban sighed. "I don't seem to be able to make myself as clear to people as you can. You say something and Normals come back with an answer that relates to some underlying thought. With me, it seems to be all I can do to get across subjects I'm concentrating on." He paused. "Maybe you have some telepathic talent you aren't aware of."

"Me?" Ten grinned wryly. "I only wish I *could* tell what Iregara think. And speaking of what people think . . . do you have any idea what's going on inside Pol's head?"

"No." Roban scratched at his wiry hair. "But I don't think it's good."

"Come home with me. Maybe the two of us can persuade him to talk about it."

They left the storefront. Ten picked up his bicycle from where it stood parked beside the door and they started through the shopping mall. Roban began telling him about the interviews with the Sealight Silents.

Ten noticed two young Iregara strolling ahead of them. The juveniles stopped at a fruit stand and one picked up a red fruit. A moment later the shopkeeper appeared in the doorway and several other adults in the area stopped to turn around, too. None of them said a word, but the juvenile returned the fruit to the bin.

Ten blinked. Had he seen what he thought? Could that be crime prevention, Egarad style?

The juveniles glanced back at him. Their fur rippled, then they broke into a run and raced off, shouting at each other in play.

Ten grinned. "Now that was very interesting."

"Frustrating, actually," Roban said.

Ten stared at him a moment before realizing that Roban

thought Ten's remark referred to something Roban had said about the day's interviews. Roban's preoccupation with recalling those interviews had made him miss the incident involving the juveniles.

Roban talked most of the way to Ten's place. Ten found listening difficult, however, despite his interest. The beauty of the late afternoon kept distracting him with details like the moisture beaded in the bottom of the funnel-shaped leaves of ganayaha trees they passed on the woods path, or the webs of the spiderlike shen fere shrouding low brush like bridal veils and the red-and-yellow bodies of sugar idi hovering above wild, purple-smelling ishasama in the meadows.

As they came in sight of Meem Shen, Roban stopped talking business and said, "I wonder why our people let themselves be shut away in stone and steel canyons."

Ten shrugged, smiling. "Different needs?"

"These people know quality of life. We should tear down Earth's cities and rebuild them like this."

Complete with igelis? Ten wondered. He also thought of the lost child he had helped hunt several days before, and finally found dead in the woods with adu tracks around the small, mauled body. "Egarad cities aren't quite paradise."

"Lushanah looks like the outskirts of hell, my grandfather used to tell me," Roban said. His voice carried a dreaming note. "He said that from the city you could look out across the dryland, flat and featureless as a plate, and the grass wasn't just brown but a golden brown, so it looked like it reflected the sun. He said you could think you were looking across a sheet of brass to a horizon that seemed a thousand klicks away." He stopped short. "There's someone in your house, Ten."

Ten saw the movement inside, too. His initial alarm disappeared a heartbeat later, though. "It's probably Brithe."

"Brithe?"

"You remember." He grinned. "The object of my fur fetish?"

To his surprise, Roban's color deepened in a sudden flush. "I remember. What's she doing here?"

"I forgot I asked her over for the evening."

"What about Pol now?"

"That's still all right. She can help. Who better to answer questions about the culture?"

Brithe was equally surprised to see Roban. She regarded

him with a still-eyed impassiveness that Ten suspected masked displeasure. "You didn't say there would be other people, too." But when Ten explained about Pol, she became immediately sympathetic. "I'll be glad to help if I can. Is he upset about the officer who was killed? I heard Ashe's head was almost twisted off."

Ten swallowed. He had not thought of the broken neck in quite those terms before. It sent a queasy wave through his stomach.

Brithe peered at him. "Are you upset, too?"

"We all are."

Ten pulled a new black-and-scarlet jumpsuit out of the closet and headed for the san to change, though he found himself reluctant to peel out of the uniform and give up its paragee shield.

Through the closed door he heard the phone chime, and Roban call, "It's for you, Ten."

It was Pol. "I'm mighty sorry, podner, but I can't make it tonight after all."

Ten wished again that the phone screen here showed faces. Pol's voice sounded unnaturally controlled. "I wish you'd try." He hunted for something that might persuade Pol. "You know you're going to have to talk to someone, and I thought you'd prefer us to Deathrage."

"Now, don't you fret, son." Pol laughed, but it sounded tight and forced in Ten's ears. "I'll just tell her the same thing I did the lieutenant . . . I'm just wore out. I'll be right as rain soon as I've had me a good night's sleep. Y'all have a nice evening, hear? *Hasta mañana.*"

Ten waved off and turned to look helplessly at Roban. "What do we do now?"

Roban shrugged. "Let him alone, I guess."

"But—" Ten began.

Roban patted his shoulder. "He'll be all right. You take the mental health propaganda too seriously." He headed for the door. "Well, since Pol isn't coming, there's no reason for me to stay."

"Why not? The three of us can do something together."

"Three's make triangles and crowds."

"But we aren't—damn." Ten sighed as the door closed behind Roban. He looked up in mute appeal to the heavens. "I don't know what's happening to everyone."

"Me," Brithe said. "He wouldn't have left if I were a Terran woman."

"It isn't you," Ten quickly reassured her.

She looked at him. "It is. I don't mean to come between you and your other friends."

Now Brithe was going martyr on him? What *was* this? "It has *nothing* to *do* with *you*," he said through clenched teeth.

She flinched. "You don't have to shout."

For god's sake. *"I'm not shouting!"*

The clap of hands sounded outside the door. Ten jerked it open. Siyan held a luras out to Ten.

Heat came up Ten's neck and face. Ruefully, he took the luras and stepped back to let Siyan in. "I'm sorry. I guess I'm disturbing you."

"Yes," Siyan said. "Loud."

Ten petted the luras. "I know. I'll keep my voice down."

"Misunderstand," Siyan said. "Scale. Loud . . . medium . . . quiet . . . Silent. Loud." Siyan pointed at him.

He sighed. A telepathic shouter. Wonderful. What could he do about that?

"Nothing." Siyan paused. "Gathering. Join?"

Ten shook his head. "Not tonight. I'm spending the evening with my friend."

"If you want to go, I'll understand," Brithe said. "Neighbors come before outsiders."

"Drana," Siyan said.

Ten stiffened. Before he could say anything, however, Siyan said, "Misunderstand."

Ten rubbed his cheek across the top of the luras's head. "I understand. Isn't the drana the different one, the odd man?"

Siyan hesitated before answering. "Yes. No. More."

Brithe put on her cape and started for the door. "Goodnight. Enjoy the Gathering."

"Wait a minute." He blocked her path. "I accepted your invitation and my father always taught me it's ill-mannered to stand up a lady."

"Shen bonds are very important, Ten."

"Important," Siyan confirmed.

"For Iregara maybe." Ten handed the luras back to Siyan. "I'll—"

"Drana important."

"Ten, I'd better go."

"No, damn it!" In a minute he was going to lose his

temper. "Quit being noble and sit down! Siyan, I can't come to the Gathering tonight."

Siyan stroked the luras, looking hard at Ten. "Misunderstand. Explain."

Did Siyan intend to explain something, or expect Ten to? At the moment, he neither knew nor cared. "Another time. Goodnight."

Siyan regarded Ten intently for a few moments, then slowly left.

Ten turned to Brithe. "So, what would you like to do this evening?"

She thought. "I know of a chorale performance. Some Terran music is on the program, including Bach."

Bach? That sounded wonderful. However, he arched a brow at her. "I thought you didn't like concerts."

"Not alone, but now there's someone to experience the music and talk about it afterward in the same terms I do."

Ten grinned. "You let me start talking about Bach and you may not have a chance to say anything in any terms." He thought briefly of Pol, worriedly, then decided that perhaps Roban was right. He would leave the Texan alone. He could see him tomorrow at briefing.

Chapter Thirteen

POL DID not appear at briefing in the morning until after Robbie and the sergeants had arrived. Ten studied him critically. The Texan looked better than he had yesterday, though Ten thought he still detected a slight ripple of tension along Pol's jaw. All through the recitation of the incident list, floating patrol assignments, and suggestions passed on from other watches for handling typical Egarad situations, Ten repeatedly tried to catch Pol's eye. The other man's attention, however, remained riveted on Robbie. Ten had to wait until the briefing ended to catch him.

"Howdy, podner," Pol said. "Sorry I couldn't make it last night."

"How do you feel today?"

"Frisky as a new baby calf. I hit my bunk right after I talked to you and slept like a log to twelve hundred this morning. I'm a new man."

Was the heartiness genuine or forced? Ten could not decide.

"Of course, I've got this." Pol pulled a piece of paper out of a thigh pocket. Ten recognized the psyman's memo form. "She wants to see me right after the watch. I'm not even supposed to come to debriefing first."

Ten bit his lip.

"Psymen have to do something to earn their work units, I guess," Pol said. "I'll do my best to entertain her." He winked. "*Auf Wiedersehen*, podner."

Pol's image vanished. Ten stared at the empty space where he had stood, hoping Pol took the visit seriously and cooperated.

However, he did not have long to worry about Pol. Iryl Consigli, who worked the Morning Watch, came in from the garage, pulling off her helmet with a tired stretch.

"New car this morning, Ten. The paragee started acting up in the Isinhar and the v-pool sent up a Chehasha as replacement. In a flat-out run, it isn't quite as fast, but it maneuvers faster. I almost put myself in the middle of the Rabala Shen bath house going down too fast, so take it easy until you get the feel of it."

"Thanks for the warning. You have a quiet watch?"

"Except for keeping an eye on a Gathering in Rabala until six hundred this morning . . . a celebration in honor of newborn twins." She grinned. "I've heard loud parties before, but the sheer decibel level of the singing and music of this one puts Terran parties to shame. Luckily, with the city built the way it is, they couldn't disturb anyone outside Rabala. The neighbors are really proud of those babies. You'd think every adult in the shen was the mother. It might be good P.R. to stop for a visit. Have a good watch."

Ten did not take the car out immediately. Instead, he started to walk through the shopping mall first, but almost before he left the storefront, the radio in his ear murmured, "North Twenty-five. Assault, Thelis industrial mall, Nubasar Printing."

He raced for the car, acknowledging the call as he ran.

Arriving at Nubasar Printing in Thelis, he found the victim, a calligrapher named Ru, groaning in the middle of the printshop. Other employees had offered what comfort they could, a blanket to wrap in and a rolled cape under the bloodied head. Ru was only marginally conscious, unable to talk, so Ten patted one furred shoulder comfortingly and examined the wound on the back of the Egara's head. The clean line of the laceration suggested it had been inflicted by something with a sharp edge. He looked around for a candidate. Before long, an Egara pointed out a metal stool with blood on the edge of the seat. Ten peered at it, but left it sitting where it had been found, before a printer computer whose large tracing screen had been smashed.

"Don't anyone touch anything," he said. "I'm bringing up a Criminalistics unit to examine the shop for possible personal traces left by the assailant."

The question was, of course, what had happened. The ambulance had taken Ru to the hospital and the C-unit arrived and started processing the shop before the questioning of the other shop employees produced a possible answer.

Ru had been scheduled to set up a long job on the printer. It was the consensus that being a conscientious person, the calligrapher had probably come early to get started. No other employees had been in the printshop at the time. Despite its size and work volume, the printshop ran only thirty-four hours a day—by Egarad counting. It shut down ten hours for cleaning and equipment maintenance. However, that rarely took the whole ten hours, usually no more than five or six.

"So someone familiar with the routine could expect to find it empty for at least two hours?"

"Yes."

It looked to Ten as though someone intending to vandalize the printshop started to make use of those hours . . . and was interrupted by Ru. The vandal hit Ru from behind and fled.

"Who would know your routine?" Ten asked.

Any number of people, it turned out: employees, clients, and employees in surrounding workshops. Ten sighed. He might have known. And of course, except for a hook high on the door to keep out children and igelis, and remind adults not to trespass, the printshop was never locked.

"I'd like a list of your employees, particularly Silents, working here now or who left or were fired for any reason in the past year."

"North Twenty-five," his radio murmured. "Vandalism, B'gen Antiquities, D'she shopping mall."

He grimaced. Another one? "En route," he replied. He looked at the shop foreman. "If you'll make up that list for me, I'll come back later after it." He headed for the car.

The vandal in the printshop had been interrupted, but the one who went through the antique shop had had time to do a thorough job and used every minute. From the door of the shop, Ten surveyed piles of broken glass and pottery, splintered wood, and twisted metal. He made his way carefully through them to a small salt-and pepper-furred Egara sitting with a black luras on a stool in the center of the devastation.

"B'gen?" Ten asked.

"Ruined," B'gen said, face buried against the luras.

Ten pulled off his helmet. "Yes." His eyes moved from the shredded remains of a tapestry on one wall to pieces of translucent white stone at his feet, so smashed he could not begin to guess what they had once been part of. "You found the shop like this when you came in to open?"

B'gen looked around. "Irreplaceable." The shopkeeper slid off the stool and wandered through the shop, still holding the luras.

"Please don't touch anything," Ten warned. "What are some of these things?"

"Sen Nuraled, seventy-fifth century," B'gen said, stopping before the tapestry. A scarlet-booted toe touched a copper platter bent almost double. "Twentieth-century Shubenad." And with a groan, the shopkeeper squatted by the translucent shards at Ten's feet. "Sith Marad urn, sixty-second century."

Ten squatted on his heels, too, feeling the other's pain. "I'm so very sorry. I've passed this shop many times and always admired the items on display in the windows. If you'll help me, maybe I can find the person who did this. Have you had any recent disagreements with anyone, particularly a Silent?"

"Brrrt?" the luras said.

Ten reached out to stroke the animal's head.

"Reason?" B'gen asked, looking up at Ten. "Reason?"

"Revenge, perhaps. We're beginning to see a pattern in these incidents. Please try to remember anyone you might have offended."

B'gen touched a delicate fragment. "Unique."

Ten sighed. B'gen appeared as incapable of answering questions as Ru. Still petting the luras, Ten tapped his ear. "North Twenty-five, Communications. Advise the C-unit at Nubasar Printing that when they've finished there, I need them at B'gen Antiquities in the D'she shopping mall."

When Communications acknowledged, he stood and walked around the shop, scanning it with his kinecorder. The destruction was not quite complete, he discovered. A few items had escaped damage. How? This puzzled him. Why should a fragile piece of glassware sit untouched while a metal goblet next to it had been pounded flat? Surely the glassware would have been easier to destroy.

B'gen's eyes lifted from the floor to focus on the glassware, then flicked toward the flattened goblet. "Shubish dynasty. Forty-two extant."

B'gen cared nothing that a piece remained untouched? The shopkeeper looked at him. "Minor."

Ten frowned thoughtfully. He eyed the other untouched pieces. "What about that stool? How valuable is it?"

"Minor."

"And that ceramic statue of an irath?"

"Minor."

Ten rubbed his thumb down the cleft in his chin. "Have only the really valuable pieces been destroyed?"

"Yes," B'gen said with a groan.

Ten sucked on his lower lip. Then whoever did this knew antiques. That should narrow the field a little. "Do you have a bitter competitor, say one who is a Silent?"

"No."

Which left him, probably, with a choice of employees and customers. With patient persuasion, Ten pulled B'gen's attention away from the broken items and put the shopkeeper to work listing people with whom B'gen remembered disagreeing. Through questions asked so they could be answered with a simple *yes* or *no*, Ten confirmed what he had observed coming through the shopping mall on the way to briefing every morning, that the shops near B'gen's all closed during the night. Probably no open shop lay near enough for the people in it to have heard noise during the time the vandalism must have occurred. Still, he wrote a note to post in the storefront, asking Dal Kiefer, the Evening Watch officer, and Iryl Consigli to talk to people in the shops on their watches and see if anyone heard or read anything.

Ten took B'gen's completed list and, after the C-unit arrived, headed back for the printshop to pick up the foreman's list. He phoned the names to Investigations, volunteering to check out the local ones and possible witnesses. That gave him plenty to do while walking through the malls and ishen. He also made a point of visiting Rabala Shen to congratulate everyone on the new babies, though he declined their mother's offer to let him hold the twins. Egarad babies, still hairless, did not look so very different from Terran ones, he discovered.

Most of the talking brought him no useful information, but in the upholstery shop across from Nubasar Printing, he found a witness.

"Saw," the witness said, casually tossing huge bolts of upholstery fabric from a paragee platform onto shop shelves.

Ten could hardly believe his luck. He stared at the

blue-gray Egara, who wore a white fan design on the forehead and another over each shoulder like epaulets. "You saw someone in the printshop or leaving it?"

"There." Fan pointed toward a small plaza area near the edge of the mall. "Read. Remembered. Looked. Saw."

Ten passionately wished he could read the thought streams and concept images behind each word. He tried for an explanation one word at a time. "You read another mind? The assailant's?"

"Ru."

"During the attack?"

"Yes." Fan never stopped working.

"Did Ru see the assailant?"

"No."

"What was it you remembered?"

"You."

"*Me*?" He may well have talked to this particular Egara before; he talked to as many people as possible in his patrol, but he could not remember what he might have said.

"Said look." Fan pointed to an eye. "Said see. Looked. Saw."

"You saw what this fleeing person looked like?"

"Yes."

A question at a time, the description emerged, a Silent wearing yellow hip boots and a red tabard, approximately three hundred twelve *hin* tall—which worked out to a hundred sixty centimeters—of medium Egarad build, red roan in color, decorated with white and black crescents.

"You saw this person *that* clearly?" Ten asked with some skepticism. The light could not have been very good at that hour.

"No. Recognized. Worked." Fan pointed toward the printshop.

The old familiar pattern. "The person you saw once worked in the printshop?"

"Yes."

Which did not necessarily mean the person Fan had seen was the guilty party; Ten refused to fall into the trap they had with Ladras over Haritheen's death, but the odds made that person a fine candidate for investigation, and that made him feel so good that when he passed Dal Kiefer in the storefront at the end of the watch, Kiefer eyed him suspiciously.

"You aren't on anything, are you?"

"Satisfaction," Ten came back, and told him about it.

Kiefer listened enviously. "I'm glad you had a good watch."

Ten regarded Kiefer with concern. The other officer looked tired and tense, as though he had already served a full watch, and a bad one. Was it related to Ashe's death? Ten wondered. Evening Watch officers must be hit particularly hard by that.

After debriefing and filling out reports, Ten caught the skyrail south to the stationhouse without bothering to change out of his uniform. His haste did not help him catch the day Criminalistics technicians before they left, but he found Bioni Elanca, the section chief, still there. He put on his most persuasive smile as he begged her for the print and antique shop findings.

Elanca had the pouter-pigeon plumpness of a middle-class matron, but her eyes gleamed hard and sharp as flint. "Don't oil me, officer. I have a son on Earth about your age who inoculated me against beautiful boys by practicing his charm on me while he was growing up. We haven't finished all the analyses yet, but if you can restrain your eagerness for a few minutes, I'll see what we do have."

She led him through the laboratory. Little of value had been found in the printshop except to confirm through blood and hair matching that the stool had been used as the weapon to strike Ru.

"But we had some luck in the antique shop," Elanca said. She showed him a holo and cast of a footprint found in some plaster dust. "There are several distinctive scars there that will help us match the boot if you find us a suspect sole."

She moved on to the micro section. "And it appears your vandal put a fist through a glass case. Left a piece of hide behind. You're looking for a suspect with a cut on one arm, a mature individual with liver-chestnut fur with a bright red design. Hair analyses show some of the hair dark and some bleached and dyed red. Meda, do you have the dye identified yet?"

A young woman with toffee-gold skin looked up from dropping reagents into shallow dishes. "Yes. I'm just trying to match it to local products. I'm pretty sure it's an Egarad dye."

That must be the director's wife, Ten thought. He had

heard she worked in the lab. He had not expected her to be so young, though, or so beautiful. She appeared to be tense, however, rather like Pol. He wondered how Pol's talk with the psyman was going.

"Call us tomorrow," Elanca said. "We'll have more answers for you then."

Ten left, heading for the firing range. Although they were no longer expected to fire anything more lethal than a sleeper, shooting qualification remained a requirement and he practiced frequently. He found himself at the barrier beside Bara Deem and nodded a greeting to her. The range master handed him a needler sidearm.

Ten concentrated on the circle in the middle of the target silhouette, staring at it until nothing else in the world existed. He was hardly conscious of raising and firing the needler. Each needle marked the target with a splash of ink. After ten shots, he lowered the needler. All the ink spots lay within the fifteen-centimeter circle. Not bad, he decided. He fired four more groups of ten, with each grouping tighter than the last, and the final round, fired with his eyes closed, all lay within the seven-centimeter circle.

"Very nice," Bara said. "You'll score well come qualification."

He glanced over at her target. "No better than you. Hand/eye coordination works again. Would you like some coffee?"

They walked around to the canteen. Ten chucked two red work unit disks into the tube beside the coffee urn and filled two cups. "I wonder how Pol and Deathrage are doing," he said.

Bara accepted a cup and sipped the steaming liquid. "I hope she can help him."

"What's wrong?"

She shrugged. "He won't talk about it. I'm sure it has to do with the Iregara; he's been tense and withdrawn ever since we went on patrol, though he tries to hide it. He has nightmares . . . sweats and twitches and groans all night. I've begged him to talk to me, but he won't. I think stubborn pride must be part of the Neo-Texan image." She paused to take another swallow of coffee. "I haven't seen him off-duty for two days now, not since you told us about Roban's case being thrown out of court. He played the jolly cowboy at the holo showing but I could tell he was upset about something. Later . . ." She grimaced. "Well, nothing went right in bed and he blamed me . . . said nothing like that *ever* happened to him with any *other* woman. He was so vicious about it, I left. Maybe I shouldn't have done that, do you think?"

"I don't know." Ten sucked on his lower lip. "I guess we'll know how it went when we see him tomorrow at briefing."

"He's off for the next two days." Bara glanced sideways at Ten. "Would you like to come over for supper? I have more Egarad wine and I feel like company tonight."

So did Ten. He accepted her invitation. For a moment, though, seeing her house for the first time, he almost regretted doing so. He had heard her say she lived in a geodesic dome. He had not expected it to be built almost entirely of Sunsorb window material and uncurtained, open to the view of the entire shen. The fact that so was every other house did nothing to lessen his self-consciousness.

"Talk about living in glass houses."

Bara frowned. "Do you hate it, too? Pol saw it once from the outside and refused to come in. He always insisted we go to his place."

"I don't insist." Ten grinned. "If Billy Pilgrim could do it, so can I."

She blinked. "Who? What watch does he work?"

His grin broadened. "He's a character in an old novel Brithe loaned me to read. Part of the time he lived on exhibit on the planet Tralfamadore."

Bara looked thoughtful. "I think I have an uncle who emigrated to there."

"This is a fictional Tralfamadore." He told her the story over supper.

Listening, she smiled. "Brithe loaned you this book? She's teaching you almost as much about your own cultural heritage as Egar's, it sounds like."

Somewhat sheepishly, Ten had to agree.

They moved into the sitting area after supper and stretched out on piles of cushions. As the light faded, the walls became more mirror and less window. Distorted reflections of the room and themselves looked back from each triangular pane.

Sipping her wine, Bara said, "I find these people a wonderful relief. Once you accept the fact that your head is as transparent as these walls, you can quit pretending. You can tear up all the masks and be what you are, say what you feel."

Ten swirled his wine in its glass. "Very nice in theory, but . . . maybe you don't have thoughts you'd just as soon no one around you knew about."

She laughed. "Oh, I have them, and I'm just as embarrassed as anyone being caught thinking them, but there are compensations. For example, today I was trying to ask this Egara some questions. The citizen had information I needed to know, but I couldn't understand the answers at all. I got madder and madder until I wanted to dent the good citizen's skull with my baton. Finally I came out and expressed my opinion of the citizen's ancestry. What would that have gotten me back home?"

"If you did it to a so-called upstanding citizen or a high holy?" Ten grimaced. "A complaint to Internal Affairs at the very least."

"Well, this Egara just looked at me with those big, unreadable purple eyes and said, in essence, that I could think what I liked, however wrong I was." She laughed. "It didn't answer my questions, but it did clear my head, and eventually we started to communicate." She paused. "You can't tell me you object very much to being read; you're the one exploiting telepathy to direct Normals how to catch suspects for you and inviting them into your head to communicate with Silents."

"But that's *business.*"

"Wouldn't you like to be able to say exactly what you think all the time?"

She had an attractive argument.

"And since I've been preaching saying what one feels," she went on, "I'll admit I don't feel like throwing you out into the cold night. I can't offer a canopy over the dome, but with the lights out, the effect is almost the same."

He looked at her over his wine glass. "What about Pol?"

"Like my mother, despite the efforts of the high holies to enslave women to men, I'm my own person. I owe Pol only loyalty as a friend, not sexual fidelity. Do you want to stay?"

Ten considered, then held out his glass for more wine. "Yes."

Chapter Fourteen

THE TROUBLE with spending the night at Bara's house, Ten decided, was morning. He hated crawling out of bed into the frigid dawn to catch the skyrail home in time to clean up and reach the storefront for briefing. All the way from the east end of the city's south leg, back around the western end of Rahelem Bay and north to Meem Shen made a long, chilly ride. However, one benefit emerged; in the hurry to avoid being late, he actually arrived at the storefront early. It left him time enough to call the station and learn that the lab had identified the dye found on the antique shop vandal's hair. Before the character forming on the phone screen could be completed, however, a Terran voice came on the line.

"This is Inspector Corine Paget. I've been assigned to the case. You have special interest in this?" She did not sound hostile, just briskly efficient.

Ten remembered her from orientation, small and compact, with the grace of a gymnast. He told her, "I'm interested in clearing anything that happens in my patrol."

"You can be a big help to me if you want, then. The dye is a local one, brand name Sushan, color name Copper Flame. It's distributed solely to those shops where the Iregara have their fur decorated."

"Decco shops."

"Right. Now, I've called the decco suppliers and obtained the names of the shops buying Sushan dyes. Would you visit those in your patrol and find out which ones have used Copper Flame on an adult with liver-chestnut fur? This vandal might very well live in your cluster."

"Give me the shop names."

In the first few shops Ten became so fascinated watching the decco artists work, he almost forgot to ask his ques-

135

tions. With the customer lying on a workbench, the artist laid out the design, outlining it first by applying dye or bleach a few drops at a time, then filling in. Soap-and-water-soluble paints could also be applied if the customer wanted only a temporary design. Beading like Brithe's was sprayed on. The average design, he learned, needed to be renewed at least once a year . . . more often if the individual shed a great deal.

Watching one artist, Ten asked, "Wouldn't it be easier if you used a mask, something like a sheet of static plastic with the design cut out of the middle of it?"

The artist looked up, regarding Ten with a stare that, however impassive, made him feel as he had when his mother caught him tracking mud across a clean floor. "Easier," the artist agreed, and without further comment returned to work.

But decco artists, he discovered, were one group who remembered what other people *looked* like. They remembered colors and designs applied as long as two years before. In fact, unlike other Iregara, colors and designs were almost all they remembered. They had difficulty recalling whether specific individuals were Normal or Silent.

"Do you remember decorating a liver chestnut with Copper Flame?" Ten asked.

Those that had, did, and eventually one shop in the Neer business mall produced a name, Anubas, which Ten also found on B'gen's list as an employee discharged just three days before the vandalism. He called Inspector Paget. Paget, however, was out. After a short debate, Ten decided to call on Anubas himself.

Ten found the Egara in Little Hills Shen. Looking at a strip of fur and hide missing from the right forearm, Ten asked, "May I look at your boots?"

Anubas appeared dazed. Mechanically, the Egara pulled off the boots and handed them to Ten, then stood back with arms wrapped tightly around a young child. On the sole of one boot Ten found scars bearing a strong resemblance to those on the print found in B'gen's shop.

"I think we ought to take your child to one of your neighbors," Ten said.

Anubas hugged the child tighter. "It wasn't my fault."

Ten's mouth thinned. "No one forced you to vandalize the shop."

"It wasn't my fault about the customers. I tried to work

with them. I tried hard, but . . ." Around the child's back, both fists clenched. "I hate them."

Ten sighed. "Let's find someone to take care of the child."

Anubas led the way to a house across the lane. The Egara who answered the door looked at Anubas, then Ten. "Understand."

Ten turned away unhappily while Anubas said good-bye to the child. He wished the vandal could have been male or a childless female. He did not like doing this to a child.

When the child had gone inside, Ten pulled Anubas's wrists behind her back and wrapped them. "Let's go."

"I don't know why I destroyed those things," Anubas said in a flat voice. "It's B'gen I hate. It's B'gen I wanted to kill. I love treasures like those. They're beautiful and unique. They can't be replaced. But I was so furious . . . it was like I stood a long way off watching myself; I couldn't interfere, no matter how much I wanted to stop what was happening."

Ten carefully recorded it all with his kinecorder and called for prisoner transport.

A few hours later he learned that the printshop foreman had identified a former employee from the description Ten's witness gave. Nevel Roche, North Twenty-four, located the suspect in his cluster and made an arrest.

Ten found himself in for congratulations and good-natured kidding both that day at debriefing and again late the next afternoon in the rear of the stationhouse after marksmanship, baton, and open-hand qualification, while waiting for their physical test.

"Lucky leo," Bara said. "Two complaints from your patrol cleared in three days and then you wrapped that proxy killer in court today."

"The Haritheen case is Roban's," Ten said, "and it isn't finished yet; the mediator only agreed to examine the evidence. We go back for formal hearing Autumnday 4. However"—he grinned—"we have high hopes."

Bara grinned back. "Why don't we celebrate your success tonight?"

"Not yet." He did not feel at all like celebrating Anubas's arrest. The recorded confession bothered him. Could it be used? How did one handle self-incrimination in a society where it could not be avoided by most of the population?

He found himself disturbed by B'gen's attitude, too. The antique dealer wanted Anubas confined to a care facility as an incurable antisocial. On Earth Ten had never questioned prison as a solution, but care facilities, he knew from orientation, were not like prisons. They had more in common with psychiatric hospitals, except that they did not extend lifelong care. No sentence lasted longer than five years. If, at the end of that time, an inmate was judged incurable, a nonproductive citizen who only caused himself and others pain, he was euthanized.

"I think the antique shop vandal regrets what happened there. I'm trying to convince the shopkeeper to drop the antisocial charge and be content with suing for reparations."

Bara met his eyes solemnly. "I'll keep my fingers crossed."

"What is this, a Gathering or physical qualification?" the trainer cried. "Come on, who's next?" Ogilvie looked at Ten. "How about you, Kampacalas? You look full of energy. The course is down the valley past the travelport terminal to the flag and back, then over the obstacle course."

"Sadist," Ten said.

"Save your breath, boy; that's eight iyah ahead of you."

"Ten. There's no such number as eight here."

The trainer rolled his eyes. "A right fly kid, aren't you? Go!"

It was a shorter distance than many of the training runs he had made, but the pace had to be faster to meet the time limit. Even that might not have been so bad, except for jumping barriers and climbing walls at the end, in pursuit of an imaginary suspect. Ten tried not to gasp too hard while Doctor Goodnight recorded his heart rate, respiration, and blood pressure afterward.

"I'd still like to see more muscle on you, officer," Goodnight said, "but you seem fit enough otherwise." He marked Ten's form: *passed*.

Ten staggered to the locker room and collapsed on a bench.

Bara came in a few minutes later. "Thank god that's over for a while," she sighed, dropping down beside Ten. She sucked in a deep breath and blew it out again. "I just passed Pol coming from the range."

Ten forgot his pain. "How does he look?"

She bit her lip. "He *looks* fine, but Trini Van Swaay was

right behind him and she says his hands shook so bad on the range he didn't have anything close to a grouping. He couldn't qualify."

Ten ran both hands through his sweat-soaked hair. "I think I'll wait for him before I shower."

"Me, too."

While they waited, officers flowed through the locker room, into the showers sweaty and groaning, out again cleaner but still complaining. Finally Pol arrived. He moved more easily than most, his breathing almost normal.

Bara and Ten exchanged glances. Whatever else might be wrong with the Texan, he obviously remained in superior physical condition.

"How are you doing?" Ten asked him. "How did the visit with Deathrage go?"

Pol turned. "Why should you care?" He spoke without his drawl.

Ten blinked, taken aback, then smiled tentatively. "Because I'm your friend."

"Friend." Pol spat the word. "Is that why the minute my back is turned you're flatdancing my woman?"

And before Ten could react, Pol grabbed him by the throat and threw him backward into a wall. The Big Bang went off in Ten's head. Through the thunder and lights of spreading galaxies, he dimly heard people yelling, heard Bara's voice lashing angrily: ". . . no brand on me, cowboy," and then, full of concern: "Ten, can you hear me? Are you all right? Talk to me."

"I'm all right." He groped for a bench and sat down holding his head. The back of it throbbed with a pain he felt all the way to his fingers and toes.

The rest of the group present had dragged Pol across the room and were holding him against the far wall, yelling at him to take it easy, but Pol still struggled, cursing Ten.

"*Stop that!* All of you calm down *right now!*" Everyone looked up to find Sergeant Brynche in the doorway. She took in both Ten and Pol with one sweeping glance around the room. "I won't even ask what this is about. If you were on my watch, you'd both lose a day!"

Ten peered up at her. Granted he did not see much of her, but did she usually react this strongly? He thought she looked unusually pale.

"While you're brawling like gutter rats, Martine Her-Many-Horses—" She broke off to swallow.

In the sudden silence, Ten heard his heart hammering.

Brynche went on in a tight voice, "We just found Officer Her-Many-Horses with her throat cut on a neck wire."

Chapter Fifteen

"I NEED more personnel," Devane said. He looked around the grouped briefing-room desks at the members of the police board, aiming urgency at each of them. "I need two-officer cars on the Evening Watch."

After all the times he had met with them, Devane still found their faces unreadable, but experience had taught him roughly how each might be reacting. Lishulir and Gemun were undoubtedly thinking *no* and *if they can't handle the job, send them home.* Anaya and Seche might be considering a *yes* vote. Ibal would be using deep-reading to probe into Devane and read underlying thought streams.

"Need?" Ibal asked softly.

Devane liked Ibal, but his feeling rode a fine line between admiration and irritation at the effect the healer's comments invariably had, that of making Devane reexamine his words and feelings.

"Need. It isn't that we can't work with the personnel we have, but I have sixty-five officers on the Evening Watch—that's a hundred and one to you—in a state of panic, afraid for their lives. With two officers in a car, they can protect each other, but I don't have enough people now to double them up. That makes more personnel a *want* that equals *need.*"

"Have," Gemun said. "Reliefs."

"I need the relief officers in that capacity. I can't ask everyone to work without time off. They work more hours and days now than they ever did on Earth."

"Reallocate," Lishulir said, and began tapping numbers into the cal-chron on one wrist. The Sebigeth Textile Mill's personnel director jotted the resulting figures down on a notepad and pushed it up the line of desks to Devane.

Devane read the calculation with a frown. "No," he said

emphatically. "This strips the other watches down to just the permanent patrol in each cluster. It doesn't leave us with any floating patrols to cover hot spots."

"Temporary," Lishulir pointed out.

"Recorders," Anaya, their lawyer member, said.

Gemun came back, "Expensive."

"Not preventative," Ibal said.

Devane strained to follow the meaning of the exchange. "Are you talking about recorders in the cars?"

Ibal said, "Rejected."

The recorders would have been better than nothing, though as Ibal pointed out, their only value came after something had already happened to the officer in the car. They hardly constituted a deterrent.

"Reallocation," Lishulir repeated.

Devane shook his head, still disagreeing. "We're finally starting to have an effect. The clearance rate is slowly increasing and the incident rate decreasing. The floating patrols and impromptus are important factors in that decrease by keeping perpetrators uncertain when a cop will appear in a particular area. Don't destroy the little progress we've made."

Gemun murmured, "Insignificant."

Seche looked up from doodling textile designs on a notepad and said in careful Translan, "I read historic police had . . ." Seche searched for the term and came up with two English words. "Ride-alongs."

Devane regarded the textile designer with delight. Seche, whose Terraphilia had led to learning Translan and producing the name *cops* for D'shenegar's police officers, kept surprising him. He could not recall ever having heard of such a thing. "Who rode along?"

Seche went back to Isegis. "Citizens. Cadets. Reserves."

Civilians? What a good opportunity to improve public relations that must have been. A pity it had been abandoned, though Devane could understand why. Few officers these days would agree to civilians in the car except as prisoners or emergency passengers. Even if they could be reassured that the citizen did not intend to back-shoot them, they would rebel at accepting the added anxiety of maintaining a passenger's safety while answering calls.

But the idea of cadets and reserves, now . . . that offered possibilities. Perhaps he could initiate a prerecruitment program, offering rides to citizens who might consider applying for appointment to the department later. That would not only give the Evening Watch officers some friendly, interested company, but would present the opportunity to learn advantages and possible problems presented by Egarad officers, suggesting how the future police training must be tailored for them.

Which brought up the question of what kind of training to give the ride-alongs. He did not want to add to his officers' worries. He would have preferred an abbreviated police course, but at this point, they had no time for that. In order to put another body in each car as soon as possible, they might have to settle for a Quickteach orientation session that outlined police duties and methods and included emphatic orders to obey the officers they rode with.

"I'll agree to ride-alongs," Devane said.

"Yes," Anaya said.

The vote went around the desks, spoken aloud principally for his benefit, Devane knew, and to his astonishment, for the first time since he had known them, the board voted unanimously. But why not? Even Gemun and Lishulir could have few objections to a program that avoided bringing more Terrans to Egar and cost the citizenry very little but their time.

Once the ride-along proposal had passed, the remainder of the meeting consisted of planning publicity and implementation.

For the second day in a row, Martine Her-Many-Horses' murder dominated debriefing. As Robbie's relief and not their regular watch supervisor, Lieutenant Jaia Dryden made no attempt to restrain them, just sat back with Cathcart and Vasja Hershey, a relief sergeant, and let them talk.

"I thought we left neck wires and other lion traps behind on Earth," Finn Hildebrand said.

"It looks like they followed us."

Ten could not see who spoke, but he joined the shudder that swept across the room like a wave. The thin, nearly-invisible monofilament wires had menaced law officers for five hundred years. They could be strung anywhere and if hit, cut through skin and muscle to bone in a fraction of a second. Defenses had been developed, the most satisfactory so far being a shield with a serpentine strand of monofilament embedded in a clear plastic matrix. A paragee field helped, too. Set at full strength, it resisted wire with detectable pressure. However, there were always a few cases every year where officers were caught without a shield, through carelessness, haste, or failure to expect trouble, and were traveling too fast to stop when the telltale rebound warned them of the paragee field meeting wire.

Ten would never forget the weed-tangled lot where he and another rookie had cornered a man suspected of beating two prostitutes to death. Crossing the lot, Ten turned his ankle in a hole and fell. That accident probably saved his life, because several strides later, crossing between two trees, the other rookie hit a waist-high wire. It sliced to his backbone and then, horribly, as he started to fall, caught up under his ribs. He hung there suspended, screaming, flailing like a spastic marionette . . . spilling entrails and what seemed to Ten like gallons of blood out onto the ground. The rookie had not lived long, not more than a minute, probably, until the aorta pumped itself dry, but Ten remembered it as hours, and hours more that he had lain on the ground retching until he found control enough to activate his radio and call for help.

And now that kind of horror had come to Egar, too, where they had no antiwire shields yet? How soon could the department purchase some? he wondered.

"Well, that must mean our killer can't be Egarad," someone said. "How would they know about monofilament?"

"Any Silent who's been to Earth could have heard about it."

"Or any Normal could read about it in our own minds," Pol said, with no trace of a drawl.

Ten watched the Texan on the far side of the room unhappily. He had been trying for two days to speak to him, either at briefing or debriefing, but since the fight in the locker room, Pol had avoided him, only glaring at Bara and him from a distance.

Mab Heier said, "Maybe, but what does that have to do with using a monofilament on Many-Horses? No Normal killed her."

"How can we be sure?" Pol asked.

Several people came back at once. "Other Normals would know. The witnesses around when she died didn't read any Normal minds with knowledge of what would happen to her."

"We have only their word for that."

Neval Roche stared at Pol. "Normals don't lie."

Pol looked back steadily. "How do we know? We can't read their minds to tell, though they can read anything they want in ours. They could all be in a conspiracy against us."

That had to be Pol's problem, Ten decided. He caught Bara's eye. Pol could not accept the telepathy. It was why he refused to enter Bara's house, and why he had gone impotent after hearing about the deep-reading talent of mediators.

"I don't think we can trust anything the furries tell us," Pol went on.

Lieutenant Dryden reacted to that. "Wassom, the director has forbidden the use of that term! And I think you're being rather free with unfounded accusations."

Pol's mouth set in a thin line. "I don't think it's unfounded. There were dozens of Normals around when Many-Horses went up the passage and hit the wire, yet all of them swear they read no other minds and didn't see whomever it was she chased. How is that possible? One of them must have seen *something*. If they all claim they didn't, they're lying."

Normals lie? Normals in a giant organized plot against Terran police? Ridiculous, Ten thought. Pol had gone raving paranoid. And yet . . . what *did* they have besides the word of the Iregara what Iregara were like? How many human telepaths existed to verify the truth? And even if what the Iregara claimed was generally true, did that rule out the possibility that the people of D'shenegar had gone anti-Terran/antipolice enough to slag cops?

Ten shook himself. What was he doing? He sounded as brainbowed as Pol. Looking around, though, he saw his new doubts reflected in sixty-eight other faces, including those of the lieutenant and sergeants. Only Bara's carried a refusal to believe such a thing.

"You're wickers, Pol," she snapped. "There's no conspiracy. There's only some vicious Silent."

"You'll probably be the next victim," Pol said, "and you'll deserve it."

If they had occupied the same room, Ten would have bounced Pol off the nearest wall. No matter how troubled in mind, Pol had no right to talk like that. Bara went white, and around the room uniformed bodies stiffened and eyes flashed in anger, informing Ten that others shared his opinion. A few started to express themselves vocally.

Dryden stopped being passive. "All right, everyone back off. Calm down. Wassom, expressing feelings doesn't include the right to gut-kick."

"I'm just trying to warn you. You all wait. The minute this ride-along program starts, the rest of the Evening Watch will be dead, too. They're all after us, prying into our heads to find weapons to use against us. You wouldn't find me taking one of them as a passenger, even if I worked Evening Watch."

The sergeants exchanged quick glances. Lieutenant Dryden looked at Pol for a moment, then said quietly, "Perhaps we can arrange that you never have to worry about that, Officer Wassom."

"He isn't responsible for what he's saying, Ten," Bara said. "He isn't rational any longer."

Ten ran a hand through his hair. "Maybe."

They walked together in the woods outside Meem Shen, through the deepening shadows under the trees. This evening, with Pol's words echoing and reechoing in his head, Ten wanted to stay away from Iregara. He did not want them knowing anything he thought or felt. If Pol was right, then he would be in danger because the plot had been discovered. If Pol was wrong . . . how could normal relations ever exist again between the police and the citizens of D'shenegar? Trust would have been destroyed. He had asked Bara to join him and headed here as soon as debriefing ended, hoping no one in the shopping mall was reading him.

He watched a thilis dart from branch to branch overhead, a red flutter of wings and a bright, trilling song. "As Pol says, how do we know?"

"*I* know."

He looked sideways at her. "How? Telepathy? Intuition? Wishful thinking?"

"You can't actually believe that three hundred thousand people are all plotting to kill us, or hiding someone who is! That's brainbowed! If they want to be rid of us, all they have to do is kick us off the planet. If they want to kill Terrans, they have plenty in the Enclave; they don't need to import any more." Her voice lowered as it increased in intensity. "If you're hostile or suspicious, everyone will know it. Don't let Pol's nightmares jeopardize your performance and usefulness here."

"I *know* they'll know it," he snapped. "That's why I'm out here, away from them . . . to try to work it out." He sighed heavily, unhappily. "I know Pol's probably talking out of the wild blue yonder. At least, part of me knows it, but the rest . . . What he says resonates."

It rang in his very bones, echoing old fears learned on Earth. It called up memories of that other rookie hanging on the monofilament, and of Oakland division citizens setting traps or waiting to attack officers coming to answer simple domestic disturbance calls.

"I know," Bara said, "but you can't listen to it. Ten, we have a chance to be something else here, not lions, not feared and hated all the time. We can be friends with these people."

He eyed her. She really believed that. He had thought so, too, when he signed up for Egar. Now—now he no longer knew. Somehow he doubted it. The gulf between the races was too wide. "I think you're dreaming, Bara. Director Brooks can call us Conservators of Peace or anything else he wants, but we still represent the 'thou shalt not' voice of society. Whatever we do infringes on someone's freedom."

She came back, "Are you saying 'thou shalt not' when you try to convince a shopkeeper to sue for restitution instead of having the vandal locked up? Aren't you saying, 'There's a better way'? By stopping to deal with a victim instead of instantly racing off after a perpetrator, aren't we saying, 'Let us help'?"

He smiled down at her. "What ever made you go into police work?"

"My father was a leo. He died saving three kids from a sniper when I was four years old . . . a hero's death. I grew up wanting to be just like him."

"I assume you were less outspoken in St. Paul?"

She laughed wryly. "Not outspoken at all. My mother was; she'd say exactly what she thought, everyone else be damned, even high holies, but I never had the nerve to do that . . . not until I came here. And now that I feel like I'm breathing free for the first time in my life"—she looked fiercely up at him—"I'm not going to let Pol turn the rest of you into raving paranoids and spoil it all for me."

Ten might have laughed if the knots in his chest and gut had been looser. "I wish there were some way to know for certain the Iregara are what they say."

"There are a few human telepaths. They've never reported inconsistencies, have they?"

"No . . ." He stood thinking for a minute, then turned and broke into a jog.

Bara fell into stride beside him. "Where are we going?"

"To talk to Brithe. I hope she's home."

She was. From the doorway she eyed the two of them without expression. "I didn't expect you tonight . . . certainly not with anyone else."

"I have a question and you're the only person I know who might be able to answer it," Ten said.

She considered for a moment, then backed out of the doorway to let them in. "What question?"

He told her about Pol's accusation. "Can he be right?"

She curled in a chair, one finger tracing the carving on a heavy wooden arm. "How can I know? I don't read minds either, remember."

"But they're your people. Have you ever seen any behavior that differed from something they told you, behavior that might suggest they lied?"

She absently brushed one hand down the fur of the other forearm, making iridescent rainbows. "No," she replied slowly. "I don't think so. In my experience, the words of Normals have always been matched by their actions.

"I don't think there can possibly be a conspiracy against you, and I'm sure no one would protect a person who had become—what's your word?—masochistic, someone who would kill for the pleasure of feeling the dying one's pain. Those deviants are always confined in care facilities as soon as they're identified."

The knots inside Ten loosened. Leather creaked as he relaxed in his chair. "You can't know how relieved I am to hear that."

Brithe's fur rippled, sending more rainbows at them. "There's only one instance I know when a Normal can lie and not be detected."

Tension tightened Ten again. "What instance?"

"If the Normal is a haban."

"A what?" Bara asked.

"Haban. It's a—" Brithe sighed, hunting for words. "It's a psychotic condition. People build model realities in their heads. Sane people have model realities that almost match outside reality, but psychotics' models match little or nothing at all. I'm told that Normals identify deviant minds by that difference. Am I comprehensible?"

Ten nodded.

She went on, "There are Normals who can impose bits of their reality on someone else. A healer does it. She builds an image of health in her own mind and convinces the patient that it is also *her* reality, and so the patient becomes cured. Now if a mind with that kind of power becomes psychotic, no one can detect the disparity between internal and external realities because anyone reading the haban mind has that reality imposed on her, too."

Ten stared at her. "Then one of them could kill and pretend the victim felt no alarm or didn't notice the killer?"

"Not pretend . . . believe. The haban has to believe her actions are something else. Even insane Iregara can't fabricate a lie."

"Could the haban imagine he couldn't be read and convince witnesses of that?" Bara asked.

Brithe considered. "I don't know. Perhaps."

Ten and Bara looked at each other. Ten felt his grimace echo hers. A Normal whose deviance could be just as impossible to detect as a Silent's. That fit. Such a Normal could read whatever information he needed from their heads, kill them, and believing he could not be read, impress his mental invisibility on any Egarad witnesses. And that meant that instead of a few hundred possible suspects, they had three hundred thousand.

"A haban," Ten sighed.

"They're named after one of our more infamous historical personalities, Haban the Butcher, who in the fifth century led the people of Yadishin against the people of Efegan. Haban so dominated the Iyadishined minds that seven hundred people died before someone in Efegan realized where the distorted vision was coming from and killed Haban."

"And there's no way to detect one of them?" Ten asked.

"A deep-reader usually can, but perhaps not always. Fortunately, it's a rare condition."

But one could very well be out there in D'shenegar now, and one was enough when the one hated police for being invaders, for interfering with personal liberty, for being members of a race whose world Silenced so many of his people . . . for whatever reason. "Why didn't anyone mention ihaban before now?"

Brithe regarded him impassively. "Perhaps everyone has been too busy blaming Silents to consider another possibility."

That stung, but Ten recognized the point as one well taken. He flushed guiltily. "Well, now that they have been mentioned, I think I ought to inform someone in Investigations. May I use your phone?"

Chapter Sixteen

"WHAT ABOUT these ihaban, doc? Are they real?" Devane asked.

Andea Deathrage looked up from her desk to Devane standing in the doorway. She pushed a straying lock of gray hair off her forehead. "They're very real. I've checked with several healers and they confirm Brithe's information."

"So we might have one running loose around here?"

"Estimations—why don't you come in and sit down, director?—estimations I've obtained put the possibility rather higher, to as many, perhaps, as fifty. That's fifty by our counting."

"*Fifty?*" Devane came in and sat down.

Deathrage shrugged. "Actually, it's a very small percentage of the population when you consider that the healing talent occurs in about one individual in seventy-five. That fifty also includes several who are confined to care facilities and those whose psychoses aren't severe enough to warrant confinement. So if we want to talk about just the undetected, severely psychotic individuals who might be capable of these killings—"

"Yes," Devane said pleasantly, "let's talk about them."

A corner of Deathrage's mouth twitched in amusement. "Then we're talking about no more than five, according to the Iregara I've consulted, which is considerably fewer latently homicidal individuals than you'd find in a comparable Terran city."

"That's five too many." Devane ran a hand over the kinky cap of his hair and sighed. "For my people's peace of mind a psychotic telepath isn't much better than a conspiring populace. Both can read our weaknesses and strike where we're most vulnerable. I don't need to tell you what's happening to morale, especially on Evening Watch."

"No." Deathrage pushed at the straying lock again. "Some of the psychological profiles are slipping badly. You have a few officers close to tipping off."

Devane sucked in his breath. "How close? Can we help them before we lose them?"

"Oh, yes. They're still functional. I think switching them to a different watch, preferably Day, would help profoundly."

"Put someone else on Evening? Wonderful. Then I'll have a new set of officers going over the brainbow."

The psyman did not bother responding to that, only raised a brow. Devane pushed abruptly up out of his chair and began pacing. The change was inevitable, of course. The question was only *when* . . . now, while the officers were still useful, whole personalities, or after they became jacket cases.

Still pacing, he asked, "Do you have any suggestions how to choose who takes their places?"

She pushed a paper across the desk toward him. "I've made a list. The first column is the officers who must, in my opinion, be taken off Evening Watch. The second column is officers who should *not* be put on Evenings. Beyond that, the choice is yours. Take Dal Kiefer, for example. Both Consigli and Kampacalas on the other watches in his patrol are psychologically healthy individuals with good anxiety tolerance. Switching with Kiefer, their stability will hold them until the ride-alongs begin, after which they should feel less vulnerable."

Maybe, Devane thought. What they really needed to cure the problem, of course, was to catch this bastard killer. Everything else fell into the class of panaceas and stop-gap measures, a treating of mere symptoms.

"Speaking of officers tipping off, have you finished your evaluation of Pol Wassom?" he asked.

Deathrage sighed. "Yes. We might as well ship him back to Earth. He isn't the only officer seriously disturbed by the lack of mental privacy, god knows. There are about twenty-five or thirty, but in most cases I'm having good luck using hypnotherapy to convince them how desirable it is to have people around who understand exactly how one feels, that in understanding, they accept the dark corners we're afraid to show our fellow humans. In fact"—

unexpectedly, she grinned, bringing a youthful shine to her face and eyes—"I almost have myself convinced of the joys of baring my soul."

Devane pursed his lips thoughtfully. "Could you work with my wife, too?"

"I'll be happy to. Have her set up an appointment with me." Deathrage frowned. "Returning to Wassom . . . unfortunately, during that ridiculous Regionalization craze, the Texans adopted an image of their concept of the old cowboy, which calls for a man to be strongly self-sufficient, admitting no weakness or pain. Wassom is caught in that image. Put that together with the fact that he lies near the bottom end of the hypnosis-susceptible curve and what I end up with is someone almost impossible to reach in any practical length of time. He can probably still function as a police officer on Earth, but he's useless here."

Devane stopped pacing at the window. It looked out into the exercise court, where three officers jogged around the track and four more played chanach. He watched them broodingly. "They're dying here, aren't they . . . one way or another? The board may not have to shut down the department; it'll die of attrition." The thought dropped the bottom out of his stomach.

Deathrage said, "Some are being injured. On the other hand, we have many individuals adjusting well to the culture and a number who embrace it with enthusiasm." She paused. "We talked about this in the beginning, remember? We knew there would be casualties."

"That doesn't make me any happier to see fine young officers destroyed." And depression threatened at even the thought of losing his department. He spun away from the window. "Let's see the list."

He took the list to Captain Titus and caught the Uniformed division chief just leaving. He glanced at his wrist chron in surprise. "Is it that late already?"

"Later," Titus said. "I'm already overtime." But he opened the door of his office again. "Come on in."

Titus was no more pleased than Devane had been to learn about the watch switches, but he accepted the necessity. Together, the two of them went down the list and made the changes, trading assignments with Day officers in most cases and, in one, with a Morning officer. Then while Titus took the list down to Lieutenant Robbie to break the news to his officers, still in debriefing, Devane saw Lieutenant La Flore and made sure Lieutenant Scott would be notified when he came on at midnight. He came back to his office to find Meda pacing impatiently around Liril's empty desk.

"I've done everything possible I can in the lab. Aren't we ever going home? You work later every night."

Would it help to point out the worsening situation? He decided, somewhat wearily, that it would not. "I know. I'm sorry."

"If you're going to be much longer, I can go on home without you."

"Please wait. I'm almost through. There's only a few more things to take care of. Don't worry; Runah is always willing to look after Gerel."

She followed him into his office. "Too willing. He spends more time with Iregara than he does with us. Have you actually stopped and listened to him talk recently? He's starting to sound just like them."

Devane knew better than to admit he had not noticed. "I don't think it's anything to be alarmed about."

"Nothing to be alarmed about! That he won't be able to communicate with other human beings?" Meda whirled and started for the door. "Stay as long as you like. I'm going home, and when it comes time for me to leave for the Enclave, if you're not there, I'll take Gerel with me."

Devane looked up in alarm. "I'm through now." He shoved a stack of hard copy into his briefcase and hurriedly followed her.

They walked to the skyrail station and waited for the train in silence. Devane used the opportunity to pull some work out of the briefcase and go over the printouts. A few items made him wince. The Quickteach session for the ridealongs would cost more than he had anticipated; the board was going to complain about that unless the program produced good results . . . Did the cars require *that* much maintenance in an average ten-day period? And he wondered if a way could be found to trim cost on the Deviant Information Exchange System that Brithe in Data was setting up to facilitate data exchange between cities with police programs. On the train, he kept working.

"We impose on Runah too much," Meda said. She spoke normally, the impatience and edge gone from her voice.

Devane stopped working to listen.

"We can't expect a neighbor to go on indefinitely being a private child care service as a favor to us."

That touched a guilty nerve in him. He sighed. "Maybe you're right."

He thought about that the rest of the way home, and when they stopped at Runah's house to pick up Gerel, he apologized for the inconvenience of their lateness. "I'll try not to let it happen again, or else we'll work out some way to compensate you."

Runah looked impassively at him. "Not inconvenient. No imposition."

"It certainly is," Meda said, "though it's good of you to think not. Gerel, put down that creature and get your jacket."

Gerel stood holding a tiny ball of black fuzz. "Mine," he said.

"Later," Runah said. "Weaned."

Meda glanced sharply at Devane. *Hear him?* her look said. "Gerel, iluras are for Iregara, not people. I'm afraid we can't accept the cub, Runah."

Gerel's eyes filled with tears. As he returned the cub to the box where Runah's luras tended the litter, he looked up at the Egarad teacher. "Parent, please."

Meda stiffened. "Runah isn't your parent, Gerel."

"Parent," Runah said. The teacher pointed to Meda. "First-parent," then waved toward the walls. "Neighbors parents."

Devane remembered when Runah and Gerel had used the term the night Ashe died. So that was what they had meant, and why Runah kept Gerel so willingly. Meda might be the first parent, the progenitor, but all the neighbors also considered themselves parents, responsible for caring, too.

Meda paled. She pushed Gerel into his jacket and toward the door. "Goodnight, Runah."

Runah looked after her. "Feels."

Devane sighed. "I know. I'm sorry if we disturb you."

The teacher looked back to him and touched his arm. "Yes."

He slowly followed his wife and son. In the house, he found Meda alone in the kitchen area, pacing.

"I've sent Gerel to his room. We have to talk, Dee. I won't have one of those luras creatures in this house."

"Meda," he began, "they're harmless—"

"I won't have Gerel going native. And I *won't* have aliens claiming *my son!*"

He sighed. "There are any number of cultures on Earth where group parenting—"

"But these are *aliens!*" she snapped at him, never stopping her quick, nervous pacing. "You'd give your child to them, wouldn't you? You would. You'd let aliens raise your son. You don't care."

He frowned. "Certainly I care; I'm just not bothered by the fact that they're different from us. What matters is how concerned they are about Gerel's welfare, and they're concerned. If you could look at them objectively for a moment, you'd see that." He took a deep breath. This seemed like as good a time as any to broach the subject of visiting Deathrage. "Meda, Andea Deathrage has been working with officers who feel about the Iregara's telepathy as you do and she's having good success helping them—"

"Brainbending them, you mean?" she interrupted in a tight voice. "And you want me to let her stir around in my head, rearranging my personality? No." She shook her head. "I'm not interested."

For an intelligent woman, Meda could certainly be stubborn, Devane reflected. He put on an easy smile and shook his head. "She doesn't want to change your personality. She'd only be helping you see other aspects of telepathy, comforting aspects, so you won't be afraid of it any longer."

Meda backed away from him. "She'd turn me into someone who doesn't care if she's doing something in public or at home in privacy. You know how exhibitionists embarrass me; I couldn't bear to be one of them!"

"Meda, that's ridiculous," he said mildly. "She'd do nothing of the kind. Look, you don't have to agree to any therapy sessions. All I ask is that you go talk to her. Talk to her just once and if you don't like what she has to offer, I'll never mention the subject again. For your sake, and mine and Gerel's, go the one time, though."

Meda bit her lip.

"Please."

She frowned uncertainly. "Just once, and I never have to go back?"

"That's right."

She took a breath and let it out slowly. "All right. Make an appointment for me."

Grinning, he grabbed her and hugged her. "Right. I'm sure you'll be glad afterward. All you really need is to give yourself a chance to know the Iregara and—"

She pulled away from him. "Like you do, you mean? You don't know them a bit better than I do! You just accept them blindly, without understanding a thing, not how or why they do the things they do, nor whether any of it is good or bad. Of course they aren't aliens to you. Terrans aren't human, either. Everyone outside the police is just a victim, perpetrator, suspect, or witness. You don't care how these people feel about Gerel, not really; you love them because they gave you that damn *job*. The *department* is all that matters to you. If they all turned into giant spiders tomorrow, you'd go on working for them without thinking twice. I think you'd live in Hell and work for Satan himself, Devane Olin Brooks, if he'd give you a police department to play with!"

She raced up the stairs and the slam of the bedroom door shivered every window in the house.

Devane sat down on the steps into the sitting area. He rubbed wearily at his temples. She made defending himself very difficult when she threw accusations that came so close to the truth. He probably would work for the Devil, giant spiders, or anyone else who wanted him to set up and run a department.

"Daddy?" said a small voice behind him.

He looked around to see Gerel creeping down the stairs. He smiled. Gerel ran to him and threw himself into Devane's lap. "Mommy's afraid. Why?"

Devane hugged the boy. The perceptiveness of children sometimes awed him. To most people, Meda would have sounded merely angry. How could Gerel recognize that the emotion covered fear? And how could Devane explain the why of that fear to the boy?

"On Earth people are alone in their heads. You remember that, don't you? It wasn't that long ago we left there."

"Remember," Gerel agreed.

"They get used to being alone, to thinking thoughts and having feelings they're afraid other people may not approve of. It's like . . . using the san. You wouldn't like having to use one that sat open in the middle of the shen."

Gerel sat quiet for a minute. "Could," he said at last.

Devane smiled. "Well, your mother couldn't. I don't think I'd like it, either. She's also afraid of losing you. You don't act like the little boy who came to Egar with us." He paused and held the boy off so he could look him in the eyes. "Gerel, I know you don't need to use whole sentences with your teachers or schoolmates, but other Terrans aren't telepathic. Neither your mother nor I can understand what you mean when you say just one word. When you're with Terrans, you have to talk like Terrans do. You have to use sentences, even though it's slower than just thinking. Promise me you'll do that. If you do, your mother might not get so upset. And maybe, if she stops being upset, one day we can talk about getting a luras."

Gerel brightened. "Tomorrow?"

"Not tomorrow. Not until I say so. Now, promise me you'll talk like a Terran around other Terrans, and especially around your mother."

"Promise," Gerel said. He looked up the stairs. "Crying."

"What's that?"

Gerel smiled sheepishly. "Mommy is crying."

The boy's ears were certainly sharp. Devane could hear nothing. He set the boy down, stood, and took Gerel's hand. "She needs some comforting. Let's go up and talk to her. You talk to her, too. It'll make her feel better." He could cross his fingers and hope, anyway.

Gerel looked up at him and smiled. "I hope, too."

Devane smiled back. "Good boy."

Chapter Seventeen

How QUICKLY the old habits came back . . . walking cat-light, nerves stretched to their taut, humming maximum, ears alert for even a whisper of sound out of the ordinary. Ten unhooked the door of a closed shop and stepped inside. He glanced around. Even in here the light augmentation of his night goggles worked well enough to turn the darkened interior into a gray twilight. Finding nothing suspicious, he backed out and rehooked the door.

How quickly he had lost the tolerance for working under such tension, however. On his third night of Evening Watch, he felt more exhausted than he had after a full week in the Oakland division of Topeka. There, at least, he had had respites, and Avel to guard his back. He had known which shadows most likely contained danger. Here . . . death might come from anywhere. Thank god the ride-alongs began in two days. He would welcome the company. Now if the police board would just authorize purchase of antiwire shields instead of insisting that monofilament was only a temporary problem here, not worth an expenditure for shields, he might be able to start breathing easily again.

Ten moved carefully down an arcade between mall sections. He kept his baton ahead of him, swinging from ground to helmet level and back down with a rhythm regular as a metronome, alert for any vibrations along it, for any resistance that might mean a monofilament wire.

The patrol looked different at night, unfamiliar, filled with strange faces and new fur patterns. D'shenegar ran around the clock, but not with the activity of the daylight hours. Where he had grown used to activity, shops sat dark and silent, and where he would have preferred to find people, even unfamiliar ones, the malls lay empty. None of

them, however, neither shopping mall nor business and industrial malls, emptied completely, and with relief he
checked the last closed shop and moved into the still-active
section of the shopping mall. He pushed up his faceshield
long enough to remove his night goggles.

Even there, though, he felt like something of a stranger.
Eventually he would know these people, but for the present, he felt as he had his first days on patrol, having to
introduce himself everywhere, explaining who he was to
faces with no recognition in them.

Most of the shops had fewer customers so late at night,
but one business increased . . . gambling. Mornings he
had found the chance house a quiet place of desultory activity. Patronage picked up after midday, but by dark the
chance house had so filled that the gamblers even took
their games to tables outside. Filled by Egarad standards,
that is, but certainly nothing like the deafening cacophony
and buttocks-to-buttocks crowd of the smoke-filled, sweat-
reeking gambling hides he had helped Vice officers wrap in
Topeka.

Some of the games he knew, Terran roulette and dice or
Egarad versions of them. Others, however, he still did not
understand: a pile of flat, colored oval disks to be moved
with the aid of only another disk, small stars tossed in a
wire basket; a ring dropped down a clear plastic chimney
filled with movable pins protruding horizontally into it.

Ten spoke to a few people there. He lifted his chin in
greeting to one patron he recognized from his shen. Then
he moved on, watching every shadow.

He still felt dazed from the shock of the transfer. It had
caught him unprepared even though everyone on the Day
Watch had known something unpleasant must be coming
when Titus called Robbie out of debriefing. Speculation
had swept the room.

"Someone else killed, do you suppose?" Josh Bridewell
asked.

That typified the consensus and they fell silent, waiting
to learn the name of the latest victim.

Robbie's face told them nothing when he came back in.
Impassive as an Egara, the lieutenant swung onto a desk
and pulled his legs up to sit cross-legged. "There's good
news and bad," he said.

The room went so still they might all have turned to
stone. Ten's chest tightened.

"The good news is, no, there isn't another dead cop. The bad news—" Robbie paused to take a deep breath. "The bad news is that the psyman wants six officers taken off Evening before they become jacket cases."

Ten stopped breathing altogether. Who would take their places?

"These five officers will report for Evening Watch tomorrow," Robbie went on. "Amaro, Flood, Jernigan, Kampacalas, and Reiss."

Kampacalas! The icy fire of fear flooded out through Ten, into his toes and fingers, then rushed back to solidify in his stomach as a petrified lump just under his heart.

Robbie sent a sympathetic glance at each of the five. "If you want to swear, go ahead. This is the place for it."

Ten had wondered if he looked as pale as Calvin Reiss. Reiss asked bitterly, "Who will our glorious leader put on the watch after *we* go over the brainbow?"

"Or get slagged," Lara Flood added.

Brandon Amaro regarded Robbie thoughtfully. "What happens if I won't do it? What if I just refuse to report for briefing?"

Sergeant Lessman shifted position restlessly. Robbie nodded at her. "Go ahead, Mete."

Rather than answer Amaro's question, though, Lessman asked two of her own. "You mean you'd refuse to do your job? You'd let a brother tip off, or leave part of this city unprotected, out of fear for your own skin?"

A flush darkened Amaro's face. "No . . . of course I wouldn't."

He might want to, they might all want to, Ten thought, but they would not. No matter how frightened, they would still report for briefing.

After the watch, Ten spent the evening with Bara, conscious that it might be the last time they would see each other for some time, and in the morning, he took his uniforms in to the station to have the paragee fields checked for operating condition. The technician pronounced their operation perfect. Even so, Ten reported for briefing that afternoon with his stomach knotted tightly and a cold prickle of sweat under his arms.

The first person he saw after switching on the holocom was Jael. She regarded him in silence for a moment, then smiled wryly. "Hi, Ten. I never thought I'd be sorry to see a friend join my watch."

He wished he could touch her. The solid warmth of another being would have felt comforting, even if the touch were no more than a playful punch or a pat on the shoulder. Instead, he stood alone, surrounded by only ghosts, shadows wearing the faces and uniforms of colleagues.

He pushed back the depression that thought threatened to bring by matching his tone to hers. "Well, I'm not overjoyed about coming in, either; it shoots the hell out of my social relationships."

"Oh, I think you'll find friends on this watch easily enough," a voice said.

Ten looked around for the speaker, and found her directly behind him, tall and fair-haired, her eyes almost on a level with his.

"Purely on the basis of appearance, you're an improvement over Kiefer," the woman said. "I think we've passed each other at the station. I'm Mirre Howe." Her frankly evaluating gaze made Ten feel like an entry in a livestock show. "A pity our patrols are so far apart. Welcome to the Death Watch."

Only then did Ten notice the tightness in her voice and body that betrayed the fear beneath her façade of predatory sensuality. He almost smelled the sharp, acid reek of it. It made him think of Bara's belief that here on Egar, masks became unnecessary. Might it be a relief for Mirre Howe and all the others here, himself included, to discard bravado and pretense, to wear their fear openly? Or would it destroy them? Would admitting fear be giving in to it, and make it impossible to leave the safety of their storefronts for whatever awaited them outside?

He was still turning the question over in his mind when Lieutenant La Flore came in with Sergeants Brynche and Gerhardt. La Flore checked the holocom network indicators on the lectern, then glanced around the room. "I want to welcome our new members of the watch: Brandon Amaro, Lara Flood, Hal Jernigan, Steven Kampacalas, Kyle Roman, and Calvin Reiss. I'm sure none of you are pleased by this transfer, but I hope you'll continue to perform as well here as your records indicate you have on your previous watch. I won't minimize the danger we're facing, but I don't think it warrants the panic I see in some of you, either. Despite everything, you're still safer than you were on Earth. We've got just one nago after us. Keep sharp, keep in communication, and you'll probably be all right. On the other hand," he went on, raising his voice, "don't take the matter as casually as Officer Casebier. Wake up, Casebier! I think you ought to hear the incident list along with the rest of us."

La Flore had a point, Ten realized, but even one killer became a serious matter when that one had managed to kill three survival-trained members of such a small department in fourteen days and to leave no real lead to his identity.

Ten pulled his mind back to the present as he finished his walk through the shopping mall and swung into his car to lift for Glade Shen. The patrol looked new from the air, too. Instead of the bright, hard glitter of a Terran city, or the familiar daytime mixture of woods and meadows, black velvet spread beneath the bright crescents of the moons, scattered with subdued patches of light. He had seen pictures of Earth's nightside from orbit and the Moon, aglow with the light of its megapolises. What would Egar look like? The lights might be hard to see from very far up; they might appear as no more than misty patches, like ghost fire.

A chime rang twice in his ear.

Ten came alert. The computer's signal. He waited for the instructions sure to follow.

"North Twenty-five, impromptu, Tharshan retreat, Sh-6," came the precise voice of the computer. A light flashed on the city grid on his control panel.

Tharshan retreat . . . a place of dark isolation. Ten's mouth went dry. He tapped his ear. "North Twenty-five, Communications. Confirm impromptu for Tharshan retreat, Sh-6."

"Impromptu confirmed," the dispatcher replied.

His hands tightened on the Chehasha's controls. "En route to impromptu now."

He landed the car in a meadow as close to the retreat as possible and climbed out cautiously. With sleeper drawn and ready in his right hand and night goggles on, he moved from the moonlit meadow into the darkness of the woods. He had walked lightly through the mall, but he tried to move like a phantom now, testing each step before moving forward. The thick, soft soles of his boots made no sound on the hard ground of the path.

His nerves sang. Through the thunder of blood in his ears, he stretched his hearing across infinity—collecting, sorting, identifying every sound he heard: wings of a bird in flight; the snuffling of an animal, probably an adu; the distant wail of a balach; the high wingsongs of moonflies; the rasping buzz of another insect in the leaves near his feet. He heard the squeak of a rodentlike ibus and the hysterical giggle of a gelis . . . all woodland sounds, all normal. From the meadow came the grunt of a grazing animal and the dry swish of grass bending to its passing. Somewhere west, a skyrail train whined past.

He had used this path often on the way to Brithe's house, but the shadows had never seemed this dark or threatening before, even when brightened to gray twilight by the wide-angle lenses of his night goggles. He turned his head constantly, piercing each shadow in turn. In particular, he peered ahead, watching every centimeter of the path and air before him, alert for any reflecting gleam in the air. He used the sleeper as he had the baton earlier, sweeping the barrel in a ceaseless check for wires. He waited, too, for any change in the feel of the paragee field around him.

He reached the retreat. Nothing so far. He stopped to push up his faceshield and wipe away the sweat that trickled down his face and neck despite the chill of this last night of summer. He took some deep breaths. Had he breathed on the way up the path? He could not remember.

Before stepping into the retreat, he squinted at the tree on either side of the entrance. And there, exactly at throat height, light reflected back at him.

Monofilament!

Now he did hold his breath. Moving to one side, he stared at the entrance again from a different angle. This time he saw the entire length of the thin, pale strand crossing the space between the trees.

Ten reached up to touch the wire with the barrel of his sleeper. No one wanting to keep fingers ever used a bare hand on monofilament. He started to draw the sleeper along the wire, to find its point of attachment to the tree, when to his astonishment the strand fell loose, adhering to the sleeper's barrel.

He stared for a moment, swearing in surprise, then jammed the sleeper into his holster and dared to touch the strand bare-handed. It glued to his fingers. A cobweb! Ten slumped against the tree, laughing weakly with relief. He had run into nothing more lethal than the first strand of a web some fere was building to catch supper.

Ten hurriedly checked the retreat, found nothing, and after reporting to Communications, returned shaking to the car. If he was like this after just three nights on Evening Watch, he thought, he would be a jacket case by mid-autumn.

Flying the car to Glade Shen, he walked through hoping to god the ride-alongs helped relieve some of the tension. If they did not, he had better find some way of coping or he would end up being shipped back to Earth like Pol. Though right now, that seemed almost an enviable fate.

Pol had left this afternoon. On the pretense of conducting interviews, Roban had checked out a car, then picked up Ten and Jael, and the three of them took Pol and his luggage to the shuttlebox in the travelport. Pol looked better than he had for many days, relaxed and almost happy.

"It's back to Dallas and the wide open spaces for me," he said.

Ten tried to find something to say. "I'm sorry."

"Sorry? Not me, podner." Pol punched Ten's shoulder playfully. "Irirath just don't look nothin' like longhorns. Besides, it isn't your fault I've got this high-level need for privacy that makes me 'psychologically unsuitable for duty among telepaths.' I'm only sorry I went after you about cutting between Bara and me. I think I knew even then you hadn't, but I was out of my head."

Ten shrugged off the apology. "I know. It's all right. You're looking forward to going home, then?"

He laughed. "I sure am. This place is going to make good story material to impress the fillies."

Jael said, "Don't forget to telscribe those letters for me."

"Rest easy, little lady; I'll send them off, and Roban's and Ten's. Hey, Ten, what's this sister Miral of yours like?"

Ten smiled. "Eight years older than I am and not easily impressed, but I'm her adored baby brother, so one way to make stock with her might be to call and talk to her about me."

Roban sighed. "Too bad I don't have a sister near his age, because I know my folks would like to hear first-hand how I am."

"And my parents," Jael said.

Soon they had him promising to make half a dozen calls in addition to telscribing the letters, and Ten was beginning to feel homesick. Living there in Topeka near his family, he had never gone this long before without seeing them.

"Soon," the gate attendant told Pol.

Cargo handlers began loading the outgoing box with crates of fabric and hand-crafted jewelry. Watching them, the smile faded from Pol's face. He bit his lip.

"Sorry to be going, after all?" Jael asked softly.

He toyed with the call and telscribe list in his hand. "I guess I am." The drawl had disappeared from his voice. "Neither of my folks were ever shipped back from any of the strange places the marines stationed them. I don't know what their reaction is going to be to this. But, it isn't just what my family might think. I wanted so much to have this job, and to do it well." He looked around the broad expanse of the travelport until he focused on Ten. "I envy you, being able to tolerate Normals peeking into your head."

"I'm not sure I tolerate them yet," Ten said. "I'm not at all happy about my neighbors regarding me as a pet freak."

He saw Jael give him a sharply puzzled glance, but before she could ask the question he saw forming in her eyes, the gate attendant said, "Ready."

They looked at each other, trying to find quick last things to say. Pol put out a hand to Jael and she reached past it to hug him. "Good luck."

Life is full of comings and goings. Had some poet said that? Ten wondered. He hated the goings, the feeling of seeing someone he liked for the last time. In his turn, he hugged Pol, too, a knot in his throat.

"Time," the attendant said.

Pol peeled loose. "Y'all take care, hear?" he said huskily.

He stepped into the shuttlebox and the vaultlike door closed behind him.

Remembering the scene as he walked through Glade, the lump came back into Ten's throat. He swallowed to rid himself of it. He should not be thinking of that now. Officers died of such distractions.

Sunstone Shen came next on the patrol. Almost without conscious volition Ten headed for Brithe's house.

"Good evening, citizen," he said when she answered the door. "Have you seen any suspicious strangers tonight?"

She regarded him impassively for a moment, then smiled. "Come in while I try to think."

He accepted the invitation gladly, even while saying, "I can't stay long, just a minute or two, but as long as I was in the neighborhood, I thought—" He broke off with a grimace. "This new schedule is going to make our evenings together few and far between."

"Yes."

"I thought I heard the Sweeny as I came up. Did I interrupt your practice?"

"Yes. Do you want to listen for a while?"

He did. Following her up to her bedroom, he pulled off his helmet and lay back on the bed. As he sank into the pile of bedding, he felt the tension flow out of him. This was what he needed to help cope. "Sanctuary."

"What?"

He closed his eyes. "Your house has just been elected a sanctuary, someplace I can relax and feel really safe. What was it you were playing? I haven't heard it before."

She did not answer immediately. After a moment, he opened his eyes to find her staring intently at him. Before he could ask if he had offended her, however, she smiled and turned away toward the synthesizer. "The title is *Rimamin*. The great Manithis wrote it two thousand years ago."

She began playing. Soon not only had the last of Ten's tension gone, but the music had picked him up and carried him soaring with it, away from D'shenegar and deviants and killers. He listened with eyes closed, letting images flow through his head. As so often happened now, he saw Egarad landscapes, this time the dryland as Roban's grandfather described it around Lushanah . . . endless rolling vistas of brassy plains, stretching to an infinite horizon beneath a vault of brassy sky. But what did that crashing sequence of sound mean?

"How do you translate *Rimamin*?" he asked.

She never missed a note. "The Rimamin is the most famous canyon in the world, the canyon of the Ayah Rasar, the Golden River. From the Great Falls it's two thousand iyah long and a yah deep, cutting down through both the Heshem and N'shan Escarpments."

Two thousand iyah? Ten translated that into kilometers and Terran numbers and whistled soundlessly. Over a thousand kilometers. And a yah deep? Almost a kilometer. Some canyon! He listened to the music with new awareness. Yes, he could see it now, another Grand Canyon but with waterfalls. He thought he could listen to Brithe play all night.

Dreamily, he said, "I'll have to see this wonder sometime while I'm here."

The music stopped. He opened his eyes. Brithe stood with fingers slack on the Sweeny's keys, staring blankly at the wall before her. After a minute, she turned around.

"You should. When is your next time off?"

He knew without stopping to think. "I have two days starting day after tomorrow . . . provided they aren't canceled because I have to work on some investigation or have to go to court."

"We could go then."

He sat up. "How far away is it?"

"Fourteen thousand iyah, but if we leave right after you come off duty tomorrow night, a highliner can have us there by morning. We can spend two days walking and flying the canyon. It would give you a change from D'shenegar."

He could certainly use that! "I wonder if Roban and Jael would like to go."

"I hadn't thought of them, but . . . all right, if you want."

"Let me call Roban right now."

Roban, still at the stationhouse when Ten reached him, greeted the idea enthusiastically. "I don't have time off; they have me talking to every Egara within five klicks of the mall where Many-Horses died, but I'll come anyway. I'll develop some exotic two-day disease. Will you ask Jael?"

"At debriefing."

"North Twenty-five," his radio whispered. "Status report."

He glanced at his chron in horror. Oh, lord, had he been here *that* long? With his transponder signal indicating no movement after this length of time, no wonder Communications wanted a status report.

"Status normal," he replied. "Concluding interview and proceeding on through the shen."

"Received. Thirty-seven forty-three hours."

Ten told Brithe, "I'll contact you tomorrow at the station," and hastily returned to patrol.

Chapter Eighteen

THE HIGHLINER came down out of Egar's upper atmosphere at dawn and broke through a thin sheet of cloud. "Rimamin," an amplified voice said.

Ten pressed eagerly against the port. It angled outward, following the curve of the bulkhead, providing a clear view of the ground. Below, the Golden River, looking gold indeed in the light of the rising sun, flowed across the drylands in a broad ribbon to disappear abruptly through a boiling cloud of vapor into a huge rent in the earth that snaked westward to the edge of the world.

"There it is, Ro," Ten said. When Roban did not answer, he looked around and shook his head. Though sitting bolt upright in one of the two seats facing Ten and Brithe's, Roban was sound asleep. Ten shook one knee. "Ro, we're here. Wake up."

"You have to apply the proper stimulus," Jael said. "Adeyanju, the sergeant's coming!"

Roban's eyes opened instantly, a smooth awakening that could only have come from long practice napping in patrol cars. "Hi, sarge," he began, then looked around, realized where he was, and frowned balefully at Jael. "Fly leo, aren't you?"

She grinned and pointed out the port. "Rimamin, sleeping beauty." She assumed a tour-guide voice. "The canyon was discovered in 2017 by the mother/daughter exploring team of Rimamin and Gira as they followed the Golden River west. Beginning with the Great Golden Falls, visible below you now, which plunge nine hundred and—ah—" She groped for the figure and failing to remember it, gave up with a grin. "It impressed the hell out of me as a twelve-year-old, I remember."

Roban winked at Ten. "The Grand Canyon is wider and deeper."

Jael sniffed. "Not by much, but it's a damn sight shorter and minus the falls and Golden River. If it's pure size you want, go visit the Valles Marineris on Mars."

Brithe eyed them. "Are they playing a game?"

Ten nodded, and peered out the port again. The shadows in the canyon made seeing into it impossible, but as the highliner settled earthward and Rimamin yawned wider and wider, giving the town on its south rim the appearance of a collector's miniature, he no longer cared that he could not see into the canyon yet, or that it was narrower than Earth's most famous canyon; it still awed him, particularly the triple horseshoe Falls with water pouring over them like molten gold.

With a happy sigh, Ten sat back for the landing. "I think I'm going to be glad we came."

Half an hour later, he was sure of it. Brithe had made reservations for them in one of the guesting houses along the rim and their room opened onto a terrace lying directly on the edge. Holding tightly to the heavy red stone parapet, Ten peered over into the bottomless shadows of Rimamin, then looked up the canyon toward the thunderous falls and the triple and quadruple rainbows shining above them.

Roban leaned on the parapet beside him. "What now? Surely we don't just stare at it from here."

"There are thousands of iyah of hiking and climbing trails," Brithe said, "but since we have just two days, we'd probably do better to rent a skimmer from the guesting house and fly the canyon."

Ten headed for the door. "Let's go."

They had a choice, they found . . . fly themselves or take one of the chauffeured group flights.

"Group tours?" Roban grimaced. "I think we can fly ourselves."

Ten laughed. If universal situations really existed, then tourism must surely be one of them. Though like Roban, he preferred to fly himself, while watching a group of some dozen Iregara climb into a clear-domed hovercraft, each carrying a kinecorder, curiosity tempted him to join, just to see how similar, or different, the tour might be from its counterparts back on Earth. In the end, however, he followed his friends to the guesting-house official in charge of skimmer rentals.

The official asked if they were qualified to pilot a skimmer, but before any of them answered aloud, the Egara looked impassively from Ten to Jael and said, "Cops? What?"

The query must have produced a very mixed collection of image replies in the three of them because the Egara stared hard at each in turn, an ear flicking as though to ward off a worrisome fly, before finally assigning a skimmer.

"I don't think that poor soul could understand what we are," Jael said. She climbed into the pilot's seat. "Because it's my second trip, I'll fly and let the rest of you look."

Buckling himself into his seat, Ten thought about her first comment. Someone who did not know what a police officer was? Ten felt a strange mixed sensation of insecurity, loss of identity, and profound relief. Then a thought struck him and he had to laugh. "If we just passed the oar test, this is definitely the right holiday site for us."

Brithe stared. "Ore? Raw mineral? I don't understand."

"*Oar* as in rowing a boat," Ten told her. "The Greek classics must be some Terran books you've missed."

"What do Greek classics have to do with us?" Roban asked.

"Maybe I'm wrong, but I think the story goes that this Greek Ulysses—maybe one of my ancestors, who knows?—wanted to find a new life. He'd been on the sea, so he put an oar over his shoulder and walked inland with it. When he came to a place where the locals had to ask what the oar was, he stopped and settled down. We've just brought our badges where they're unknown objects." Leaning back in the seat, Ten stretched, feeling giddy and gloriously free. Here he was just another Terran. "All right, Jael, fly on. Show us this wonder."

Ten found Rimamin every bit the wonder promised. As the bronze sun rose higher, shadows retreated deeper and deeper until they vanished altogether. This close to the equator, the sun shone almost directly down into the canyon for most of its passage. Jael followed one of the prescribed flight paths down the canyon, flying high and then low, letting them see the walls in all their variety. Rimamin had fewer different types of rock formations than Ten had seen in pictures of the Grand Canyon, but in compensation it offered the awesome rise of its walls and vivid colors. Most of the rock seemed to be sandstone of either yellow or red, and with the sun shining on it, the stone looked gold or scarlet. The rock lay in layers . . . horizontal, tilted crazily sideways, or rippling and sagging like material stretched so far it was unable to snap back to its original tautness. When the skimmer flew near the floor, along the river, the walls towered above them toward heaven itself. Ten found the river interesting, too. Even down here, away from the sun, the water still looked gold.

By midday they had reached the end of the upper canyon. Brithe suggested, "Let's go back to the falls. The lower canyon is just more of the same."

Jael turned the skimmer around just outside the upper canyon, giving them all a view of the Heshem Escarpment before plunging back into Rimamin. The escarpment was a bit overwhelming, too, eleven hundred meters of weathered rock, left when the ground fell toward the Sirithamir Sea. And the N'shan Escarpment lay only a bit over another thousand kilometers west? Ten thought. What must early explorers have thought, following the Golden River and finding these two giant steps leading down to the bottom of the world?

But he soon forgot explorers and escarpments. The Golden Falls lay ahead, and nothing in Ten's experience matched, or even approached, their impressiveness. Small at a distance, they grew as the skimmer flew up the canyon toward them, rising even higher into the sky and stretching out wider with each passing minute. Their sound grew from a low, distant murmur through a gradually increasing roar to a sound so great that when Jael grounded the skimmer at the foot of the falls at mid-afternoon, it had become so tremendous, so overwhelming, that it swallowed even itself, leaving only a numbing void in the ears. Ten stared breathlessly up at the seven-hundred-meter-wide curtain of molten gold plunging down toward him from the rim nearly a kilometer above. The world disappeared, lost in the assault the falling tonnes of water made on his senses, in the boiling vapor that stung exposed skin on his face and hands like countless icy needles, and in the all-consuming sound.

Then, suddenly, the falls spun bottom-end up. Ten found

himself head down, looking past a bright green tabard to the ground moving backward past yellow-booted feet. He blinked in astonishment. What was he doing slung over Brithe's shoulder?

Trying to ask was out of the question this close to the falls; Brithe could not possibly hear him. Instead, he rapped on her back to attract her attention and arched his back to bring himself upright, thinking to slip off her shoulder. However, she held him fast with a grip on his hips and legs. All he accomplished was a vantage point that allowed him to see the few Iregara in the area turning to stare at him. He felt like a fool.

Then he saw Roban and Jael walking off to the side. Jael grinned wickedly at him.

"You!" he yelled at her, and was just able to hear himself. "You're responsible for this, aren't you? Put me down, Brithe!" He thrashed around on her shoulder. "*Put me down!*"

Brithe dumped him unceremoniously on the ground. Ten rolled to his feet and charged Jael, who jumped behind Roban. "Protect me, officer!"

Roban stepped aside, shaking his head. "This was your idea."

She shrieked and evaded Ten by dodging around a large boulder.

"What the hell were you trying to do?" Ten yelled over the roar of the falls. He went around the boulder after her.

She laughed, moving to keep the rock between them. "You have to be the world's easiest hypnosis subject!" she shouted back. "You were so mindwarped just watching the water you didn't feel me tap your arm or anything! So I thought we'd better save you from yourself!"

"By having me carried away like a sack of grain? I'm going to get you, Meadin! I'm going to get you and throw you in the river!"

"You'll have to catch me first!" With a whoop of laughter, she leaped a low thicket of brush and raced down the riverbank.

Ten went after her.

She ran like a hare. If they had not both run the same courses at home under Ogilvie's training whip, he would have had no chance of catching her. As it was, the chase became less a matter of speed than endurance, endurance well-tried by the deep sand along the riverbank and the obstacles presented by frequent rock outcroppings and brush. As a course, Ten reflected when his breath began burning like fire in his lungs, it would have warmed Ogilvie to the core of his remorseless soul. Then Ten found his second wind and forgot everything but the woman fleeing ahead of him and the exhilaration of the chase.

It ended abruptly. Jael stepped wrong, turned her ankle, and fell face-first into the sand. Ten dived on her.

"Default, default," she gasped, rolling away kicking at him. "Help, rape!"

He scrambled after her. "No fair asking aid," he told her, gasping too. "If you want to rape me, you'll have to do it by yourself."

She kicked at him again, but this time feebly, laughing, then gave up altogether and went limp. "Surrender. I'll leave your virtue intact if you forget to throw me in the river."

"Agreed." Ten flopped on his back and for a while they did nothing but lie panting side-by-side on the sand. After several minutes, however, Ten sat up. His gaze traveled across the sand, down the riverbank to the waters of the Golden River itself.

"It's really gold. I thought the color was just due to the sun shining on it this morning, but it's really gold water, isn't it?"

Jael sat up, brushing the sand off her jumpsuit and jacket. "Amber, anyway. When I came here as a kid, they told me the water is stained by mosses and other plants it flows over crossing the drylands."

His eyes came back to the sand, red and yellow like the rock of the canyon walls. He dipped into it and let the damp grains run through his fingers. "Nice beach, too." He heaped up a little mound and patted it into a firm pyramid. "I've never been on one like this before. The beaches around lakes in Kansas are either pebbles or mud."

Two Iregara passing on the hiking trail just off the beach regarded them expressionlessly. Jael waved. Ten went on playing with the pyramid. With a little coaxing, and more sand, it became a square tower. He pressed his finger into the sand at intervals around the top, making rough crenellations. "A person could build a nice sand castle out of this."

Jael grinned. "Or two persons could."

By the time Roban and Brithe arrived, Ten and Jael had

two sections of wall built and were working on a corner tower.

"Hello, children," Roban said. "Are your mommy and daddy around?"

Ten grinned sheepishly but went on smoothing the tower wall.

"Don't act so disgustingly adult and professional, Ro," Jael said. "Come down here and help us."

"I'm afraid I don't have much experience in castle building, but I'll watch here with Brithe while you two finish your therapeutic sandbox session."

"Is this another game?" Brithe asked.

"Yes," Roban said. "The human is the only known species that continues to play after it ostensibly becomes adult."

Jael grimaced. "Listen to Grandpa. Ignore him, Ten."

"I am."

"What is the structure?" Brithe persisted.

So while she and Ten worked, Jael launched into a lecture on medieval fortifications. Brithe asked a question from time to time, but for the most part listened in silence . . . amazed silence, Ten assumed, or perhaps puzzled silence, because one of her remarks was: "I can understand physical exercise; that strengthens and tones the body. Mental games supple the mind, but this . . ." She came over to walk around the castle, studying it.

They had it almost finished. Ten sat back on his calves for a moment to admire their handiwork. For his first effort, he thought it had turned out very well. He sighed happily and leaned forward again for the last smoothing.

"Why are you doing this?" Brithe asked.

Ten shrugged. "I don't know. I never have before and the sand was here and I had the time . . ." He laughed. "It's a human kind of thing to do."

"It's a change," Jael said. "It's something different, something to exercise different skills than usual, to add a new and interesting flavor to life. It's—it's drana."

The word caught Ten like an electric shock. He stared at her. "What?"

Brithe, leaning down to study the castle more closely, bumped against Ten and lost her balance. She clutched at him to save herself but succeeded only in taking him with her and they both fell full length across the top of the castle. Ten yelped in dismay as the walls and towers, built with such careful, loving labor, crumbled under their weight. In the process of trying to find her feet again, Brithe rolled over and knocked down the one tower the fall had not demolished.

She scrambled up full of apologies. "Oh, I'm so sorry. Your castle . . . This is terrible." She helped Ten to his feet. "I should have been more careful."

"Yes," Jael said.

Ten exchanged a helpless glance with Jael, then stared sadly down at the ruin. He shrugged. "It's only sand. Don't worry about it."

He brushed sand off his clothes. What a lot of it clung to him. It seemed to be everywhere, all over his jumpsuit and hands. He even felt it on his nose and one cheek.

"Let me help you," Brithe said. She brushed at him.

Ten winced. "Not so hard," he protested. Her pats came with almost enough force to knock him down.

She eased up immediately with another apology.

Cleaned off, the four of them headed back up the canyon . . . taking the hiking path this time. Jael and Roban walked ahead, arms around each other, and Brithe followed. Ten trailed behind, looking back toward the beach.

The sand lay in a shapeless heap, bearing no resemblance to the proud form it had held so briefly. Mere sand or not, losing it hurt, he had to admit. He did not blame Brithe, but somewhere inside him, he felt a sharp pang of loss. The castle had not even had the chance to be finished and admired properly, and now it was gone. The accident cast a small shadow on what had otherwise been a perfect day.

"Ten? Coming?" Brithe called.

With a sigh, he turned away and followed the others back toward the falls and the skimmer.

Like their room, the guesting house dining room overlooked the canyon. In addition, the projecting section of rim on which it was built provided an unobstructed view of the falls. The Sunsorb ceiling and walls blocked out some of the sound, however, reducing it to a muffled rumble that Ten barely noticed. After the hours they had spent much closer to the falls, he had trouble hearing any sounds. He felt as though the noises and voices around him came through a thick layer of cotton.

At the moment, though, he had no interest in the scenery nor concern about his hearing. A ravenous appetite had focused his entire attention on the dishes of food being placed in the center of the table. He recognized the plate of bread for what it was, even though this loaf came heavy and black where the bread in D'shenegar was brown, and the vegetables looked distinctly mushroomlike, but he had no idea what the main dish might be. The dining room provided no menu. The attendant simply counted heads and brought out the food. Ten sniffed the dish as Brithe passed it to him. It smelled good, though at this point almost anything would have appealed to him.

He helped himself and passed the dish on to Jael. "Ah, food like Mama used to make."

Jael snorted. "I'll bet your mother never cooked duserihach."

Ten speared a piece of food with his prong-ended spoon. "No, but the philosophy is the same: 'Here it is; eat it or go hungry.' What is it?"

"Shredded fish baked with fruit and nuts," Brithe said. She pushed at her portion. "*My* mother used to cook a *great deal* of it."

In a fishing industry city like Subath, Ten imagined so. "Well, Iregara may not be gourmets, but what they cook, they cook well." His stomach welcomed the fish and fruit. Then he sipped his tea. "Except tea. I think I need water to thin this enough to make it drinkable."

The attendant appeared with small pots of hot water and set them down in front of Ten and Jael.

"Me, too," Roban said, but the attendant did not appear to hear. Roban had to repeat his request. He sighed as the water finally arrived. "It keeps happening. The slightest thought and Normals react to everyone else, but I have to concentrate."

Brithe said, "Some Normals broadcast faintly. You must be a Terran Quiet."

"I wonder if that's good or bad."

"Better, maybe, than being a Loud and having everyone in the area grabbing a luras whenever you happen to get excited," Ten said.

Jael suddenly gasped in delight. "Look, everyone."

They turned to follow her pointing finger. The rays of the setting sun shone up the canyon to the falls, picking out every subtle shade of red and yellow in Rimamin's walls, lighting them until the rocks seemed to glow from within. At the head of Rimamin, the sun's rays fell full on the Great Golden Falls. The water drank the fiery light . . . captured it, held it, reflected it, until the falls ceased to look like water at all and became, instead, a sheet of shimmering, blazing incandescence, blinding in its glory. The portion of *Rimamin* Brithe had played on the Sweeny replayed in Ten's head.

Food forgotten, they stared at the sight. As the sun sank lower, shadow crept up the walls, its darkness slowly devouring the color and fire. Finally only a thin line of brilliant light remained across the top of the falls, then even that disappeared.

They returned to their meal, now cold. No one spoke for several minutes.

Jael finally broke the silence. "There are times I wish I was a painter or something, so I could take that away with me to show others."

"We need to be poets," Ten said. "Can you think what a good poet could do with a golden river and an incandescent waterfall? We'll just have to suggest that the rest of the department visit here and see it for themselves."

Jael nodded.

Roban, however, scowled. "You let a bunch of Terrans come trooping around here and soon it won't be worth visiting any longer."

Ten sat up indignantly. "What? What do you think is going to happen . . . that they'll kick in the side of the canyon? We're Terrans and we didn't hurt anything, did we, just built a sand castle?"

"Sooner or later Terrans always destroy what they touch," Roban said sourly. "Look what we did to Egar before we ever put a foot on it. The three of us are here now because of what our ancestors did to the Iregara. Much as I'm enjoying being on Egar, I can't help but think how much better it would be if Iregara and Terrans had never met."

"You meant if they hadn't, I wouldn't exist?" Brithe asked.

"Exactly. Terra Silenced your trade delegation and started the whole problem we're dealing with now."

Jael sighed. "Roban, can we not—"

"What is it with you?" Ten demanded. "Why are you so anxious to make us the bad guys? I think the fault for what happened to the trade delegation can be divided. Neither side thought to learn enough about the other. And Terrans haven't created the problem here now. No Terran is stopping Brithe from receiving the professional recognition in music she deserves to have!"

"Ten!" Brithe cried angrily.

Ten flushed guiltily. He knew how personal she considered her music. "I'm sorry; it just slipped out." He looked back at Roban. "Terrans aren't shutting Silents out of society, Normals are. In seventy-five years the Normals haven't made any significant concessions to Silent limitations."

"There would be no need for concessions if we—"

Jael interrupted. "Stop it! Stop it, both of you! I came on this holiday to forget my job. If you two want to argue, you can find another place to sleep. If you stay here, I'll break the jaw of the first person who mentions one more word connected with work."

Her vehemence startled Ten. He shrank down in his chair. "Yes, ma'am."

She stared hard at Roban. "Will you agree to that, too?" she demanded.

Roban scowled, but nodded.

"Very well, then. Brithe, would you like to hear a theory I have about Silent destiny?"

Brithe regarded her solemnly. "Very well."

"I think Silents are an evolutionary necessity."

Brithe blinked. "Evolutionary necessity?"

"For racial survival in an interstellar civilization. Normals can't go charging out to the planets of newly-met races. Look what happened to them on Earth. Also, Normals might be too candid for their own good when dealing with strangers. Silents, however, can't have their brains picked and they can keep their minds intact when dealing with aliens. I believe Silents are the Egarad diplomats of the future." Jael grinned. "You who are downtrodden now may yet be the saviors of your planet."

Brithe stared at her. "That is a very interesting theory."

"I'll entertain other opinions on the subject." But no one seemed moved to debate and Jael sighed. "Well, I tried. Brithe, you suggest something for us to talk about."

Brithe looked past Ten at the red moon Nishim rising in the west. Her coat rippled, throwing off rainbows. "Would you like to hear the old legend speculating why the moons travel in different directions?"

"Yes," Jael replied quickly, before anyone could say otherwise.

Brithe's eyes looked through everyone into the distance. "In ancient times in the Seyehna Dryland, which is the birthplace of the People, there may once have lived a hunter named Sh'har who used the *thi* with such skill that her fame was known throughout the world."

"What's a *thi*?" Ten asked.

"A hunting tool," Brithe said.

"Like a bolas, thongs with three weights," Jael added.

"Sh'har would have been so proud of her skill that she would let it be known she thought she could out-throw any other hunter in the world, and even Husagir." Brithe paused. "Do you know Husagir?"

"No," Ten said.

"The last of the Giants," Jael said. "Legend says that once there were—excuse me, Brithe; I'll keep it in your style—once there might have lived a race of Giants called ihusagir. It was once thought they built the world, piled up the mountains and scooped out the seas. If they lived, they're all gone now, all but one, and the sometime trembling of the earth might be from when she walks. Thunder might be the sound of those footsteps. The seas might be Husagir's footsteps, filled with her tears of loneliness."

Brithe regarded her impassively. "Then you know the story of the moons."

"But they don't." Jael pointed at Ten and Roban. "Please go on."

"If Husagir truly lived, she would have heard of the brag, and she would have come in rage to challenge Sh'har. The two would have gone out and hunted all day long. If Husagir won, Sh'har would have been destroyed, smashed by the Giant, but if, after throwing their ithi all day, Sh'har brought down more game than Husagir, then she would have won, and Husagir might have become so enraged that she threw her thi at the hunter. Sh'har, being very agile, would have ducked, and the thi broken apart from the force of the throw, the stones flying away, two in one direction, the third in the opposite direction. The moons we see every night might be the stones of Husagir's thi, thrown so hard they are flying yet."

It was the first time Ten had never heard a legend told that way, as mere possibility, in no way claiming to be truth. "Is Husagir a figure in many legends?"

"Many."

They moved from the dining room to their sleeping room and Brithe told them a dozen more stories about the last Giant. Like legends on Earth, they dealt with explanations of why various aspects of the world existed the way they did, but unlike Earth, every story was presented as speculation only. Still, that destroyed none of their interest nor dimmed the vivid detail with which Brithe could tell the stories. When they finally went to bed, unfolding chairs into sleeping mats, Ten dreamed of a Brithe tall as a Colossus, the rainbows from her coat making the aurora borealis. She strode across the face of Egar, leaving seas where she walked, stepping down the escarpments like stairsteps, and building mountains as lesser beings played with sand castles.

Chapter Nineteen

THE HIGHLINER did not leave until twenty-four-forty, which gave them over half a day yet at Rimamin. Rather than rent another skimmer, they decided to hike, taking one of the trails down the canyon wall.

Brithe cautioned them, however. "We'll need to be careful. People are hurt and killed on those trails every year."

Ten blinked. "And people are still allowed to use them?"

She regarded him solemnly. "Of course. If people understand the danger and still want to go, why should anyone try to stop them?"

Ten grinned. "Not me, but it's certainly a different philosophy than I'm used to."

"A much saner one, I must say, than outlawing anything with a shred of risk in it," Roban said. "It forces people to accept responsibility for their actions and the consequences."

Ten bit his lip to keep from saying that he had noticed Iregara were able to find as many excuses as Terrans did for their behavior, and most of the excuses put the blame on someone or something else. The grim set of Jael's mouth warned him she would still make good her threat to break jaws at any mention of police work.

The trail started at the guesting house, an easy walk at first. It followed a path cut just below the rim. As it neared the falls, however, and began to angle downward, the path grew harder. Or perhaps treacherous would have been a more descriptive word, Ten thought. Moisture from the falls coated everything and at this hour of the morning, with the sun just starting to shine into Rimamin, that moisture still remained frozen from the nighttime temperatures. Jael and Brithe each slipped once on patches of ice. Ten moved with increased caution. There were, he noticed, no handrails, only notches cut into the rock at steep and tricky points.

"Can you imagine what this would be like on Earth?" Roban asked. "It would be stepped, paved with waterproof, nonskid footing. We'd have a plastic railing every centimeter of the way, molded and colored like wooden poles, of course, and there would be chain and wire mesh to keep us away from the edge. And of course there would be permaplast placards to inform us when we'd reached a 'sceneview area' or inform us that this is a rock and that a patch of moss and that a rodent hole." He shook his head. "It would be spoiled."

Keeping his voice carefully neutral, Ten said, "I don't think a few safety precautions would spoil anything."

Roban turned on him. "I suppose you'd rather have it government sanitized, inspected, and watchdogged?"

Ten's mouth thinned. "I didn't say that. How I'd rather have it, though, now that you bring it up, is without the anti-Terran commentary."

The skin across Roban's cheekbones darkened. He opened his mouth to say something, but Ten, with a quick glance at an icy-eyed Jael, quickly apologized. "I'm sorry. That was unnecessary. Let's just enjoy the hike, shall we?" He went on around Roban and down the trail.

Next to the falls, the path gave up all pretense of being a trail and became a blatant climb, nearly vertical in many places and all damp. Still, Ten enjoyed it. The falls shone golden ahead of him and the air tasted moistly clean . . . and the roar of the falls made any conversation or commentary impossible.

The trail snaked its way down and around rocks, parallel to the edge of the falls. About midway down the wall, though, it suddenly flattened horizontally to dive behind the water. Following it, they found a grotto cut into the rock, dim in the dusky gold light filtering through the water, with stone benches offering a place to sit and rest.

They sat down, but not for long. Jael held out her wrist and pointed to her chron. The morning was half gone; they needed to start back soon if they were to reach the travelport in time to catch their highliner flight.

The climb back had one saving grace—that looking up kept the glory of the falls almost constantly in view. With the sun shining down into Rimamin, the rocks had warmed, making the contact with them a bit less chilly.

Tomorrow he might pay for this climb with sore muscles, Ten suspected, but today it seemed worth the price. With the one section of *Rimamin* he knew playing in his head, he scrambled up a piece of trail so steep it seemed more a ladder than a path. This was the last of the difficult sections. Beyond here, the way grew easier, flatter.

He reached the ledge, panting, and grinned at the others, then turned to look up and down at the golden cataract, committing it to memory. He would not be seeing it again this close before he left.

Someone bumped against him. He hastily stepped back to put more distance between him and the edge, but in the process, he bumped again and this time lost his balance. His feet slipped on the damp stone. Something hit him on the shoulder. The next second the edge went by and he was falling, sliding down the water-slimed wall with nothing between him and the canyon floor below but seven hundred meters of sheer rock. He twisted desperately, clawing at the rock for purchase somewhere . . . anywhere.

One hand caught, then the other, but he felt the precariousness of the hold. His fingers would not be able to grip the wet stone for long unless he managed somehow to take the bulk of his weight off them. That meant finding a foothold, but the stone around his feet afforded nothing. His searching boot toes found only a smooth, slick surface. Gritting his teeth, he dug into the stone with his fingers and looked back up the way he had fallen.

Roban and Jael peered over the edge of the ledge above, mouthing words he could not understand. Where was Brithe? Then he saw her. She had shed boots and tabard and was climbing down the wall a few meters to his right. As she came even with him, she braced her feet, took a hard grip on the stone with her right hand, and extended her left hand to him.

Ten fought panic. Surely she did not mean he should let go with one hand and reach for her? If he missed, he would almost certainly fall, and even if he did not miss, what chance did she have to keep hold of him, and what were the odds of his weight pulling her loose so that both of them fell to their deaths?

Brithe beckoned to him.

He felt his grip slipping and thought fast. Not to try reaching her meant certain death, and in the next minute or so. Swallowing, gripping so hard with his left hand he felt as though the bones of his fingers were coming through the skin, he eased his right hand loose and down across the rock face toward Brithe's extended hand. Their fingers touched, then fingers touched palms, and finally her fingers locked around his wrist . . . just as his left hand tore loose.

With a gasp, he dropped, but Brithe's grip held. She pulled him across the rock face toward her and rougher stone. When he found holds of his own and his feet and hands were all well-placed, she released his wrist. She climbed ahead of him, frequently glancing back to be sure he still followed, and after they reached the ledge, she reached over to grasp both his hands and pull him up to safety.

No one tried to talk into the roar of the falls, but Roban and Jael raised brows inquiringly at him. He shrugged in reply and leaned his head against Brithe's shoulder, not caring that the beading on her fur scratched his face. When his knees felt strong enough to support him again, he stood, and they all made their way back up to the rim as fast as caution would let them.

Ten found himself the center of a concerned group at the guesting house.

"Fell. Read," Iregara said. They looked at Brithe. "Brave."

"We're lucky she was along," Roban said. "Jael and I could never have done what she did. Without her, we'd have lost him."

Ten nodded. "Thank you, Brithe."

She stared at him without expression, only an ear twitching, but eventually she smiled faintly.

In response to everyone's queries, Ten insisted he was all right, just fine. He did feel all right, at least until they boarded the highliner; then, watching Rimamin and the falls drop away below them, weakness swept through him. He began shaking uncontrollably.

"I'm going to be in some condition for patrolling tomorrow," he said wryly.

"Why don't I bring you some tea from the galley?" Jael suggested. "Are you sore any particular place? Would you like your neck rubbed?"

"Don't smother him," Roban said. "All he needs is rest. You sleep and you'll be fine by the time we get home, Ten."

"I'll be fine," Ten repeated, like a child reciting a lesson. Lying back in his seat, he closed his eyes.

For a while, he listened to the three of them talk, their voices distant and echoing, as though coming to him down a long tunnel. Presently Brithe's voice stopped and he heard only Roban and Jael, speaking English.

"For someone who claims to have enjoyed this trip, you were certainly unfriendly last night," Roban said in a petulant voice.

"We weren't alone, Ro. I can accept my neighbors being aware of what I'm doing, but I'm not ready to flatdance in front of eyewitnesses yet."

"Ten and Brithe were both asleep. They wouldn't have witnessed anything. I know you by this time, Jael; you were mad at me for some reason. Why?"

Her sigh echoed down the tunnel to Ten. "If you must know, I'm sick of hearing you worship the Iregara and blame the Terrans for every problem on Egar."

"What? I thought you were as much an Egaraphile as I am."

"I am; however, I don't consider them saints the way you do. They're people, ordinary organisms, imperfect just like we are. They're just as fallible and thoughtless. Only you won't see that."

"I can see that you've become very cynical. When did this happen?"

"During my adolescence here. I learned to know the people very well then."

"My grandfather—" he began, voice rising.

"Your grandfather is your whole problem," she interrupted. "How old is he?"

"Eighty-three, but what—"

"The trade delegations were repatriated seventy-five years ago. That means your grandfather couldn't have been more than eight years old when he left Egar. You've spent your life hearing about Egar as remembered through the eyes of a child. You see it as innocent, idealized, and unrealistic."

Ten heard Roban's angry intake of breath. "You've never said anything about it to me before."

"I kept hoping experience would override the stories and mature your viewpoint, but it hasn't."

"You're calling me immature? Thank you so much."

"I'm not—" she began in protest.

He interrupted her. "Maybe we'd better reconsider our sleeping arrangements. I don't want you to feel you're committing statutory rape," he said acidly.

Her breath hissed through her nose. "And maybe *you'd* be happier dancing one of your precious Egara, if it can be done!"

Roban's voice went glacial. "I think I'll follow Ten's example and sleep all the way back to D'shenegar."

"Ro." She said his name with a note of apology, then muttered, "Bastard," and fell silent.

Ten opened his eyes. He saw them both lying back in their seats, eyes closed. Brithe had gone. He closed his eyes again but even without his friends arguing, he could not sleep. In memory, he fell again, over and over again. He felt his feet skid from under him and gravity pull him down the rock face. He hung on the rock, fingers slipping while Brithe strained to reach him.

Sweating, Ten gave up trying to sleep. At least with his eyes open he did not keep seeing the side of Rimamin. What he needed, he decided, was a tall glass of something highly alcoholic. He doubted any existed on the highliner, however. Lacking that, tea—full strength—might do. He stood up and climbed the ramp to the observation level.

He found Brithe there, staring out at the white sea of clouds below them. She glanced up, then away again, lost in some private world.

He sat down in a chair next to her. "I couldn't sleep."

She said nothing.

Another of her moods? If so, he would do best to leave her alone, but he could not make himself leave, nor sit silent. He recognized the sign; he had seen it time and time again in people following some harrowing experience . . . an uncontrollable compulsion to talk. "Ironic, isn't it? I come on holiday to escape from danger and I almost get myself killed. Thank you again for being there."

"Yes," she said, without looking away from the clouds.

"Any Normals around me the next time I hear *Rimamin* are going to read some very different images than the composer meant to evoke, I'm afraid."

She said nothing.

He sighed. "What's the matter? Why do you go off and close the doors between you and other people?"

Brithe looked around slowly. "When you spend your life alone, sometimes you come to like and need solitude."

"You want me to leave?"

"Not this time. This time I was thinking." She looked out at the clouds again, but he felt a difference in the action. It no longer shut him out. "I had a thought when I was climbing down after you. You bumped against Roban and slipped. It was an accident, but I thought, what if it weren't?"

Something cold crawled up his spine. "What?"

She looked into his eyes. "The second bump, when you slipped, he made a grab for your jacket, but if he wanted, he could have been pushing you instead."

Ten could not even begin to imagine what she was talking about. "*Push* me? *Why?*"

"Not him . . . the killer. I thought, someone like Roban, a Quiet, who thinks Terrans have harmed my people, someone like that who's gone deviant could be killing the officers."

He stared at her incredulously. "You think the killer might be a *Terran?*"

Her violet eyes remained fastened on his. "It could be."

"But—" He shook his head. "That won't work. It has to be someone who knows police, and in particular, this department. The other Terrans in D'shenegar have almost no contact with us. The only way it could be a brainbowed human is if—" Somewhere in his chest, a knot interfered with his breathing. He fought to ease air past it. The one condition under which a Terran could fit their killer's role was if the person worked in the department. Ten shied from that possibility. "It can't be anyone in the department itself."

"You're probably right," Brithe said. "They're your people and you know them better than I do. Still, Pol Wassom had to leave because he unbalanced, didn't he? Why couldn't there be someone else unbalanced, but not seeming so because she has adopted Egarad ways, which is what Director Brooks wants?"

"She?"

She looked at him. "You have three pronouns; I choose to use *she*. Is it impossible for a Terran to be homicidal? The old mystery novels are full of such people."

"It does happen," Ten admitted. *All the time on Earth,* he added silently.

"Then your killer could be Terran. You could have brought her with you."

Ten eyed her. "You'd rather the bad guy be one of my people than one of yours, wouldn't you?"

"Of course."

And she could be right. Unfortunately, she could be very right. A Terran, who knew human psychology; a member of the department, who knew police; a Quiet, someone who could not be read or not be read clearly by any possible witnesses; and an Egarad sympathizer, who blamed Terrans for Egarad ills. He thought her theory unlikely—his vote still went for a *haban*—but he knew he would have to mention it to someone when they reached home.

Where was the attendant? He needed that tea more than ever now.

Chapter Twenty

"DEATHRAGE," DEVANE said, "tell me about Kampacalas."

The psychiatrist leaned back in her chair and regarded him across her desk. "You want a thumbnail sketch, or an account of his sexual habits and partners, his intelligence and adaptability index, his current frustration threshold? What?"

"What goes on in his head? This is the second time he's offered us an alternative identity for our cop killer and this time he's proposing that we're harboring the nago right here in the department. What's he trying to do, make us afraid of each other? Does he want to destroy morale so we'll all be sent back to Earth?"

"Oh, come now, director. Kampacalas is very much the type of officer you wanted to bring to Egar: young, bright, idealistic, and conscientious. He's exercising that last trait by passing on what was suggested to him. He very properly brought the information to Mete Lessman, who passed it up the line to you. I talked with him just recently when he came in for his routine visit. At that time he'd just been transferred to the Evening Watch and was somewhat frightened and distressed. Also, one of his best friends was Pol Wassom, and we were preparing to ship Wassom back to Earth. Still, every answer he gave me indicated a balanced, stable personality. I had Abin reading from the other room, too, and deep-reading verified my findings."

Devane tugged at an ear. "How is having an Egarad assistant working out?"

"It's certainly the answer to overcoming reticence like Wassom's, but I think we ought to be open about having a deep reader present during the interviews . . . as I've already mentioned a time or two. If we're caught at being covert, I believe we'll pay a heavy price in lost trust."

Devane shrugged. "All right. From now on, keep Abin in the room and let everyone know the reason. What about this idea of a psycho Quiet in the department being involved in the killings?"

"It's a valid possibility. Abin tells me the broadcast power percentages follow our old familiar friend, the bell curve, with a few Louds, a great number of individuals in the Medium range, and a few Quiets. The human curve is probably about the same, with the addition of some natural Silents below the Quiets."

"Then let's look into this quickly and quietly. Use Abin to screen our personnel—call all of them in on some excuse or other—and let me know how many fall in that Quiet range. We can check those officers out and maybe we'll never have to let anyone know we ever suspected our own people."

Deathrage sighed. "That's wishful thinking, surely. You don't for a moment think there's any way to keep the grapevine from learning about this and spreading it, do you? Director, do I have to remind you that this isn't Earth? D'shenegar isn't a place to keep secrets, so why don't you get in practice for the time you have Egarad personnel and not even try?"

"Because these aren't Egarad officers," Devane said. "I don't want to spread panic. If we don't feel we can trust each other, we're finished as a department."

Deathrage just looked at him. For a moment, Devane felt disoriented. He knew that expression, but with violet eyes, not blue ones. When he realized why, he caught his breath. Ibal, the healer on the police board, looked at him that way from time to time. He found himself reacting to Deathrage as he reacted to Ibal, too, listening more carefully to his own words and rethinking what he had just said. And what would happen if the field officers did not feel they could trust their command officers? he thought.

"On the other hand," he said aloud, "if we go ahead and check everyone's broadcasting power, and deep-read the individuals in the Quiet category, we don't have to wonder if we can trust each other because we'll *know* if anyone is guilty or not."

Deathrage beamed at him like a mother taking pride in a particularly clever child. "We can have this question answered in less than two days."

Devane eyed her. "Sometime I'll have to introduce you

to a certain member of the police board. I think you'll find yourselves kinfolk under the skin."

She chuckled.

They went to work on the logistics of the screening and were just finishing when the intercom chimed. In response to the psyman's activating wave of one hand and brisk, "Yes?" Liril's voice said, "Devane, tour."

Devane sat up. "My son's school. I almost forgot. I'll be right there, Liril." Waving the intercom off, he stood and started to leave the room, then paused at the door. "Oh, make another appointment for my wife, will you?" He said it with some embarrassment. His own wife, and he had less influence over her than he did over the other three hundred and some Terrans in the department. "This time I'll see that she keeps it."

Deathrage shook her head. "Don't do that. Missing two appointments tells me she doesn't really want to talk to me. You might force her to come, but you can't force her to listen, and if she's here under duress, she's less likely than ever to be receptive to anything I might have to offer."

Devane frowned. If Meda would only come, he felt sure she would stop being afraid of the psyman.

"She has to come on her own or it's a waste of both our time," Deathrage said.

Devane eyed her, then grinned. "Now I'm convinced you and Ibal are related."

Still grinning, he hurried to the reception area. There, Runah and Ilidin, the First-Level school's other teacher, waited with two dozen children ranging in age from what on Earth would have been three to seven years old. Gerel and D'ne charged out of the group toward him, Gerel shouting happily, "Daddy!"

D'ne said, "Parent."

Bending down, Devane included both in his hug. He straightened again, taking each child by a hand. "I'm glad you could bring them this afternoon, Runah. While we're going through the station, all of you keep in a close group. You're so much smaller than everyone else here, I don't want someone stepping on you, thinking you're igelis."

Gerel giggled and the visible fur of the children and two teachers rippled.

Devane found it one of the easiest tours he had ever conducted. At each point, he needed only a few words of explanation, and from the expressions and comments of the young Iregara, he gathered that they understood most of what he meant. Which was better than some of the VIPs did whom he had had the dubious privilege of showing around the Bryant Street station back in San Francisco. Here he had trouble only when Terran and Egarad concepts differed radically.

Gerel, who had been to the station before but never actually gone through it, reacted with as much excitement as the other children, especially in the exercise room. Only Devane's firm grip on their hands kept Gerel and D'ne from swarming over the exercise equipment.

Ogilvie, the trainer, watched the children, grinning. "Have I been invaded by Little People?"

"Yes," several of the children replied in unison, fur rippling.

The dozen or so officers working out laughed. With patient good humor, they lifted the children onto and down from the equipment and showed them how it all worked. Then the children discovered the track and chanach courts outside.

"Play?" Gerel asked.

"No," Devane replied firmly.

Someone behind him murmured, "Good. I've seen the kids play in my shen and those little bastards are damn *fast*. I'd hate to be shamed in front of brothers by a bunch of kids."

A howl of outrage from inside the building sent Devane running for the locker room. There he found one furious, wet, soap-covered female officer clutching a towel about her and chasing wide-eyed children out of the shower.

"Well, soap and water *don't* destroy *my* weatherproofing. What the hell is going on? What asynaptic let this damn rat pack in here!"

"Me, Officer King," Devane said, "but we're leaving now." And he herded the children out, leaving the officer staring open-mouthed.

After that, the rest of the tour seemed anticlimactic. As far as the children were concerned, at least, the exercise room had been the high point. Devane did not bother taking them down to Data. He did stop in the lab, however, and he held his breath until Gerel, seeing his mother, burst into a voluble stream of chatter, telling Meda about all they had seen and done. His monologue hardly slowed, let alone stopped, from the time Meda joined them until the group left the station.

Standing at the door with Devane, watching them scamper across the court and down the path toward the skyrail, Meda laughed. "You can certainly tell which one is our son."

At least until Gerel left Meda's hearing distance, Devane thought. The boy had taken his father's advice to heart. What chameleons children could be. "I guess we can stop worrying about him going native."

She glanced at him, then turned away from the door. "May I buy you coffee, Director Brooks?"

"I never decline a lady's invitation."

They had it in the canteen, looking out into the little courtyard garden between the E and I wings. Meda sipped hers nervously. "Did you make another appointment for me with Deathrage?"

Devane shook his head.

She sat back in relief. Something continued to disturb her, however. She toyed endlessly with her coffee mug. "Dee," she said at last, "can we talk?"

Now? He thought of the work waiting on his desk, work he had already delayed in order to play guide for Gerel's school. "Do you want to go to my office?"

She looked around. "I thought . . . maybe here would be better. Being in public will help keep us calm and rational."

He dreaded conversations she started that way. He sighed. "All right, what do you want to talk about?"

She sipped her coffee. "Gerel. I don't know what's happening to him."

Cautiously, Devane said, "He seems happy and normal to me. First you were upset because you thought he wasn't talking enough. Now he's talking. What's bothering you this time?"

"He talks, but only around me or other Terrans—most other Terrans. When he thinks he's alone with you or with D'ne or other Iregara, he's an entirely different boy. I've watched him. Maybe you're so used to Iregara you don't notice that he talks like they do. I think he's trying to be a different person to fit each group he's with. What kind of psychological damage must that be doing to him? He must have trouble knowing what and who he's supposed to be."

Was that all? Devane smiled. "You don't have to worry about that. Working the streets I saw children from Hispanic and Chinese families doing it all the time. At home they spoke their ancestral language and followed ancestral customs, but they looked and acted like the rest of their peer group the minute they left the house. They weren't confused; they could live in both worlds."

"But"—a frown creased Meda's forehead—"Iregara aren't Gerel's peer group. Terrans should be." She leaned toward him. "Dee, let's go home. This world will destroy us if we stay here. Look what it's already done."

He forced himself to breathe slowly. What could he say to her? That he had a contract and moral obligations to fulfill? That having waited so long for this kind of chance, leaving the job would kill something in him? No, he could not say that. Above all else, he had to avoid the issue of choosing between Meda and the job. He wanted and needed them both.

"The world won't destroy us, Meda. It's a good world. These are fine people. You've been visiting the Enclave every few nights for most of the summer, riding your bicycle back and forth alone at night. Where on Earth would you dare do that? Certainly not in San Francisco. You worry about Gerel going native, but you've never had to worry about him being molested. We have a lock on the door that we don't really need. Think about that," he said softly. "We can be safe here. While Gerel's still young and impressionable, he can be secure, and grow free of people trying to force him into a system of religion and behavior just because *they* believe that way. The only high holies here are in the Enclave."

She bit her lip. "I—yes, I guess it's true. I hadn't thought of that before."

He reached out to take her hand. "Then please do. Think about it, and then if you'd still rather live on Earth, we'll . . . talk about going back. Agreed?" He made himself smile at her.

She squeezed his hand. "Agreed."

"And now," he said, standing up, "Director Brooks had better apply himself to his desk chair and get some work done."

He leaned down to kiss her but she evaded him. Rather than press the issue, he touched her cheek and headed for the door. There he paused to look back. Meda sat with hands pressed to her cheeks, staring thoughtfully off across the canteen. What was going on in her head? He could ask Liril, of course, but watching Meda, he rejected the idea. Give her her privacy. Let her tell him her thoughts in her own time. He only hoped he had given her something positive to consider.

Chapter Twenty-one

A CHEERFULLY insulting chorus greeted Ten and Jael at briefing. "They're back. That proves they aren't so bright; if they were, they would have kept on going."

"How was the trial today?" Nilc Parctski asked.

Ten and Jael looked at each other. "You tell him," Ten said.

"Well, as a trial," Jael said, "Egarad appearances have to rank as the most boring in the galaxy. They consist mainly of the mediator staring at the witnesses. The one time we actually had any kind of extended question-and-answer series was when Roban examined Ladras for the mediator. And even that turned out dull. The only excitement," she said with a wicked grin, "came when Kampacalas went to sleep and fell out of his chair."

Ten stared at her indignantly. "I never—" He broke off, glaring. "Next time I *will* throw you in the river."

"The important question is, did we win?" Delores Kirschner asked.

Ten shrugged. "When we're investigating for both city and defendant, how can we say? It's yes and no, whatever the decision. Society won, I suppose. Nafee ordered Ladras to a care facility for observation and prognosis, and when and if released from there, Ladras will owe reparations to Shumar and Haritheen's children."

"So now the fun's over and it's back to work," Paretski said.

"It's been very quiet the two nights you were gone," Lara Flood remarked. "I don't know if that means anything significant or not."

Ten shook his head, grinning. "Everyone on this watch thinks he's a comedian." A buzzer sounded somewhere. Ten raised his brows at the others. "What's that?"

"One of us has someone at the door of the storefront. It's probably a ride-along."

More buzzers sounded. Ten crossed to his door and checked the observation screen. Outside stood a dun-colored Egara with face marked by red and blue streaks like ancient Terran Indian warpaint.

"Identity?" Ten asked.

"Darith. Rider," the Egara replied, and stretched out the left arm, exhibiting an armband bearing the police yin-yang insignia.

Ten let Darith in. Around the room, he watched the images of other Iregara appear among those of the uniformed Terrans. "Welcome," Ten told Darith. "I'm Ten Kampacalas, your officer." He eyed the facial design. "That looks like temporary paint. Did you mean to come dressed for battle?"

Darith stared at him, reading, Ten felt sure, the images of old Terran Indians in his mind. Darith's fur rippled slightly. "Coincidence." The Egara reached up to touch the warpaint designs. "Appropriate?"

Around the room, other Iregara asked, "What?"

Ten glanced toward them. "Is there a problem?"

His colleagues grinned. "One of communication. The ride-alongs can't understand you or what your ride-along is talking about directly. They have to read it out of our heads, and sometimes if we don't understand, either, that can be confusing."

Yes, a broadcast conference would provide definite problems for the Iregara, Ten decided, like vid without the text strip. With that thought came an idea. Broadcasts might be utilized to demonstrate a Silent's viewpoint of Normal conversations. It could prove enlightening and instructive to Normals.

"Is," Darith said.

Ten raised a brow. "You've had two nights of it already, so I expect so."

Lieutenant Dryden mounted the dais with Brynche and Gerhardt. She checked the holocom network indicators on the lectern. "It looks like all the storefronts are on the network. Has everyone's ride-along shown up?" When no one indicated a negative, she shuffled through her notes. "Before we start, I have a small task for the ride-alongs. It seems someone has suggested that our killer might be a

Terran with a minimal broadcast level, working in this department."

Ten felt his face heat up. He glanced around to see if anyone showed signs of knowing who made the suggestion. The the room erupted into angry and profane protest, but only Darith reacted to Ten, turning impassive eyes on him.

Dryden rapped a fist on the lectern. "All right. That's enough. Director Brooks feels the possibility is so remote as to be ridiculous, but in order to settle the question, so we can all go back to hunting the Silent or haban who's the real killer, the director has asked me to classify the broadcast level of all officers. As I go down the role, will the ride-along tell me whether that officer is a Loud, Medium, Quiet, or Silent? Officers in the last two categories are asked—that's *asked*, not ordered—to submit to a deep reading at the station tomorrow." She looked around the room. "According to the director, there's no penalty for refusing the reading, but I think we all understand that any officer who declines had better have good reasons for doing so. All right . . . Amaro."

The roll call produced just one Quiet, but Dene Baker did not appear alarmed at being a potential suspect. "Certainly I'll take the deep reading. I had to stretch to meet the minimum height requirement in Winnipeg. I'm almost flattered to have the brass or anyone else thinking I'm able to break Ashe's neck that way." She held up her hands, hardly larger than a child's. "Besides, I was on duty during every one of those killings and Communications can testify to my location."

Everyone sat back. The tension that had gripped the room since Dryden's announcement faded. The lieutenant quickly read the incident list, then had Sergeant Brynche pass on some procedure suggestions before dismissing the watch.

Ten caught Jael's eye. "Round up Roban after the watch and meet at my place for food."

She grimaced. "We've had a fight and he's still sulking. I'll try to talk him into it, though."

Outside the door, Ten and Darith met Dal Kiefer coming in. During the few words of greeting and patrol information they exchanged, Ten noticed that Kiefer no longer looked exhausted or tense. The change in watches had obviously helped him.

"Be careful. Keep sharp," Kiefer said in parting.

Ten smiled. "I'm not worried; I have my trusty shotgun rider to watch my back."

Darith assumed a posture of someone holding a long weapon and peering around watchfully. Ten's smile broadened to a grin. The Egara had copied the image in Ten's head. Darith glanced at him and the Egara's fur rippled.

They were off to an auspicious start, Ten thought. Aloud he said, "Let's go to work."

They started a walk through the shopping mall. As they walked, they both talked to shop employees and mall patrons. Here in the remaining hours of daylight, the shops were still open and populated. Ten stopped at B'gen's Antiquities, too.

The shop still had an empty look, but some new items filled the space left by the destroyed antiques. B'gen puttered among the new acquisitions, arranging and rearranging them. As Ten came in, B'gen turned and stared hard at him. "No."

Ten sighed. "Please reconsider. Reparations should be penalty enough. You know confinement in a care facility can be the same as a death sentence."

"Yes," B'gen said.

Ten regarded the shopkeeper with a frown. "You're being very vindictive."

"Yes."

"Don't your neighbors find your emotion painful?"

B'gen paused only a moment before replying shortly, "Justified."

Ten stared at the graying Egara a minute longer. What now? Maybe the shopkeeper would relent in court. "Very well. I'll see you before Mediator Huthe day after tomorrow. Don't forget you have to appear to testify about your disagreement with Anubas."

He left the shop. At his shoulder, Darith said, "Change doubtful."

Ten smiled thinly. "B'gen is obstinate, but don't be so sure seeing Anubas won't bring a change of heart. Even if it doesn't, I can always hope the mediator will consider my opinion before making a judgment."

"Reason?"

"Aside from the fact that I feel euthanasia is too severe a penalty for vandalism, I don't think Anubas is an incurable, or even very antisocial. She regrets what happened, and I saw her love for her child. I hate to see the two of them separated."

"Parents."

Ten glanced toward Darith. "Intellect tells me, yes, the neighbors care just as much and can parent just as well, but"—he shrugged—"my Terran-raised heart doesn't accept it. I believe in families."

Flying from mall to shen to other malls, and walking through each, the two of them talked. Ten did most of it, carrying on a monologue about Earth and Topeka, about working there, comparing it to D'shenegar. He knew he was talking too much, but he seemed unable to stop, as though a plug had been pulled in him, compelling him to empty himself out. He had missed having a partner, he knew, but not until now had he realized how much.

They walked the Crafter's industrial mall. Darith moved as Ten's shadow, pacing him and listening patiently. Then they checked the Third-Level school and several more ishen before moving on to the Thelis industrial mall. There, with the evening faded into the blackness of night, Ten slipped on his night goggles under his helmet. Without being told to do so, Darith dropped back half a step, letting Ten check passages and openings with his baton for wires before they moved through. Ten nodded approval. This telepath learned fast. They might have been working together for months or years instead of merely hours. If not quite safe, Ten felt at least less vulnerable.

"I've talked enough," he said as they checked the closed shops. "Now it's your turn." He grinned. "Tell me all about yourself in one word or less."

In the gray twilight of the goggles, Ten saw Darith's fur ripple.

"What kind of work do you do? Why are you interested in playing cop?"

Before the Egara could answer, however, Ten waved a hand for silence and held his breath, listening. Something or someone moved around the side of a carpetmaker's workshop. "Read anything?" he whispered to Darith.

"No," came the reply, so soft as to be almost inaudible.

Animal minds broadcast, too, so if something live occupied those shadows, the mind must be a Silent one. What Ten would like was for Darith to make vocal noise, as though the two men had stopped for a bit, while Ten himself slid up to the corner.

Darith waited for Ten to flatten against the front of the shop, then shuffled around, muttering. Ten drew his sleeper and eased along the wall cat-silent. At the corner, he stopped, then dived around the edge.

An Egara with a black-spotted face jumped away from an open window.

"Cops," Ten called. "Come here."

The Silent bolted backward.

Ten ducked under the lower edge of the open window to give chase, but the Silent ran toward a passage between buildings, and Ten thought with sudden fear of Martine Her-Many-Horses' last chase. Instead of running after the Silent, he pointed the sleeper and fired. The Silent went down, skidding forward on momentum before coming to a stop in a crumpled heap.

Ten tossed Darith the wrap strap, picturing its use in his mind. "Wrap Spotted-face there, hands behind the back. I'll check to see whether we interrupted an entrance or an exit."

The front door had the usual hook set high enough to keep igelis from reaching it. Nothing had disturbed the hook. Ten flipped it open and stepped inside, looking around the workshop. As far as he could determine, everything seemed in order, but he decided the owner or supervisor should verify that.

He tapped on his radio. "North Twenty-five, Communications."

After a short delay, the reply came. "Go ahead, North Twenty-five."

"Data should have a record of who owns Ananad Carpets in the Thelis industrial mall. Find out who it is and ask that person to meet me at the shop. We have a possible break-in."

"Will do. Thirty-six fifty-three."

Ten glanced at his wrist chron. That late already? Only five hours until midnight. The ride-along's presence was shortening the watch.

While he waited, he continued checking the workshop, looking over the looms and finished rolls of carpet, but carefully touching nothing. He examined the open window, too. It had not been forced, of course; it had no lock to need forcing. It simply lifted up and swung out, a combination of movement that could be accomplished just as well from the outside as inside but was complex enough to defeat igelis. The radio in his ear murmured a constant stream of acknowledgments from Communications as officers all over the city notified the dispatcher of each new location and activity.

Hands clapped twice outside the front door. Ten went to open it. Outside stood Darith, carrying the Silent. Darith laid the Silent on the ground and handed Ten a short Egarad knife.

Ten clucked his tongue. "Where did you find this?"

"Cape."

"Wonderful." He knelt to search the Silent thoroughly.

A familiar number brought his attention to the radio. "Cleared for a personal, North Seven." That would be Jael. He wondered what she was up to.

"Personal?" Darith asked.

Ten felt every centimeter of the Silent, running fingers through the fur, checking the cape and tabard, pulling off the boots to search them, too. "It's time out from duty for a personal errand, usually a trip to the san or a stop somewhere to pay a bill, though I've known officers who used them to visit women or make sure a wife wasn't entertaining visitors."

Darith regarded him impassively. "What?"

Before Ten could try explaining marriage and infidelity, the Silent regained consciousness. As Spotted-face's eyes opened, Ten asked, in Translan, "What's your name?"

"I want to sit up."

Ten helped the Silent into a sitting position. "Did you open the window of the workshop?"

Spotted-face tested the wrap strap. "This is tight."

"What were you doing at that window? Why did you run when I told you who we were?" Ten held up the knife. "We found this in your cape. Why were you carrying it? Were you planning to vandalize the carpet shop?"

Spotted-face replied with a suggestion that widened Darith's eyes and left Ten wondering whether the physically improbable but entertaining idea had been invented by Spotted-face or adapted from Terran profanity.

Ananad, the shop owner, arrived shortly. Hurrying up to them, the Egara looked at the Silent and answered several of Ten's questions in one word. "Yath!"

"You know this person?" Ten asked.

"Yes."

Questioning produced a now-familiar story. Yath had

been employed by the shop but dismissed a short time before for fighting with other employees. In this case, the Silent had actually struck one of the loom technicians.

At Ten's insistence, Ananad checked the shop. Nothing had been disturbed or damaged, which meant they had probably caught Yath on the way in. That presented a problem. If the Silent had not actually entered the shop, no offense had been committed. Carrying a weapon was not forbidden, nor was walking around the mall at night. Running when ordered to come forward by a cop might be suspicious, but not grounds for arrest. Ten could think of no valid reason for holding the Silent, however positive he felt that Yath had been about to vandalize the shop.

With a sigh, he slid the depolarizer from its case on his equipment belt and ran it over the wrap strap. The strap dropped off Yath's wrists. Recharging the strap and coiling it to put it in its case, Ten said, "I'm letting you go."

Yath regarded him without expression.

"But only because nothing has been damaged. I'm filing a report on this incident, though. Your name, description, and address will be in our computer, and if there should be any vandalism connected with this shop in the future, you'll be the first person we come looking for."

Staring after the departing caped form, Ten hoped the experience had cooled the Silent's anger, but thinking of the difference between Yath's—sullen?—silence and the stunned, sleepwalking reaction exhibited by Anubas after the antique shop incident, Ten suspected not. They would hear more from citizen Yath. He made a mental note to warn Consigli and Kiefer that the shop should be given extra attention for a while.

He bid Ananad goodnight and resumed the patrol with Darith. "That's a situation I hate even on Earth, and there we can find all kinds of excuses to hold a subject if we want to. We can be positive about what the subject intended to do, but . . . intent is criminal only after the crime has been committed. We—"

In his ear, a flat voice in Communications said, "Repeat. Unable to read you." After a pause, the dispatcher went on, "Identify yourself, please."

Ten stopped to listen.

"All units, hold traffic. Will the unidentified unit please repeat your transmission? I'm unable to understand you." The voice remained without expression.

"What?" Darith asked.

Ten shook his head. "I don't know. Trouble."

The voice on the radio switched to Isegis. "Name? Identify."

Ten wished passionately that he could hear the other's transmission. Speaking Isegis could only mean Communications was talking to an Egara, a Normal, and Ten could think of only one group of Egara with access to a police radio, and one reason to be using it. He waited anxiously for the dispatcher to go on.

"Say problem, Hedee," Communications said.

Another long pause dragged on while Ten bit his lip in an agony of fearful impatience.

"Wait, Hedee." The dispatcher switched back to English. "Communications, North Seven. What is your location?"

Jael's location? What was wrong with looking at the board?

"North Seven," Communications said again, the voice never losing its flat precison. "Communications to North Seven."

Fear leaped in Ten. *Answer, Jael,* he prayed. *Roger the call, damn it.*

"North Seven, please respond." After another pause: "North Seventeen, proceed to F-12. Meet ride-along Hedee and attempt to locate North Seven. I have no signal from the personal transponder."

"Come on, Darith!" Ten ran for the car, tapping on his radio. "North Twenty-five. Request permission to assist North Seventeen."

Communications did not answer immediately. Ten clenched his fists. *Come on, you bitch,* he thought, *and don't you dare tell me to stay on patrol.* The hell he would keep shaking doors and wait for someone else to find out what had happened to Jael. He would go even if it meant disobeying orders.

"North Twenty-five," Communications said at last. "Permission granted."

With a sigh of relief, Ten ducked under the door of the car and pulled it down tight behind him. Darith dived into the other side. Ten lifted the car and sent it south at a speed that red-lined the panel gauges and rammed both him and Darith deep in their seats.

In less than three minutes he had covered the ten kilometers to the location where the signals on his panel's city grid indicated the location of Jael's and North Seventeen's cars. He grounded the Chehasha in a meadow beside the other vehicles and swinging out, raced toward the woods, startled ichehasha scattering before him and leaping high toward the silver moons.

"Casebier!" he shouted. "Casebier, it's Ten Kampacalas! Where are you?"

Rudi Casebier, North Seventeen, appeared out of the shadows at the wood's edge. "I haven't found her yet."

Ten flashed his hand lamp past Casebier, onto two Iregara standing among the trees. "Which of you is Hedee?" he demanded. "Why the hell weren't you with her like you're supposed to be?"

Casebier caught Ten's arm. "Hedee isn't a bodyguard and you know it. Calm down."

Ten shook off Casebier's hand but dragged in some long breaths. "All right." More reasonably, he asked, "What happened?"

"Hedee was just telling me that Jael asked for and received permission to take a personal."

"I heard that on the radio. She was taking it here?"

"Retreat," Hedee said, pointing into the woods.

"What for?" Casebier asked.

"Meeting."

"Whom was she meeting?"

"For god's sake, details can wait," Ten snapped. "So she was going to take a personal. She went to the retreat. Then what?"

"We," Hedee said. "Both. Walked." Hedee headed along a path into the woods, showing them, then stopped. "Here. Sleeper."

Ten caught his breath. "Jael went down?"

"I. Woke. Gone."

"Did you hunt for her?"

"No reading. Radioed."

Ten shined his light into the woods, first on one side of the path, then the other, fear running like icy fire in him. "No reading at all? Could she be unconscious, with her reading covered by animal minds?"

The Iregara looked at him. Darith said, "Possible."

"Then let's look for her. She might be close. Be careful. Check for wires."

The five of them fanned out through the trees in serpentine paths. Ten moved cautiously, alert for any glint in the air as well as for tracks on the woods floor or broken branches that might indicate someone's hurried passage. Jael's abductor might well have left traps for anyone following.

"North Seventeen, North Twenty-five, status check," Communications said.

"This is Twenty-five. We haven't located North Seven yet."

"Do you need assistance?"

They would need an army to search these woods, or good old-fashioned woodsmen. Trying to pick out a track in the jumble of dead and live vegetation on the woods floor was more than he could do. Where could Jael have been taken? Suddenly, a thought struck him, an idea where she might be.

"Respond, North Twenty-five," came the voice from his radio. "Do you need assistance?"

"No," he replied.

He wanted to run, but he forced himself to walk, still checking for wires, straining to detect that telltale rebound of his paragee field. Why had he thought of the retreat? A hunch? It was easy to reach by the path . . . though why she should have been taken there or anywhere else puzzled him. It was not the killer's previous pattern.

He checked the entrance to the retreat and found it free of wires. Stepping into the clearing, he glanced around . . . and froze, staring at the bench in the center.

For the first moments, he felt nothing but a sense of unreality. Medieval images and the strains of "Greensleeves" clashed in Ten's mind. Stripped naked and laid out on the bench with hands folded across her chest, Jael looked like a marble effigy on top of some ancient tomb. In the twilight of his goggles' vision, her skin shone pale gray and flawless.

"Jael?" he said.

Slowly, he crossed the retreat toward the bench. He felt as though he were watching himself through a telescope . . . remote, detached, insulated from all feeling by that sense of watching a play or dream.

He said again, softly, as though not to startle her, "Jael."

Then he stood beside her, looking down, and the dreamlike quality shattered. Her hands, crossed so decorously, had been bound at the wrists by a wrap strap, and the left side of her head, which he had not been able to see until now, showed as black pulp, the blood robbed of its color by the night. Small wonder her transponder did not function. It must have been destroyed by the blow that killed her.

He tapped on his radio. "North Twenty-five, Communications." The words, calm and measured, reached him as though spoken by someone else. "I've found Officer Meadin. I need a supervisor and C-unit."

"Supervisor and C-unit dispatched."

"Oh, my god," came a whisper from behind Ten. He turned to find Casebier and the three Iregara in the retreat entrance. "They said they heard you screaming," Casebier said, goggle-covered eyes on Jael's body.

Screaming? Ten blinked at them. Not aloud, he knew. It must have been in his mind.

With that thought, the distance between himself and the scene collapsed. He catapulted headlong into the middle of it. As the landing shattered his insulation, anger ignited deep in him. He walked out of the retreat, onto the path, pushing the others ahead of him. Softly, he asked, "Who was she meeting here?"

Hedee regarded him with pupils dilated. "Person."

"People have names. Didn't she think about it?"

"Not name. Image."

"Describe the image."

Hedee stared hard at him. "Thin. Fur, eyes color." The Egara pointed at Ten's black equipment belt. "Skin color." The Egara touched Darith's dun-colored fur.

"Height?" Ten prompted. "Was the shape like Jael's or mine?"

Hedee held up a hand higher than the top of Ten's head. "Shape . . . you."

A male, then, about a hundred eighty centimeters, with black hair and eyes and light brown skin. The familiarity of the description hit Ten. "Was the hair wiry, like an Afro's?"

"Image," Hedee said. "Same."

Casebier looked questioningly at Ten.

Ten took a breath. "I just thought of Roban Adeyanju. That's who she expected to see. The killer lured her here by making her think she was going to meet Roban." He looked back at Hedee. "When did she receive word to meet him?"

"Briefing."

Ten frowned. "Someone at the briefing told her—"

"Note."

Ten blinked in disbelief. Someone at briefing gave her a note? That was impossible!

Hedee sighed. "Found. Bulletin board."

Ten heard Casebier exclaim sharply. His own chest felt suddenly tight. "She found it on the bulletin board? *Inside* the storefront?"

"Yes."

"That can't be," Ten said. "The door only opens for people with authorized palm codes."

In a tight voice, Casebier said, "Maybe the person who left the note *had* a palm code."

Ten bit his lip. Could Brithe be right after all? He did not want to think so. "Maybe the killer persuaded the Day Watch officer to post the note."

Noise sounded down the path. Sergeant Brynche and Lieutenant Dryden came toward them, followed by a Criminalistics team. At the retreat entrance, Brynche shone her hand lamp in and drew a sharp breath. After a quick look toward Jael's body, Dryden said, "All right, what happened?"

Ten looked back into the retreat, where the C-unit team were setting up their field lights, making the clearing an oasis of brilliant light. In the glare, Jael no longer looked like a marble effigy. Now she could be seen for exactly what she was, a naked young woman, flesh bleached by death, nothing at all like the friend who led him on that chase down the beach of the Golden River just two days ago, or who laughed up at Roban from the other side of their sand castle.

Ten's breath caught, stuck at a tight constriction in his throat. He gasped, struggling to breathe.

"Kampacalas!" Dryden snapped.

Ten dragged his eyes around to her.

"You tell me about this. How did it happen? Come on, Kampacalas, *report!*"

Ten reported, somehow, forcing the words out. He paused frequently, but at each stop, Dryden nodded encouragement, and he went on. Eventually, she knew everything Ten did and he smiled a faint thank you at her. Her insistence on his reporting had kept him from falling apart.

"We can ask Bill Chen if an Egara asked him to post that note for Jael," Casebier said.

"We will." Dryden turned toward Hedee. "Did you actually see the writing on the note?"

"Yes."

"How were the characters drawn? Were they the complex ones a Normal would use, incorporating thought-stream elements, or a Silent or Terran's simpler forms?"

"Simple," Hedee said.

"Was the note signed?"

"Yes. Alien." Hedee squatted down and used a forefinger to trace lines in the dust of the path. The two resulting letters were not perfect. Rather, they looked distorted in the same way Ten thought he might reproduce a word in Arabic that he had seen only briefly. Still, the forms were recognizable: *Ro.*

"Whoever forged his name knew his signature and nickname," Ten said.

Dryden eyed him thoughtfully. "Maybe it wasn't forged."

Ten gave her a puzzled frown. "It was a genuine meet that the killer knew about and intercepted Jael on the way? Then where's Roban?"

Brynche said, "Your psychological profile says you're very loyal to friends. Are you blindly loyal as well? Adeyanju is a Quiet. We classified him this afternoon."

Ten's frown changed to one of uncertainty. He tried to read Brynche's and Dryden's expressions, only dimly visible in the light shining out of the retreat. "I know he's a Quiet. What are you trying to say, that *Roban* killed her? That's wickers!" His voice rose.

The conversation with Brithe in the highliner came back to him abruptly. Someone like Roban, Brithe had said, a Quiet Egarad sympathizer, but even she had not suggested that Roban himself might be guilty. Roban had attempted to grab him when he fell at Rimamin.

Then without wanting to, Ten remembered other words of Brithe's: *If he wanted, he could have been pushing you instead. Could* Roban have pushed while appearing to try to save him? Guilt stabbed Ten instantly, but the question lingered. They *had* had a near fight the night before, and a few words that morning.

Suddenly, he remembered the fight Roban and Jael had had on the highliner. His breath caught. The two of them fought one day and Jael died the next evening. No. No, he would still not believe Roban could have had anything to do with—he glanced back into the retreat—with that.

"Fights?" Darith said. "Fall?"

"What?" Dryden asked.

"It's nothing," Ten said, silently swearing. Never any privacy. "Roban may be a Quiet, but he isn't guilty of killing any cops, let alone Jael. The deep reading will prove that."

Dryden sighed. "The trouble is, you see, Adeyanju won't be having a deep reading. When asked to submit to one this afternoon, he refused."

Chapter Twenty-two

No MATTER how long he worked, the stack of hard copy demanding his attention never seemed to diminish, Devane reflected. He had never dreamed running a department would be this much work. Still, even with paper piled up to his ears, he normally enjoyed it. Tonight, however, he could not concentrate. After reading a column of figures for the fifteenth time and still not understanding what he had read, he leaned back from the dining table, groaning and rubbing his eyes.

Meda looked up from where she curled in a pillow chair with a book viewer in her lap. "Why don't you stop for the night?"

He shook his head wearily. "I have to have these statistics ready for my meeting with the board tomorrow afternoon."

But he could not make himself care about it. Instead, his mind slipped back to a period earlier in the evening, when he and Gerel had taken a break from their respective homework for a walk around the shen together before Gerel's bedtime. They had not talked much. Occasionally they broke into a jog, racing up the steps with Gerel's short legs pumping hard to match his father's stride, but for the most part they just walked, enjoying each other's company. A last run took them most of the way up the hill and they sat on the steps to catch their breath, blowing thick steam that swirled around their heads before dissolving in the chilly autumn air.

Devane looked out over the sunset-reddened waters of Rahelem Bay. What a beautiful world, he thought. He rarely found himself comparing D'shenegar to San Francisco these days. It was so very different, in architecture, feel, smell, and general atmosphere. Only the similarity in landscape really linked the two, and the temperature, Devane added wryly. He wondered if some Egarad writer or visiting Terran had ever paraphrased the sentiment that Earth's classic humorist Mark Twain expressed about San Francisco and said, "The coldest winter I ever spent was a summer in D'shenegar."

Gerel giggled. "Funny."

Devane cocked a brow at him. "What's funny, cub?"

" 'The coldest winter I ever spent was a summer in D'shenegar.' "

Shock jolted Devane. He stared at the boy in breathless astonishment. "Gerel . . . did you read that from my mind?"

Gerel's eyes widened fearfully. He started to back away, but Devane pulled the boy to him, hugging him hard. "It's all right, cub; it's all right. I'm not angry at you, just surprised. *Did* you read me?"

Gerel's voice came muffled. "Yes."

"How long have you been able to do it?"

"A little while."

This was something Devane had never expected. Could people learn telepathy? He needed expert advice.

So he took Gerel's hand and they had gone to visit Runah.

The teacher had few answers for Devane except that no, telepathy could not be learned. One had to be born with the capacity. Gerel apparently had been. There was no way of knowing when or if he might have ever developed that rare human capacity to receive if he had remained on Earth, where communication did not require it, but here the boy had quickly learned to use his talent. How much more it might develop and in what directions, Runah did not know, either. His perceptive range had not quite reached that of the ordinary Egarad mind, but Gerel appeared to have the surprising ability to read selectively, blocking out what he did not want to hear.

"Wish," Runah said.

Devane nodded. Yes, he imagined Iregara would like to be able to do that, too. It occurred to him that if Gerel could find a way to teach Iregara to block, Earth would no longer be closed to Normals.

And now all the questions about Gerel and his unexpected talent jostled together in Devane's mind, coming between him and the column of statistics. The foremost question, of course, was when and how should he let Meda know? Glancing at her reading her book, he sighed.

She laid aside the viewer and came up the steps to massage his neck. "Why don't you read something recreational for a change?"

Warmth spread through him. She had not done this for a long time. This was almost the old Meda. He bent his head, happily submitting to her kneading fingers. Had their conversation this afternoon started a turnaround? He passionately hoped so.

"All right. What are you reading?"

Her fingers worked out along his shoulders, smoothing the knots from his muscles. "Not something recreational. It's a history text Runah loaned me. I thought—I thought I'd try to learn more about the planet."

He spun in his chair to regard her with surprised delight. Grabbing her hands, he kissed both of them. "Thank you."

Perhaps this *was* a turnaround. If so, Gerel's talent might be just what they needed. Meda could hardly fear telepaths when her own son was one of them.

"Meda," he began.

The phone chimed, interrupting him. Answering it, he forgot all about Gerel. He listened bleakly to the voice from Communications delivering news he had come to dread hearing.

Meda read his face as he waved off. "Oh, no! Not another officer dead!"

He nodded wordlessly. "A car is coming after me." He went for a jacket and kissed her. "I don't know when I'll be home."

From the entrance to the retreat, Devane watched the Criminalistics technicians work around Jael Meadin's body. Helpless anger filled him. She looked so young stretched out there. They all looked so young—Meadin, Cole, Casebier, and Kampacalas—hardly more than children. What he done to them, bringing them out here to die on an alien planet?

He turned to look at Kampacalas. The officer slumped against a tree on the edge of the path, eyes fixed on the helmet dangling from his hand by its chinstrap, guilt and misery etched into his face. "Come on," Devane told him. "If Adeyanju killed Meadin and the others, he's no friend and you haven't betrayed him by talking."

Kampacalas watched the helmet, spinning first one direction, then back the other. "If."

"We have enough against him to make him a good suspect," Captain Titus said. "He refused the deep reading; he fought with Meadin; and he has access to the storefronts to put up that note. Chen's told us no one asked *him* to post the note. Do you know any more than what you've told us about Rimamin and the flight back?"

The trouble with trying not to think, Ten reflected, was that more memories came bubbling up out of his mind, all the anti-Terran sentiments Roban ever expressed, about Silencing Iregara and importing the barbarity of bars and cages to Egar. And seeing the director, another incident surfaced, too.

"Ashe," Darith said.

Devane did not miss the angry glance Kampacalas sent the Egara. With obvious reluctance, Kampacalas said, "The night Ashe died Roban was furious about being clawed over by Director Brooks because our case against Ladras was kicked out of court. He even turned on me, wouldn't talk to me or go anywhere with me that evening, just wanted to be left alone, he said. The next day he . . . evaded when I asked what he'd done with the evening. In the same conversation he told me he didn't believe anyone had killed Ashe or Wofford, but that they'd killed themselves by being careless." He watched the spinning helmet. "That's all I know."

Devane pursed his lips. "I guess we'll have to force a deep reading on the inspector. Find Adeyanju, Titus."

Titus glanced at Lieutenant Dryden, who tapped on her radio and asked Communications for Inspector Adeynaju's transponder coordinates. Presently she reported, "He's in the south leg of the city, director. Communications, contact the inspector and have him meet me at this coordinate."

Ten listened to Communications call Roban. He spun his helmet harder on its chinstrap, torn by conflicting emotions. It seemed like a dirty trick, having someone report to be arrested, and he, Ten, had helped do this to Roban. But, a voice in him whispered, what if Roban *had* killed Jael?

"Why do you suppose he laid her out like that?" Ten heard Casebier ask. "None of the others were."

"Communications, supervisor," the radio murmured.

"Be advised Captain Basanites is en route to your location."

"Officer's night again," Titus said, then frowned. "Director, this *is* a break in the pattern. I hope it doesn't mean we're dealing with two different killers."

"You mean, maybe Adeyanju killed Meadin but not the others?" Brooks asked.

"It's happened before, one killer imitating another. Then again, maybe the difference is his relationship with her. This might be a kind of bizarre expression of grief. Sometimes killers do contradictory things."

"It isn't something an Egara would do," Brynche said. "They don't lay out their dead; they cremate them and spread the ashes around the shen."

"May I go back to my patrol?" Ten asked. If he had to stay much longer, he would either burst into tears or start breaking heads. They sounded like they had already tried and convicted Roban.

"Don't leave yet," Titus said. "We want you to repeat what you know for Captain Basanites."

"But my patrol—"

"Dene Baker is covering it. Maybe you didn't hear her ordered up there while you were telling us about Adeyanju."

"Disassociate," Darith said. "Arrest."

For once, Ten understood immediately. Yes, he supposed he wanted to be gone when Roban arrived, in order to disassociate himself from the arrest, though Roban could probably guess who told the brass about his fight with Jael.

Everyone went on talking while they waited for the investigations chief and Roban, the Terrans in one voluble group and the Iregara, outwardly laconic, in another. Ten joined neither.

When Basanites arrived, Ten resignedly repeated everything, quote by quote and detail by detail. Then Titus said, "Shouldn't Adeyanju be here by now?"

Dryden called Communications.

"Our map showed him at your location, but he's now moving south, away from you," Communications reported.

Brynche swore. "He must have been coming in and heard us talking. I told you to watch the path, Casebier."

"I was, sarge. I swear he didn't come up it."

Dryden looked at the Iregara. "Didn't any of you read him?"

Hedee pointed at Ten. "Blocks."

"Well, no matter," Brooks said. "He's running, and that's as good as a confession, I'd say. Ask Communications to track him, Dryden, and let's go after him. Kampacalas, you can remain here to secure the area until the C-unit is finished."

Ten bit his lip. Running did not suggest innocence, certainly. His mouth thinned. "Sir, I'd like to come along, if I may. If he's headed south, he may be going home."

Leaving Casebier and his ride-along behind, the rest of them hurried for the cars. Communications posted them on Roban's movements. He did appear headed for home. He kept going south until Communications reported that the transponder signal came from the coordinates of Seba Shen. They landed the cars around the perimeter of the shen and converged on Roban's house on foot, sleepers drawn.

Almost at the house, however, an Egara intercepted Ten. "Gone."

Ten quickly checked with Communications. Roban's car remained parked on the edge of the shen and his personal transponder still broadcast from inside the area.

"Gone," the Egara insisted.

Ten abandoned stealth and charged the house. "Roban?" he called, flattening against the wall outside the door. "Ro, if you're in there, better come out."

Silence answered him. With the others covering him and Lem Cole backing him up, he pushed open the door and leaped in through the opening. The sitting area was empty.

Searching the house took only a minute and as the Egara had predicted, Roban was nowhere to be found. However, Ten did find a tiny radio lying on the kitchen table. He regarded it unhappily. By removing the radio, Roban had made it impossible to track him electronically. A further admission of guilt?

A grim Cole appeared in the bedroom door. "Get the lieutenant," he said.

A few minutes later he showed them what he had found. Hanging among the other uniforms in the closet was one that was dusty, stained, and demonstrably smaller than the others. A pair of boots on the closet floor did not match the size of the civilian-style boots alongside them, either. Ten sighed. He could have accepted the possibility that Jael might keep an extra uniform here at Roban's house, but not a dirty one, and like the rest of them, she owned only one pair of uniform boots.

"Get the C-unit down here when they're finished at the retreat," Brooks told Brynche. "Have them package these boots and this uniform for processing. And broadcast a pickup on Adeyanju."

Overhead all three moons shone, lighting the meadow with their multiple splendor and surrounding Ten with shadows as he rode his bicycle along the path toward home. Surrounded by shadows. That characterized exactly how he felt. He glanced at his chron. The glowing Egarad numerals read: 0306. Late. He felt reluctant to go home, however. Despite exhaustion, he knew he could not sleep.

What a count for the night: one friend dead and another wanted for the murder, both fellow officers. No Silent was involved in the cop deaths, it appeared, no haban, just a Terran preying on other Terrans. Maybe Roban was right, and speaking from experience . . . Terrans destroyed whatever they touched . . . planets, aliens, each other. He was glad making out reports and a formal statement had taken so long that he missed debriefing and escaped the questions the rest of the watch were sure to have asked.

He stopped the bicycle and stood leaning on the handlebars, wracked by homesickness. In Topeka, he could have sat down for a long, comforting talk with his father, or cried on Miral's shoulder. God, he missed his family. He even missed Avel. He could just hear what she would say in his situation: "Trade me a sidearm needler and clip of explosive needles for this damn sleeper and I'll bring the bastard in!"

Ten would like to bring Roban in, too. Where could the Afro be? In a city where news of his crime and the hunt for him could leap from mind to mind, spreading far faster than a man could travel on foot, where every Normal would know who and what the fugitive was, where could Roban expect to hide?

Ten started forward again, sorting through the possibilities. The path entered a band of woods that blocked out the moonlight. Ten switched on his bicycle light. As the beam leaped out, a sound caught his attention. He looked around quickly, attempting to locate and identify the source, and when his eyes came back to the path, Roban stood squarely in the middle.

Ten froze but made his voice casual. "Hello, Ro. What are you doing here?" He reached for his collar, as though to touch his paragee control plate. From there, he eased his hand up to scratch his throat, moving toward his ear.

Roban brought up the sleeper he held. "Put both hands on your handlebars."

Ten did as ordered. His chest tightened. "What are you planning to do, knock me down and smash in my head, too?"

The beam of the bicycle light did not reach Roban's face. Ten could not see the Afro's expression, but he heard a sharp intake of breath. "Too? Is that how Jael died?"

"As if you didn't know."

"I didn't. How could I? I heard Basanites talking on the path, but I never saw Jael. Ten, I didn't kill her. I swear."

Ten bit his lip. Roban sounded sincere. "Then why did you run?"

"Because to prove I'm innocent, I'd have to take a deep reading."

"So?"

Roban groaned. "I—I can't do that."

Ten frowned. "Why not? What *are* you guilty of?"

"Nothing criminal, believe me."

Ten wished he could see Roban's face, but it was only a blur above the bicycle beam. "Then it can't possibly be as serious as looking guilty of killing cops."

"Oh, yes it can."

The bitterness startled Ten. He eyed Roban. "Why come to me?"

"I wanted you to know I didn't kill her. I need help, too. In one way, being a fugitive in this city is easy, but only as long as I stick to the woods and meadows. I don't dare go in anywhere. You can."

"How?" Ten asked. "I'm a Loud. Every Normal in range would know I've seen you."

Roban said desperately, "I don't have anyone else. Ten, I need proof, physical evidence, that will eliminate me as a suspect without having to resort to a deep reading."

Ten hesitated. "It might be hard. Your movements can't be accounted for. As an investigator, your location on watch isn't monitored like mine is."

"I swear I wasn't anywhere near any of them when they died. Tonight I was in the far southern leg. You heard Communications say so."

Ten shook his head. "That's no alibi. At top speed, a car can make that trip in ten minutes, fifteen max, and it was longer than that between the time Jael died and you were called."

Roban jammed his sleeper into his holster. "*I didn't do it!* I cared about Jael."

"Except when you fought."

"Everyone fights once in a while. Fights don't have to end in murder."

"Sometimes they do, though, don't they?" Ten took a breath. "There's physical evidence against you. She was stripped naked and we found her uniform in your closet."

"Stripped—" Roban's voice sounded like that of someone going pale. "Oh, god. But that doesn't mean anything. I have no lock on my door. Anyone could have put it in the closet."

How many times, Ten wondered, had he heard the complaint: "*It was planted on me, officer,*" told with a straight face and earnest voice? He sighed. "Ro, why don't you just turn yourself in and take the reading? Once it's over, you'll be cleared."

"I *can't!*" Roban exclaimed in an agonized voice.

Patiently, Ten tried again. "Look, you went to court today, or rather, yesterday. The mediator is a deep-reader. You didn't object to that."

"The mediator passed over everything irrelevant to the case."

"So will the deep-reader at the station."

Roban hissed. "Oh, god, can't you understand? This *is* relevant. It's my alibi for Ashe's death . . . but I don't dare tell anyone."

"Why not?" Ten demanded in exasperation. "What were you doing, dancing some high holy's wife?"

Ten meant it sarcastically, but Roban reacted with a start. "Not . . . exactly," he muttered. He shifted position, breathing hard. "Ten, if I—if I show you I had nothing to do with Ashe's death, will it help you believe I didn't kill Jael, and do you think you can bury the information somewhere very deep in your mind? My neighbors know already, and none of them has said anything, so maybe they have no judgments on it, but . . . I don't want any other Terrans to know."

Although itching with curiosity, Ten began to wonder if

he wanted the responsibility of a secret Roban feared that much. "If you come in for the reading, maybe the reader won't give details, just say yes, you did it, or no, you didn't."

"You can't guarantee that." He kicked at a pebble on the path. "It only happened because I was drunk. I was so chapped about Brooks clawing me that I came home and started drinking, hating every command officer and every Terran in existence. I was going down fast when—" He took a breath. "A neighbor came over with a luras."

Ten knew that pattern.

"I invited her in—I know she's female because she has three kids. We started talking and I babbled on and on about how much I love Egar and despise what Terrans have done to Iregara. Understand how far gone I was, Ten, almost obliterated. I was drunk, and she understood *exactly* how I felt. Maybe she was a bit curious, too; I don't know. Anyway . . ." His voice trailed off.

Ten waited for him to go on. When he did not, Ten prompted, "Anyway what?"

Roban groaned. "Do I have to draw you a picture?"

"Yes. *I'm* not a telepath."

"I wasn't dancing a high holy's wife that night, but I was . . ."

This time his meaning sank in. Ten felt his jaw drop. "You mean that you and she—they're another species, Ro. Is it physically possible?"

"No . . . well, yes, sort of." He swallowed audibly. "Now do you understand why I can't tell anyone?"

Ten tried to imagine a Terran/Egarad coupling, but his imagination failed him. Then he began examining his own reactions. He found surprise but no shock. He was not repelled by the idea. Iregara were people, after all; it was not in quite the same class of behavior as a prostitute he had known in Topeka who was fond of saying, and demonstrating, that the more she knew of men, the more she loved her dog.

"We've been on Egar over three hundred years. People being people, this probably isn't the first experimentation, Ro, and I don't suppose it'll be the last. And don't you think the brass have seen just about everything? You won't shock them."

"But what a locker-room item it'd make, and a nice

note, too, in my personnel jacket and psych records. Can you imagine what that would do to me when I want another job on Earth?"

The high holies would be screaming *abomination*. Ten sighed. "I'll try to help you."

Even as he said it, though, he wondered what he could do. How did one prove a negative, a lack of guilt? Maybe the lab would turn up something that might give him a lead.

"Where were you planning to spend the night?" he asked.

Roban shrugged. "Out here."

In the cold? With wild animals for company? Ten shivered. "Go to my place. Almost everyone is asleep now. Since you're a Quiet, you won't disturb anyone, and they may not even notice you tomorrow."

"*Go*?" Roban asked. "Where will you be?"

"Running against the clock, doing my best to help you before you're caught."

Roban reached out to put a hand on Ten's arm. "You don't have to do it all. I'll come with you."

"No." Ten shook his head, smiling wryly. "You remember that old saying about walking into the lion's den? That's exactly where I'm going. I'll call you when I have anything."

Chapter Twenty-three

TEN HAD never come into the stationhouse at this hour before. Except for fewer personnel, it seemed little different than it did on other watches, but he found no comparison to the same watch in a station on Earth. Instead of the flotsam and jetsam of night people cluttering the reception area, seedy, disreputable, often drug- or liquor-intoxicated, space stretched clean and empty before him. Personnel, sworn and nonsworn, moved with measured efficiency, and although nearly empty, the laboratory in Criminalistics blazed with light. Walking in, Ten nearly ran head-on into Bioni Elanca and Lieutenant Hasejian.

He started. He had not expected to find either of them here. "You're here late," he said in surprise.

"Yes," Elanca replied wryly. "Something I can do for you? Kampacalas, isn't it . . . antique shop vandalism and printing shop assault?"

Ten wondered fleetingly if one of Brooks's requirements for supervisory personnel was instant and total recall. "Yes, ma'am. I was curious about what you found processing Jael Meadin's uniform."

"Too impatient to wait for the grapevine?" Hasejian asked.

Ten put on his most boyish grin. "Yes, ma'am."

Elanca exchanged a glance with Hasejian. "I love beautiful, polite boys . . . even when they're jooking me. All right, whatever your real reason for having to know right now, we've matched dirt on the uniform to the woods path and retreat but haven't found anything else, no hair or other dust that might tie it in to whoever took it off Meadin. The killer must have been very careful, obviously familiar with Criminalistics and what we look for."

Ten took a breath. Like Roban, they must mean. "I

wonder why he carelessly hung the uniform in his closet."

The two women glanced at each other again. "Are you hinting that maybe someone else hung it there?" Hasejian asked. "Don't you give me credit for considering that possibility myself?"

Ten flushed. "Yes, ma'am, I just—"

"I remember you from orientation. You, Meadin, and Adeyanju were all part of a little group. Are you here to play defendant's investigator because you're afraid we won't?"

Ten felt his flush deepen under the sting of her sarcasm. "Like you said, Meadin was part of our group. I have to know in my own mind whether Adeyanju killed her or not. Please, if you've asked his neighbors whether anyone could have planted that uniform, I'd like to know the answers they gave."

Hasejian's expression softened. "So far, the answers have all been negative." She paused. "I know how you feel, but why don't you let me handle the investigation? Believe it or not, I'm just as anxious to find evidence that someone else did the killing, and as much as I detest a lion killer, or a leo—cop turned killer, if Adeyanju looks guilty, he'll still have the benefit of defense investigation . . . like any suspect."

Ten looked at Elanca. "Did you find anything useful in the retreat? Did you find the murder weapon?"

"No murder weapon. As for the rest"—she shrugged—"we don't know if it's useful yet. What we've found is mostly hair." She rolled her eyes. "Lots of hair. It's dawning on me more forcibly all the time how much hair a furry race leaves behind. Come here." She led him to a workbench where an Egarad technician sat placing sample after sample under a small laser. "Aburin has been checking hair with laser diffraction for the past three hours. I think half the population of that cluster must have come through the retreat at one time or another. We have almost any type of hair you care to name, short or long, silky or wiry, all colors plain or dyed. We even have beaded hairs." She pointed to a transparent sample envelope containing some black hairs tipped by tiny glittering beads. "This is a case of find us a suspect and maybe we can tell you if there is a reasonable chance he helped contribute to the collection. The only bright ray is, the laser hasn't identified any human hair yet . . . if a negative can be said to prove anything."

"You didn't find the note? Hedee said she put it in a thigh pocket."

Elanca shook her head. "No note." She pushed a straying gray lock off her forehead. "Now, be a good boy, will you, and get out from under our feet?"

Resentment flared in him. She had no right to treat him like a child crashing an adult party. "I'd just like—"

"We're the ones under orders to work around the clock until this thing is wrapped, not you. No sense in all of us missing our beauty sleep."

Hasejian snickered. "Even though she needs it more than you do."

Elanca eyed her. "I love you like a daughter, lieutenant. I used to put a foot in my Caerin's rear for remarks like that."

The Egarad technician looked around at them, eyes wide. *Puzzled at the Terran play*? Ten wondered as he left.

In the corridor outside he stood looking around him. What now? His eyes fell on the U wing roster on the far side of the reception area. Maybe that was something to try. He crossed the reception area and walked down the corridor to Communications.

Two dispatchers staffed it, a sloe-eyed Oriental-looking young woman Ten vaguely remembered having met once during orientation and an Egara with silky, golden chestnut fur. Seeing the Egara, Ten's breath caught, then eased. Any Egara in Communications must be a Silent. His thoughts were safe.

The city map filled the entire wall above their consoles, glittering with indicator lights in half a dozen colors. Ten found his own cluster and watched Consigli's red light move away from the car's blue indicator into the circle representing Lus Shen.

"Good morning," the young woman said in Translan. "May I help you?"

Ten looked at the map. "That isn't everyone in the department."

The sloe eyes widened. "Of course not. Can you imagine the confusion that over three hundred indicators would make? That's just the Morning Watch."

He had dated a dispatcher his probationary year. What was it she had told him about map operation? He had only half listened then, and in class when Communications operations was covered as well. How it worked had never seemed important as long as it worked. "The computer runs the map, doesn't it? Does it automatically show the present watch?"

"No. We have to ask." She pointed to a keyboard. "Every transponder has a code number. We can punch in individual code numbers or feed in a rollcall card, but until we do, the map won't display the indicators."

Ten rubbed a thumb down the cleft in his chin. "A few hours ago we wanted to locate a certain investigator. Are investigators on the board, too?"

The Silent said, "Not usually, unless they ask us to keep track of them."

"What is it you need to know?" the woman asked. "Maybe I can save you some questions."

"I'm not quite sure what I want. The map displays only the transponder signals you want. Does the computer receive all the signals; that is, is the potential for display always there, or does it ignore some signals until they're asked for?"

The dispatchers looked thoughtful. "The computer receives all the signals all the time," the woman said.

Hope stirred in Ten. Maybe he had found something helpful. "All right. I know the computer records the displayed signals. If I want to see the display for the Morning Watch yesterday, it can be recalled and played on a computer screen. What I need to know is, does the computer record all the signals it receives or only those actually displayed? If I replayed a section of a watch, could I punch in the codes for transponders not displayed and put them on the map, too?"

Now the sloe eyes went blank. "I really don't know. I've never tried it before. I don't have a screen here for playback, but there should be someone down in Data who can help you."

Ten manufactured a smile for her. "Thank you very much."

He left, but did not go to Data. He knew from Brithe that all Egarad computer technicians aside from her were Normals. Asking about the map recordings might betray why Ten wanted to know, and even give away Roban's present location. Ten had no desire to spoil his record with a charge of harboring a fugitive. He only hoped no Normal in the station now was paying particular attention to his mind. He left before he attracted any attention.

Walking toward the skyrail station, he wondered whom he could go to. He needed that information. A moment later the obvious solution struck him. Brithe. She knew more about the police computer than anyone else. She might even be able to make it perform a function it had never been intended to.

The problem, of course, was: what kind of reception would she give him at this hour? He could well imagine himself slashed and bleeding on her doorstep, psychologically if not physically. Waiting until morning would be safest, but did he have that much time? How much information about Roban had leaked out of him to Iregara in the station? By morning, Roban might be in detention, being forced to undergo a deep reading.

Ten took a breath. For Roban's sake, he would just have to take a chance on waking Brithe.

His knock on her door produced no results. Ten considered knocking louder, but he did not want to wake anyone else. If he stepped inside the door and clapped, Egarad-style, would that have more effect? In the end, though, after consideration, he decided against even that little bit of trespass. He walked around the house, up the slight slope, and rapped on her bedroom window.

Brithe responded the third time he tapped, pushing the window open so suddenly it almost hit him in the face. Through the narrow opening, she blinked at him. "Ten?"

"Yes. I have to talk to you."

"What about?" She sounded groggy but not hostile, which encouraged him.

"Jael was killed tonight. Roban is the chief suspect."

She seemed to have trouble absorbing that news. Five or six seconds passed before she said anything. "Roban killed Jael? How terrible."

"I don't think he did it. That's what I want to talk to you about. May I come in? It's cold out here."

"Oh, of course." All trace of sleepiness had disappeared from her voice. "Go on around. I'll be right down."

Before long he sat in her sitting area in a chair of woven leather straps with his hands wrapped around a mug of hot tea. Brithe curled in a chair opposite him, her coat throwing rainbows at him. "Tell me everything," she said.

Between sips of tea, he gave her a detailed account of the entire night, including meeting Roban. Brithe listened intently, saying nothing, with only an occasional coruscating play of light to indicate that she even moved.

At the end of his recital she asked, "Then what you want to do is replay the map at the time of the murder and display Roban's signal to show where he is?"

He nodded. "Can we do it?"

She sighed. "No. We can program the computer to do that, and we may, after this, but the present program records only the actual display."

Of course. If the computer could be used to locate everyone at a particular time, it would have been done before now. "Well," he said with a shrug, "it was a thought."

"I'm sorry."

He sipped the tea. "So we can't prove he was somewhere else during the killings. Maybe we can think it through from a different direction. Someone lured Wofford out to the textile mill with a phony complaint. Anyone could have done that. Almost anyone could have set up a meet with Ashe. How about Many-Horses, though? That monofilament had to be strung up just before she came running down the passage. Put it up too soon and someone else might have walked into it. How could anyone know she was going to be in the mall at just that time? We don't follow a schedule."

Brithe yawned. "The killer waited, perhaps. Many-Horses would have had to come through that mall sooner or later."

Ten frowned. There must be a better answer than that. The simplest, of course, was for someone to contact Communications and ask for Many-Horses' location, but the dispatchers would remember if anyone had done that. On the other hand . . . "The computer knows where everyone is. Could someone query the computer through one of the remotes and receive an answer?"

Brithe stopped yawning and sat up straight, making rainbows between them. "If the person knew the code for Many-Horses' signal, yes."

"Try this, then. The person queries the computer, perhaps from Many-Horses' own storefront remote."

"Or her own tie-in," Brithe suggested, looking at Ten's belt buckle.

He glanced down. "Or that," he agreed. "Then the killer

goes to Many-Horses' location and kills her. My question is: would the computer remember being asked?"

Brithe considered. "It should."

"Can I ask it through my tie-in?"

Her ear twitched. "It's too complex a question. We'll have to use the remote in a storefront."

"Then let's go." He set aside his tea and pulled on his gloves and helmet, then smiled. "As long as we're both already awake."

She smiled back. "Terrans are—how do you say it?—wickers."

Still, she put on a tabard and her hip boots and wrapped up in a cape. In minutes they were riding their bicycles south toward the D'she shopping mall, their breath white clouds on the night air.

"I appreciate this, Brithe."

"You aren't counting too much on it, I hope."

"No. If the computer says no, or it doesn't remember, Roban may just have to submit to a deep reading, no matter how much he hates the idea."

"I—" Brithe began, and broke off.

Ten glanced toward her. Despite moonlight filtering down through the trees, he saw only a shadow behind her bicycle headlamp. "What?"

"Nothing."

They came out of the woods, crossed a meadow between Namarad and Chalu Sheu, and entered another band of woods. Nothing moved around them but leaves whispering in the night breeze. Distantly, a cheneg screamed a hunting call. Ten sensed something bothering Brithe. Half a dozen times he heard an intake of breath, as though she were about to speak, but each time, she let it out again.

Finally Ten braked his bicycle and grabbed her handlebars, halting her, too. "What's the matter? Tell me."

She sighed. "Ten, I don't understand why anyone would refuse a deep reading that would prove him innocent just because he's afraid of people knowing he tried to couple with an Egara. There's nothing shameful in that. Since I've known you, I've been curious about it, too."

Ten choked. With embarrassment heating his ears, he tried to explain his society's viewpoint, but failed. The cultural gap yawned like a chasm between them. Finally, he said, "Mistakenly or not, some of my people, the ones in power, unfortunately, believe it's wrong, no better than bestiality. With miscegenation on his record, Roban could never find a decent job on Earth again, or at least, not in North America."

"Still, have you considered the possibility that the real reason he doesn't want a deep reading might be because it would *not* prove him innocent?"

"No." Ten shook his head emphatically. "He told me he's innocent. I believe him. I think I can tell when someone is lying."

In a shaft of moonlight, her arm shot sparks at him. "But so much fits him."

"Except the uniform," Ten said. "Don't you think he would be smart enough not to hang it in his own closet?"

She shifted position restlessly. "Maybe he's smart enough to do exactly that."

He blinked. "You just confused me."

"It's simple. Evidence exists. Trying to destroy it is usually futile. Instead, why not dispose of it by leaving it in such a way that it looks as though someone else left it to place the blame falsely?"

Ten felt his jaw hanging and closed his mouth with a snap. "Where do you find ideas like that? In those Terran mysteries you're so fond of?"

Her arm moved again in the shaft of moonlight, shooting sparks at him. "Is it impossible?"

It was complex, and in Ten's experience, simple stratagems worked better than complex ones. A better question might be: did Roban's mind work in such convolutions? Could he have lied so convincingly, and made such a fool of Steven Kampacalas?

"If the killer isn't Roban, she has to be another officer. No one else has access to the storefronts," Brithe said.

"Wait." Ten started pedaling again. "Someone else has to have access. The supplies and report forms don't appear by magic, and someone must service the computer remote and holocom. How do service personnel get in?"

"Any Terran could do it, anyone with a palm code for the computer to read."

"An even simpler method would be to program the computer to open the doors for any individual meeting some predetermined criterion, like carrying an electronic device radiating on a specific frequency."

"But none of the service personnel would know Roban's signature."

A good point. How could someone learn Roban's signature? Well, for one thing, it appeared on every report he ever wrote. Anyone with access to the computer could learn it just by asking for a hard copy reproduction of one of those reports. But that would be a full signature, not the nickname. It came back to someone who knew Roban well enough to know the shortened name.

It also came back to the computer, he reflected. The use of it ran like a thread though this thing. The computer could tell a killer where Many-Horses was. It could give the killer Roban's signature and let the killer into a storefront. It could even, he thought suddenly, order Ashe on an impromptu and then, if told to do so, forget its order. Ashe's log could have been accurate after all! He bit his lip. Could their killer be a haban working in Data?

"Brithe, have you noticed how often our killer uses the computer?" he asked. "What if it's someone in Data? Is that—"

He never finished the sentence. A hard blow from the side knocked over his bicycle and sent him flying from it into a tree along the path. His helmet saved his head and face, but pain lanced through his left shoulder.

What the hell?

Then something tugged at his right hip. He felt his sleeper pulling loose, and suddenly, sickeningly, he knew what the hell was happening. He rolled onto his back, grimacing, holding his injured arm, and stared up at Brithe. A shaft of moonlight coming through the trees lighted the barrel of the sleeper pointed at him.

He groaned. "You? It's been you all along?"

In reply, something tickled his brain, and blackness blotted out all sound and sight.

Consciousness returned suddenly, without any intermediate borderland between sleep and awareness, nothing to cushion the shock or prepare him for the pain. He opened his eyes to find himself propped in a sitting position against a tree—the same one he hit? he wondered—his hands secured behind his back with his wrap strap. The pain in his shoulder came in stabbing thrusts that echoed through the rest of his body and turned his stomach, threatened to make him vomit. He fought the nausea, but it was only a minor annoyance compared to a sharper pain in his head and the greater sickness of shame. He had worried that

Roban might have made a fool of him. What did he call what he had let Brithe do to him?

He looked around for her. He found a large, sitting shadow among the other shadows on the path, a specter without face or definite form. "Why did you do it, Brithe? Do you blame Terrans for your Silence?"

The specter spoke. "I blame everyone." He would never have recognized the flat, toneless voice as Brithe's.

"So you take it out on cops?"

"Them, too."

Too? He tested the wrap strap. It had been applied properly and held his hands securely at the wrist. The effort, however, sent new pain through his shoulder. He bit his lip until the spasm passed, wishing he could activate his radio. "I think I've broken my collarbone."

"It won't hurt long."

He could guess why not. A chill creeped up his spine. He swallowed. "I'm surprised you haven't killed me yet."

"I'll do it in Meem, where Roban can take the blame for it, too."

"Wrapping the case . . . until the next time you kill."

"That won't be here. I'll quit the job, grief-stricken, after my best friend is killed."

Anger vied with fear and shame. "I guess you *have* found some ideas in those Terran mysteries. I suppose they told you about Criminalistics and monofilament."

She did not reply.

Knowing about her explained some of her previously mystifying behavior, like the days of sharp irritability followed by days when she almost purred with friendliness. Several of those changes, he recalled, had occurred over nights when officers died. Her hidden hatred explained, too, the remarks she made, the things she did, that wounded feelings or set people around her arguing. Divide and injure. Knowing did not explain everything, though.

"You smashed my sand castle, then turned around and saved my life at Rimamin," he said. "You risked your own life to do that. Why didn't you just let me fall?"

She did not reply for a minute, then she said softly, "I don't hate *you*. You're the first person I've ever been able to share my music with." She paused. "I've been killing since adolescence. The first time was in Third-Level school, an accident. A student broke her neck falling down a ramp where I'd spilled a chemical, but it made me feel so good I started constructing other accidents whenever I could. Your death is the only one I won't enjoy." She stood up. "Enough rest. We're almost at Meem." Grabbing him by the front of his collar, she pulled him to his feet. "You can walk the rest of the way, or until we're close enough that I'll have to knock you down again. Why did you have to be the one to put all the pieces together?"

He laughed wryly. "I had the pieces, but I didn't know what they meant. I was thinking in terms of a haban. I didn't know they meant you until you hit me."

She made a sound like a stifled groan. Taking his good shoulder, she pushed him up the path. Ten moved obediently, then as her pressure on his shoulder eased, he spun on his left foot, swinging the right leg high and hard. He kicked her square in the middle of her torso. Brithe doubled with an explosion of escaping breath, and Ten bolted.

During school and his probationary year on the force, he had heard continuously how impossible it was for a prisoner to run with his hands wrapped behind his back. From observation, it appeared true; the two attempted escapees he had helped run down had been caught with little difficulty. Now he had the opportunity to discover how it felt to be on the other side.

His instructors had been half right; running was difficult, but not impossible. Fear helped keep him going even when not having his arms for balance threatened to send him headlong onto his face. He could never out-run her, he felt sure, but he hoped he did not have to; he should only need to keep away from her long enough to come within telepathy range of someone.

Ten left the path to plunge straight through the woods, taking a straight line toward the nearest habitation. That would be the shopping mall. He could count on finding people awake there.

Behind him, he heard Brithe call, and then the sound of her crashing through the brush. He strained to run faster but quietly, giving himself every advantage possible.

His toe caught on something. He fell rolling. As his weight came down on the injured shoulder, new agony burned through him. He clenched his jaws to keep from crying out. Despite the pain, as soon as he stopped rolling, he struggled to his knees, then his feet, and ran on.

He heard her after him. She did not call to him again, but he followed the sound of her passage. She, undoubtedly, was doing the same to him. And from the sound of her, she had shortened the distance between them.

How much further to the edge of the woods? Not far, surely. From there, it was a clear run across the meadow, a matter of just keeping ahead of her until the cavalry arrived.

Come and get me, citizens. Officer in trouble.

A high, hysterical giggle sounded to his right. He dodged left automatically, but an instant later identified the call of a gelis. By that time, however, he had lost his balance again. He did not fall this time, but he did bounce off a tree, striking his injured shoulder and staggering half a dozen steps before steadying.

Behind him, Brithe sounded still closer. Ahead lay the meadow, only a few meters away, and at the bottom of the meadow, the shopping mall. He kept running.

He passed the last tree and broke into the open. Glancing back, though, he saw Brithe coming into the meadow off to his left. She angled to intercept him. He was not going to make it, he thought bleakly. Once she had her hands on him, he stood no chance of fighting her greater strength. She would kill him out here, alone and unheard.

"Consigli!" he yelled, calling the Morning Watch officer in one last, hopeless, defiant plea for help.

Brithe's hand smashed hard between his shoulder blades, sending Ten onto his face. As he skidded to a stop in the sweet-smelling grass, her knee came down in the middle of his back, just below his hands. Reaching up to his head, she released his chinstrap and pulled off his helmet. She grasped him by the chin and back of the head.

"I'll make it quick," she promised.

"I won't," he came back through clenched teeth.

She was going to have to fight to tear his head off . . . if he could find a way to fight. He could not resist the grip she had on his head and was in no position to reach anywhere vital on her with either his hands or feet. Then he remembered an attempted suicide he had once pulled out of the Kansas River. He had had a similar hold on her chin, keeping it above water as he swam them both toward shore, when she decided to resist being saved. She had very nearly gotten her wish to die. What worked for her, he decided, could work for him. As Brithe's hands tightened to snap his neck, he opened his mouth and sank his teeth into her hand. He tasted the bitter salt of her blood.

Yelping, she let go. Her weight lifted slightly off his back. Before she came down on him again, he rolled away from her and lunged, somehow, to his feet.

She pawed in her cape for his sleeper. "You can't escape."

He had no intention of running. Instead, Ten charged at her, head down. When he butted into her, they both fell, but he managed to land on his knees and while she was still fighting to take a breath, he brought one knee up under her chin with every gram of strength he still had. Her teeth cracked together and she went limp.

Ten sat down on his lower legs. Closing his eyes, he threw back his head and gulped air in great sobbing gasps.

"Ten!"

He opened his eyes. Iregara were running up the meadow toward him and a police car settled to the ground near him. Consigli vaulted out under the door and raced to him.

"Kampacalas, are you all right? Someone in the shopping mall called the station. They said they read you yelling for help all the way in the woods."

He wished they had responded faster, but then realized that they had probably come as fast as they could. Only his subjective viewpoint turned the few minutes of the chase into an eternity. That was not important any longer, though. He had survived. He was alive. Right now, nothing else mattered.

He carefully avoided looking at Brithe.

Chapter Twenty-four

FROM THE moment he entered the briefing room, Devane felt something different about the police board. Their faces never showed expression but this time, somehow, the lack of expression seemed all the same, on Friendlies and Unfriendlies alike. The printouts of the summer statistics lay before each. Sitting down at one end of the grouped desks, a prickle of apprehension touched Devane. Did they disapprove? Were they about to issue termination orders?

Something flowed between Iregara. Devane felt it in a way he could not accurately identify or describe. Then Seche's fur rippled. Devane's brows rose. What amused the textile designer?

"You have something to say to me?" he asked.

Seche's fur rippled again, and in careful English, the Egara said, "Attaboy."

Devane stared for the full minute it took for the meaning of the word to sink in. "You're commending me for catching our killer?"

He would have liked to accept it; he could use a pat on the back. No one around the station had back-patted much today. The prevailing mood had been one of mixed relief and chagrin rather than jubilation, subdued because although the killer had turned out to be a Silent rather than a cop, she was still too close for comfort, a peripheral member of the family they all knew and trusted. He felt sorry for Kampacalas over in the infirmary, to whom she had been even more.

Devane shook his head in regret. "Thank you, but we were slow. Ashe's death should have put us on the right track. Logging an impromptu as a cover would have been such a foolish lie that we should have at least tried working on the assumption that his log was accurate and extended our investigation from there."

"Misunderstand," Anaya said. "This." The lawyer tapped the printout.

Seche's comment referred to the statistics? He had not expected *that*. He leaned forward. "You find those figures satisfactory?"

"Good," Lishulir said.

Devane sat upright. Coming from an Unfriendly, that was high praise indeed. "Well, we're gradually learning how to handle your people, and they're learning how to help us. Both are important factors." He paused. "I hope you've noticed that of those incidents cleared, an increasing number have been mediated on the spot by the responding officer, without an arrest and formal charges, and that of those sent to adjudication, the final judgment is rarely confinement to a care facility. The usual outcome is a requirement that the defendant make restitution to the victim or pay reparation."

"Yes," Ibal said.

Gemun shifted position with a jingle of the body chains the jewelry crafter wore. "Sufficient."

The comment did not quite fit with Ibal's, so Devane waited for Gemun to explain.

"Personnel," Gemun said. "Number."

Devane smiled wryly. "Yes, we did manage to make do with three hundred officers. Somehow we have always managed to make do with what city administrations dole out to us. You want to be careful, though, Gemun. There's a limit somewhere. It could be like the Terran peasant who came on hard times and thought he'd save credit by feeding less hay to his donkey. He cut the ration in half. The donkey went right on pulling his cart and plow, so the peasant cut the hay ration in half again. When the donkey still worked, the peasant stopped feeding it altogether. Then one morning the peasant found the donkey dead. He swore and grumbled to his wife, 'Of all the rotten luck. It was just learning to work without food, too.' "

Ibal and Seche's fur rippled, but Gemun looked back inscrutably and said nothing. Devane reflected that as disgusted as he became with the board sometimes, he did not know a single counterpart in his position on Earth able to be so candid with an unfriendly superior.

"No cuts," Lishulir said, and handed Devane a sheet of paper.

Devane scanned the characters quickly, then went back to the beginning and studied each more closely, his eyes widening. No cuts, indeed. Instead, the memo covered a discussion between the police board and the Traffic Department on the possibility of consolidating the two at the end of the year, if Devane's group continued to perform well and passed their probation. An estimation of credit saved by the consolidation would permit the hiring of thirty additional officers besides allowing Devane to use or replace Traffic's present agents.

Devane sucked on his lower lip. It depended on some *if*'s, but the mere fact that consolidation was under discussion indicated a favorable attitude toward the department. He looked up. "I apologize, Gemun."

"Yes." Although the single syllable carried no inflection, Devane felt a shrug in it, typifying the ease and brevity of apologies here.

"More," Anaya said.

Devane went on reading. Also under discussion was a change in the service contracts, to be instrumented at the end of probation as well. When renewal came up in ten years—five Terran years—all personnel, Devane in particular, would be given the option of remaining another ten years or taking an indefinite contract. He looked up. "You mean you'll offer us lifetime service, if we want?"

"Yes," Ibal said.

In Translan, Seche said carefully, "You show we cannot . . . communicate to Silents. You are . . . capable to communicate to Normals, to Silents. You are . . . bridge."

"Bridge," Lishulir echoed in Isegis.

Devane read through the section again. This did not have to be a temporary job. It could be permanent. He might never have to return to Earth.

He considered the implications of that after the meeting, while walking the boardmembers to the skyrail path. Never have to go back to Earth, never fight administration to keep police officers human instead of allowing them to be turned into repressive robots . . . never subject Gerel to USNA society.

He lost no time visiting the lab and inviting Meda for a cup of coffee. They drank it at a table out in the garden, with the cool, golden afternoon sunlight filtering down through the bronze leaves of a medehela tree. How well matched they all were, Devane mused, sunlight, medehela leaves, and Meda's toffee-gold skin.

Her face took on some of the glow of Egar's sun, too, when he told her about the "ataboy." "Dee, that's wonderful. It'll look very good on your record when you go back to the SFPD or apply for a position in some other department on Earth."

He grinned. "If I can keep collecting them, I won't have to worry about finding a job on Earth."

Her glow faded into a wary frown. "Why not?" she asked, and looked horrified as he told her. "Oh, no, Dee! Live here all our *lives*? Never see Earth again?"

"Of course we can see Earth. We can visit any time."

"I don't want to visit; I want to live there." She reached across the table to cover his hand with hers. Her hand felt cold. "I can live here for a few years, I think, but . . . not a lifetime."

He turned his hand over, lacing his fingers through hers. "It's a good world. It's good for us, and good for Gerel."

She frowned. "Other children manage to grow into decent human beings on Earth; Gerel can, too."

"Most Terran children don't have Gerel's needs." Now was the time to tell her about Gerel. He did, finishing with, "So we can't take him back to Earth. Can you imagine what his life would be like?"

She jerked her hand loose. "It isn't true! You're lying to me just because you want to stay here playing police director!"

He looked her in the eyes. "I'm not lying."

"Then that's all the more reason for leaving, and leaving right *now*, before he learns it any better." Her voice rose, shrill. "I won't have my son prying into people's minds, Dee, violating privacy. I won't have him like these people."

This was not the reaction he had anticipated. Keeping his voice calm, he said, "Telepathy isn't learned. Gerel was born with the ability. Whether we stay or go, his ability will continue developing now, Runah says."

"Oh, no." She covered her face with her hands. "And I've been around him day after day. He knows what I think, and everything I feel. Oh, no!"

Devane forcibly pulled her hands down. "What are you saying? You talk like he's some kind of monster. He isn't."

He had to talk her out of this. She could not go around Gerel feeling this way. It would destroy the boy. "Meda, he's our son, just as he's always been. He's the same little boy you brought into the world and nursed and changed diapers for. This talent doesn't change that. It doesn't change the fact that he needs us to love and care for him, that he needs his mother."

But she did not appear to have heard. She stared through him, eyes blind. "He knows everything I think." She pushed to her feet. "I have to think about this. I have to get away somewhere and think."

He stared up at her in disbelief. "You can't leave. We need you."

Her eyes focused on him. "I wonder. You have your job and Gerel has a shen full of parents. I don't know what you need me for," she said bitterly, and turned for the building.

He ran after her. "Meda, don't be ridiculous. The job has preoccupied me up until now, but with this killer finally caught, everything will settle down. We'll have some time together. We can take a holiday, maybe visit that Grand Canyon/Niagara Falls place people have been talking about."

She kept on walking, showing no sign of having heard a word he said. In the lab, she collected her coat, then walked down the corridor and across the reception area toward the front door.

Devane stayed at her shoulder, pleading. "Meda, he's your son. You can't abandon him."

A tear gathered in the corner of the eye closest to him and spilled down the golden cheek. "And I can't live with him." She looked around. "I can't bear the thought of him knowing what's in my mind. I won't hurt him the way I would if he reads me feeling this way, either. Maybe after I've had time to think, I'll feel differently."

Devane grasped at the straw. "That's right. You'll feel differently after you've gotten used to the idea. Why don't you go back to Earth and visit your parents? Stay in the Enclave until you leave. We'll be waiting for you to come back."

She nodded.

He watched her cross the courtyard and take the path into the woods toward the skyrail. She would change her mind, of course. Thinking would change it. No woman as intelligent as Meda could abandon a husband and child who loved and needed her. A trip to Earth ought to help her see how much better Egar was, too. Meda would be back.

"No."

He turned to find Liril behind him. "What?"

But Liril did not answer his question, only said, "Officers' meeting."

Devane ran a hand over his hair. He had almost forgotten. Thanking the secretary, he hurried back across the reception area to the U wing and down its corridor to the briefing room, which this time was filled with his division captains and lieutenants. He found them in the middle of a thoughtful discussion.

"But are they capable of learning another language?" Captain Titus asked.

La Flore said, "I don't know why not. All of us are multilingual."

Hasejlan put in, "I had a partner who even knew sign language for talking with deaf-mutes. This is a comparable situation."

"Exactly," La Flore said. "If Egarad officers are ever going to take over the job we're doing, they must learn to communicate with Silents, and they should be able to use the radio as well. It's much faster than writing on a telscreen."

Devane looked at him. "What is it you're proposing?"

La Flore looked up. "That we ask ride-alongs to volunteer for Quickteach lessons in Translan and that for the remainder of the current ride-along program they use Translan during the watch, to talk to their partners and to talk to Silents. Then I think we'll have a better idea about the abilities and difficulties of Egarad officers, and even if Normals *can* become useful officers."

"I think it's a good idea," Basanites said.

"Me, too," Devane said. "Ask for volunteers tonight and have them report to Data for Quickteaching tomorrow. All right, the meeting appears to have opened without me, so we'll go on from here. I think you'll like what the board had to say today."

But while he went over the business of that meeting and watched pleasure light their faces, he thought of Meda. She would come back. She must. Would it help to visit her in the Enclave and plead his and Gerel's case some more? He would try. He had to, because—for the first time, he thought of Liril's remark in the reception area and allowed himself to consider the possibility that Meda might *not* come back—what would he do without her?

"Director?" Tova Craig said. "Did you hear?"

He pulled his attention back to the meeting. "I'm sorry. Please repeat that." And Meda slipped from his mind as he became engrossed in the problem of transferring officers from other watches to even the shortage the deaths had left.

Ten insisted on being discharged from the infirmary. "It's just a minor shoulder separation. There's no point in lying here like an invalid. I want to go home."

Or maybe, he thought, as Bara and Roban flew him home in an Investigations car, what he really wanted was to go *home*, back to Earth and Topeka and his family. He could not sort through the mixture of emotions seething in him, battling for expression.

He was only dimly aware of Roban saying, "I'm transferring from Investigations back to patrol. I spent most of last night while you were gone thinking about Jael. I realize now that she was right about my viewpoint of Egar. I think I can learn some truth and perspective on patrol, and I'm in just the right location to take Jael's place. On the other hand, son, you did pretty good for a green kid. Maybe you ought to ask to be considered for Investigations."

"Good?" Ten said bitterly. "I nearly got myself slagged because I couldn't read a Silent correctly. I don't deserve to be an inspector. I wonder if I even deserve to be a cop."

Bara came around on him. "Don't be so hard on yourself. None of us read her, either."

Ten looked down at the woods and hills passing below them. "I wonder what's going to happen to her. A care facility? A diagnosis of incurable antisocial? Euthanasia?" He leaned his head back against the seat and hugged his slung arm to him. "I can still hardly believe that anyone who can play a synthesizer like she can could—" His voice caught. He swallowed and said wistfully, "On Earth, she could have been one of the best in the business."

Bara said, "Phaedra will be back from the Ginim Sea in a few days. Why don't the four of us plan on doing something together then?"

Ten shrugged his good shoulder. "We'll see."

Roban landed the Isinhar at the edge of Meem and he and Bara walked Ten to his door. "You get some rest. Don't forget you have a court date tomorrow. I'll pick you up. It's your last chance to keep Anubas out of a care facility."

Anubas? Ten had trouble remembering who that was. "Yeah," he said indifferently.

Roban eyed him with concern. "I wish I could stay a while, but I have to get into uniform and report for the Evening Watch briefing. Bara, why don't you spend the night?"

"I won't be any kind of company," Ten said, "but stay if you want. I don't particularly like the idea of being alone." He pushed open his door and walked inside.

Bara followed, but only to kiss him lightly. "I don't think I need to stay. I'll see you tomorrow." She waved as she left.

He stared after her in bewilderment and pain. She was abandoning him when he needed someone most? How could she do that?

Hands clapped from the doorway.

Ten groaned. What he did *not* need—

But Siyan came in. "Need. Bara thought."

For a moment, anger rose. How dare she sic an Egara on him? Then he sighed and shrugged with his good shoulder. Chances were his neighbor would have shown up even without Bara's prompting. He looked at Siyan's empty hands. "No luras?"

"Share," Siyan said. The Egara came down into the sitting area and steered Ten to the couch. "Sit."

Ten lowered himself carefully to avoid jarring his shoulder and lay back. Siyan disappeared up the steps into the kitchen and came back a short time later with two steaming mugs of tea.

"Feel." Siyan handed Ten one mug and sat down in another cushioned chair with the other.

Tea, the omnipresent cure-all. Ten sipped. The acid bit at his tongue. "I don't know what I feel."

"All."

He considered. Yes, he did feel everything at once: angry, sad, foolish, used, betrayed. He hated the killer and grieved for his lost friend. While all his professional training told him that someone who had been killing in cold blood since adolescence must be incurable, the musician in him cried out against destroying Brithe's talent. A part of him raged at her for creating pain and death when instead it could have been musical beauty, when her genius could have moved an entire population and generations of people to come.

"Waste," Siyan agreed. "Tragic."

Ten's eyes met Siyan's violet ones, startled. For the first time since his arrival on Egar, he felt what it was to have someone knowing his *exact* feelings, understanding as no other Terran, not even a brother officer, could . . . understanding even when the reasons for Ten's feelings lay outside of Egarad experience and perhaps outside of Egarad comprehension. For the first time, too, he wondered why Siyan chose to share Ten's feelings rather than avoid the distress of them by avoiding him.

"Aren't my emotions painfully intense for you?"

"Accustoming," Siyan replied. "Need . . . share."

Ten stared. "You need to share my emotions? Why?"

"Drana." Then quickly, as Ten stiffened, "Misunderstand. Not freak. Counterpoint. Variety. Spice. Harmony." Siyan's ears twitched. "Capstone."

Ten struggled to understand. "You mean drana is something special to you, something necessary?"

"Yes." Siyan's ears twitched again. "Outcross. Hybrid. Infusion."

Ten's mind churned. He was *necessary* to the shen? He was—what?—a new viewpoint, a fresh set of impressions and experiences to stimulate thought and creativity in the homogenizing blend of their minds?

"Yes," Siyan said. "Yes."

He shook his head. "All this time I thought—" He sighed. "Brithe twisted that, too."

But she had only helped, he realized. As with so much she said, her remarks on the subject could be interpreted several ways. They were all half-truths. He had chosen the meaning most uncomplimentary to him. Fault for the alienation lay as much with him as with her.

"Past," Siyan said. "Join?"

He tried to imagine what being a true member of the shen would be like, being part of a group other than the fellow officers who lived his daily experiences with him yet who nonetheless understood perfectly, who accepted and wanted his differences and all that he was. It would be like a family, perhaps, only bigger.

Thinking of family made him think of his own, and wonder how much it might cost to bring them out for a visit. Miral would love his hobbit hole.

Suddenly Siyan sat up, head tilted, then stood, reaching for Ten's good hand. "Need."

Siyan led him outside and across the shen. He soon saw who needed him, and why. Two Iregara stood amid carpenter tools, one yelling at the other. The one yelling stopped, seeing Ten.

"A cop. Just what I need," the Egara said in Translan. "Will you explain to this . . . individual that I'll be happy to install any new cabinet desired, if only it's made clear to me exactly what's wrong with my proposed design?"

Ten looked around. "I need an artist with paper and a scriber, please."

One of the gathered neighbors stepped forward with a sketchbook.

"Gee," Ten told the artist, "you draw what Senehar pictures. Senehar, show Gee what you want."

The artist sat a moment, then began sketching. Peering over Gee's shoulder, the Silent carpenter nodded. "Yes. Understand. Yes."

Ten stood watching them, making sure the exchange proceeded peacefully and fruitfully. He wished that all similar disputes could be resolved as easily. Perhaps, one day, they would, he mused. The time might come when instead of reaching for a blunt instrument or plotting revenge, a frustrated Silent would automatically call for a cop. And when that happened, the department would really be worthy of the title Conservators of Peace. Would it ever come, people—even Iregara—being people, unpredictable and imperfect?

"Hope," Siyan said.

Ten smiled at his neighbor. "Oh, yes, we can always hope."

In the meantime, he watched with contentment the bit of restored peace in his part of this world.

About the Author

LEE KILLOUGH is a tall redhead who sometimes feels that it was inevitable that she write science fiction. As the daughter of a newspaperwoman and a high school Spanish/English teacher, she grew up with words and the fascination of creating stories. As chief technologist in the Department of Radiology of the Kansas State University College of Veterinary Medicine, her days are filled with the problems of strange and nonhuman species.

She had never considered writing professionally, however, until meeting Pat Killough while in school at Fort Hays Kansas State College. He encouraged her to begin submitting for publication and, since the appearance of her first short story "Caveat Emptor" in *Analog* in 1970, he has been not only chief critic and cheerleader for her writing efforts but also her live-in lawyer and business manager. Her first novel, *A Voice Out of Ramah*, was published in 1979. Pat also first introduced her to the science-fiction conventions and fandom. Lee and Pat attend conventions when their work schedules permit. At home in Manhattan, Kansas, they share a hillside redwood house with a proliferating library and a highly autonomous Burmese cat named Phaedra.

CLIFFORD D. SIMAK

His worlds are prehistoric, futuristic and fantastic!